FULL ENGLISH

RACHEL SPANGLER

Ann Arbor
2018

Bywater Books

Copyright © 2019 Rachel Spangler

Print ISBN: 978-1-61294-155-4

Bywater Books First Edition: February 2019

Printed in the United States of America on acid-free paper.

Cover designer: Ann McMan, TreeHouse Studio

Bywater Books
PO Box 3671
Ann Arbor MI 48106-3671
www.bywaterbooks.com

For Susie,
I'm not sure what made you decide
to take such a wild and wonderful adventure with me,
but number fourteen wouldn't exist if you hadn't,
and this is all your fault.

Acknowledgments

My family and I had the extreme blessing of living abroad for nine months last year. While we were able to travel to Ireland, Italy, France, and Spain, the bulk of our time was spent in Alnmouth, England. The little seaside village on the far north of England's east coast became so much more than a base to us; it became home. Thanks to our friend Kelly Smith, we were able to rent a place much like the one Emma lives in during this book. We spent our Friday nights at a local pub with a wonderful group of friends and neighbors. We reveled in learning to drive on the left side of country roads, and ate more scones than any people had a right to. We made some of the best memories of our lives during those idyllic times in our beloved village. This book is part romance novel and part love letter to the place that stole such a big part of our hearts. It is my honor to share a little bit of them with all of you.

I'd like to thank all the people who made our time in England so enjoyable, and by doing so lent a great deal of authenticity to these characters. Thank you to Kelly, Jane, Hilary, Kirsten, Max, and the Red Lion Friday Club for welcoming us into your circle. Thank you, Joanne, Barry, and Ethan for taking us under your wing and sharing so many wonderful experiences with us. Thank you to Velvet for being such a stellar host. Thank you to the Alnmouth Cricket Club community, the badminton "badders" boys, and the bouldering group at Willowburn Sports and Leisure Center, who kept my son active and involved with the most wonderful group of kids any parent could ask for.

But like the characters in these pages, this book itself is part British and part American, and while the writing was done entirely in England, the work of editing and production saw the effort come back across the pond. Thank you to the amazing Bywater Books team for making all that happen in double time. Salem West, Marianne K. Martin, Elizabeth Andersen, Nancy Squires, and of course Ann McMan, Famous Designer (who never ceases to amaze with her covers) all turned this one around quickly and beautifully. Again, my longtime friends and beta readers Barb and Toni gave me wonderfully loving feedback. Lynda Sandoval flew through a sharp set of edits without making me cry once! Finally, a great group of buddies from all walks of my life came together to proofread the final typeset, including Ann, Marcie, Susan, and Diane. I also need to thank Will Banks, aka Big Papi, without whom I might never be late. And throughout the entire process of writing this book, Melissa Brayden kept me moving on this story while I traveled, and Georgia Beers kept me from getting too down on myself when I didn't hit my word goals by saying helpful things like, "But did you see a castle today? Well there you go. It all evens out!" In short, I have the best friends ever.

Last but never least, I cannot ever put into words how indebted I am to the best travel partners in the world. Susie and Jackson were with me every step of this life-altering adventure. I simply wouldn't have taken it without them. The time we spent together learning, exploring, playing, and growing offered me some of the best days of my life, and I will cherish those memories almost as much as I cherish the two of you. To Jackson, you inspire me every day with your willingness to jump into new situations and experiences with such open and accepting wonder. I am thankful every day for the blessing of watching you grow into a young man of the world. And to Susan, you are my rock and my roots. I cannot ever repay you for the way you steady and save me time and time again. No matter where we go, I am home as long as I am with you, come what may.

And as always, I cannot thank anyone for anything without acknowledging that each blessing I receive is ordained by a loving creator, redeemer, and sanctifier. *Soli Deo Gloria*

Author's Notes

Full English is told from the point of view of two characters, one American and one British. Many of their words were chosen with each character's nationality and regional dialect in mind. For instance, the American character might use the words "gas pedal" while the British, "accelerator." The same would be true of "rain boots" and "wellies" or "mom" and "mum." These were conscious choices made with the help of several British friends. Initially I'd planned to do the same with spelling of words: a "neighbour" to my Brit would be a "neighbor" to my American. However, the actual practice of spelling the same words differently from one scene to the next ended up being confusing to readers, editors, spellcheckers, and proofers alike. The differences within the document also ran the risk of complicating printing and formatting as well. In the interest of streamlining these issues to create the cleanest, most readable book possible, we were forced to pick one set of spellings and stick with them, and since the book opens in the American's point of view, we felt it most reasonable to carry that through. I know this choice may not please some of my British readers, but I hope you will forgive me, as I promise to you that if I ever write a sequel, I'll make sure to open in a British point of view and carry those spellings throughout!

Also, while the settings of this book are very much *inspired* by the places my family and I lived in and explored around the North East of England, I had to take a few liberties with the towns and the cast of characters that required I create a fictional village, dukedom, and castle. I hope those who know the area will still see the places and landmarks they love reflected in the story that follows, while understanding why the legalities of writing around them required me to change a few names and places.

Pronunciation Guide

After a few readers from each side of the sea got early looks at this book, it was brought to my attention that a pronunciation guide might be in order. I'd love to say this is definitive, however, seeing as how where you live might affect how to read even a pronunciation guide, this the best I can do.

Amalie: AHM-a-lee, Emma's ex-wife.

Amberwick: AM-ber-ick, the "w" is silent, the town where most of the story occurs.

Aoife: EE-fa, an Irish name, Brogan's sister.

Aubergine: OH-bur-zheen, which is eggplant in America and Australia.

Bairn: bern, Child or baby in Scotland and North East England.

Ciara: KEE-rah, an Irish name, Brogan's sister.

Courgette: cor-ZHET, this is a zucchini for the Americans.

Daideó: DAD-doh, which is "grandpa" in Irish.

Eoin: For Americans, just go with "Owen" here.

Haar: Har, this rhymes with "far" in American English, and it means sea fog.

Liam: LEE-um, an Irish name, Brogan's nephew.

Maite: MY-tay, a Spanish name, and also a tourist in town.

McKay: This is Brogans's surname, and in the part of England where she lives, it's most commonly pronounced Mick-KY, which rhymes with Pie.

Siobhán: Shi-VAWN, another Irish name, Brogan's sister, are you seeing a trend yet?

Volant: Vo-LAWN, this is a French surname for our American protagonist.

Zucchini: Zoo-KEE-nee, that's an aubergine for folks in the United Kingdom.

There are many others, so just pronounce the rest phonetically.

Chapter One

Northland Street was dark already, with sparse lights managing only to throw shadows across the black pavement. The headlights of the cab offered glimpses of stone buildings streaked gray by time, before sweeping out into a vast darkness over what she assumed was shrouded beach, then the North Sea.

Looping back toward the town center on the one-lane road that appeared to circle the village, her driver slowed, then stopped in front of a low, white, one-story cottage surrounded by a small, stone garden wall.

"This the one?" he asked.

Emma squinted through the dim light emanating from a neighbor's window. The cottage was the right size, but then again so were most of the neighbors' homes, and she couldn't quite make out the color in the dark but it was probably white, or maybe gray, or perhaps a light yellow. And the bushes were bigger than the pictures she'd seen online, but they were in roughly the same place, probably. "Um, it might be."

The cabbie raised an eyebrow at her via the rearview mirror, and she suspected his patience might be running thin with her lack of certainty. She understood his frustration as a little voice inside her whispered, *What have you done?*

She fought back the wave of nausea that always accompanied the question and tried to sound more confident as she said, "Yes. It's the right address, so it must be the right house."

"Good," he said, not unkindly, but with more than a hint of relief. She suspected from his multiple comments about the remoteness of the village and her need to pay for his return fare to Newcastle that he didn't get many clients inquiring about transport from the airport all the way up to Amberwick, much less having the means or the willingness to pay the cost. Maybe he didn't even fully expect her to pay, as he made no move to exit the cab before clearing his throat and saying, "That'll be one hundred pound fifty."

"One hundred pound fifty," she repeated, unsure of whether he meant one hundred and fifty pounds, or one hundred pounds and fifty pence. She could give him one hundred fifty pounds and call it a tip, unless, of course, the actual cost was one hundred fifty, in which case she'd made him drive her an hour outside the city late at night, and then didn't tip him a single cent, or pence, or whatever he'd call it. Either way, he was still waiting, his arm stretched across the back of the passenger seat with a forced casualness that allowed him to watch her more fully now. The poor man was clearly nervous as she rummaged through unfamiliar bills before finally pulling out some purplish ones and handing him two of them, mumbling, "Keep the change."

His eyes went wide, and he nearly strangled himself with the seatbelt as he tried to scramble out the door. "Let me get your bags, ma'am."

She supposed she'd answered the cost question. She'd clearly paid him double his already high rate. She would've smiled at his attempt to overcorrect his attitude if she weren't so exhausted. Instead she said, "Thank you," as he handed her a piece of carry-on luggage and struggled to hoist the larger suitcase from his trunk.

"I can carry this one up for you," he offered, suddenly more genial.

"No," she said, "I lugged it all the way from New York. I can get it to the door."

"You sure?"

"Yes," she said, glad to have a definitive answer for the first time in days, if not weeks. "Drive safe."

"You, too," he said enthusiastically. Then with a sheepish grin that showed his crooked teeth for the first time all night, he corrected himself. "I mean, stay safe on your holiday."

She stood awkwardly between her suitcases as he drove off, but once the taillights faded, she became aware of a distinct chill in the air, or maybe from somewhere inside her own chest.

"Holiday." She repeated the misnomer as she stood alone in a strange, dark town in the rural reaches of a foreign country where she didn't know a single living soul.

She turned wearily toward the house, her house, and tried to fight back the refrain that had dogged her for weeks with an internal whisper: *What have you done?*

Hefting both suitcases so they wouldn't drag noisily across the gravel driveway, she staggered under their weight toward the door. Then she stopped abruptly as she reached it.

She didn't have the key.

Why in the name of all things holy hadn't she realized that, until this moment? She was supposed to have stopped by the real estate office when she got into town. She was also supposed to have arrived in town at 10 a.m. instead of 10 p.m.

She didn't glance up and down the street to see if any of the stores were still open, because they clearly weren't. She did, however, pull out her cell phone to confirm her American plan had no service in the far north of England.

What have you done? The voice wasn't quite a whisper anymore. Her heart rate accelerated, causing her pulse to pound through her ears. The panic would overtake her soon if she didn't act. But where could she go? What could she do? There was no one around. And even if there were, what would she say to them? "I bought a house sight unseen, and I think it's this one, but I don't have a key, do you?" Maybe she could also add, "I've been traveling for thirty-two hours solid, and I'm exhausted and heartbroken and cold and lost and lonely."

Her bottom lip twitched as she realized she was no longer practicing a sad speech to garner sympathy so much as stating the facts of her life.

Swallowing a sob, she made a desperate grab for the door handle and gave it a downward yank. To her vast surprise, it pushed all the way down with an audible click, then swung open a few inches.

Her heartbeat didn't slow as she stared at the open space she'd created. Either someone had left her house unlocked, or she'd broken into someone else's.

"Hello," she whispered, not sure the noise would've been enough to wake anyone sleeping inside. Then again, if someone were sleeping inside, she didn't want to wake them.

Maybe she should close the door and knock. Then at least if she were at the wrong place, she wouldn't actually be inside someone else's home when she found out.

"No. This is my house," she whispered, fully understanding that she was whispering because she wasn't at all certain of the truth of the statement. So she did what any reasonable human would do and backed away slowly, pulling the door with her.

"Okay," she said, no longer even trying to pretend she wasn't talking to herself. "You're a writer. Write your way out of this."

Closing her eyes, she pictured a romantic lead, strong, confident, able, walking up to a door in the dead of night and rapping on it with purpose. Once no one answered, she would stride in and claim it as her own, a modern-day Columbus in this new land. *Except Columbus was a raping, murdering bastard who landed on the wrong continent, and nope, too far with that analogy. Just knock.*

Before she lost her nerve, she quickly lifted her hand and rapped on the door lightly. Then she counted to ten. When no one answered, she knocked a little harder. Another ten-count later, with the tightness in her chest loosening almost to the point where she could draw a full breath, she knocked one more time, loud enough to be heard by any neighbors who happened to still be awake. Ten, nine, eight, seven, six, five, four, three, two, one, and she swung wide the door to her new home.

Then she screamed in the face of the person standing directly on the other side.

The dark form in front of her returned the scream in kind, only

4

its shriek resonated with a disconcertingly high tone that seemed entirely out of place from such an imposing figure standing in a dark hallway.

"You're a woman," Emma blurted, not stopping to process why the thought mattered enough to be verbalized.

"Bloody hell, really?" The person doubled over. "Is that how you fucking greet women in your country?"

"What? Oh no. I mean, I'm sorry. I didn't mean to startle you."

"Well, here's a tip, not letting fly a blood-curdling scream on sight is a good way to not startle someone."

Emma's stomach did a little somersault. "Oh, I'm sorry. I'm the worst. And I pushed into your house and everything."

"My house? I sort of hoped this was *your* house. Holy shite, if you're not Emma Volant, this just got a lot weirder."

"No, of course I am, but wait, so this *is* my house?"

"Yes, but why do I get the sense you thought you were walking into someone else's during the black of night?"

"I wasn't sure, and . . ." She shifted from one foot to the other, then took an abrupt step back, causing her suitcase to topple over with a dull thud. "Hold on a second. If this is my house, then who are you, and why are you in there? Oh my God, am I getting robbed before I even move in? I have some money on me. You can have it, but I—"

"Hey, slow down. I'm not robbing you. I mean, I get the whole Irish ruffian stereotype has made it to America, but I'm not robbing you."

She had only the fleeting wherewithal to realize the woman sounded more English than Irish, but amid the myriad confusing notes to this experience, the comment barely ranked.

With a sigh, the woman in front of her flipped on a hall light, casting a fluorescent sheen on rich, ginger hair and a pale complexion offset by the most breathtakingly beautiful, sage-green eyes. For the second time in as many minutes she stepped back, startled by the appearance of the woman before her.

"No need to back away again. I'm Brogan," the woman said with a placating smile. "Come on in and let me explain."

Grabbing the bigger suitcase beside Emma without asking, she retreated into the house and flipped on another light as she went, revealing a cozy living room with a small armchair and love seat opposite an old fireplace. "I'm your property manager. I didn't mean to frighten you. I was only waiting here to give you the keys."

"I thought someone named Edmond McKay had my keys."

"Edmond's my brother. He's got a baby on the way, and his wife is in that uncomfortable stage of the pregnancy, so I told him I'd stay and wait for you."

The completely reasonable answer made every other thought she'd had over the last five minutes seem downright silly. "I'm sorry I kept you out so late."

"No worries." Brogan waved her off amicably as she set the suitcase down next to an old oak table, then with a slight flush in her cheeks added, "Sorry I screamed like a small girl who's spotted Prince Harry."

Emma smiled for the first time in who knew how long. "I wasn't going to mention it, but I suppose I should apologize for screaming, too. I wasn't expecting anyone to be in my house."

"Which you weren't sure actually was your house, but you walked into anyway," Brogan teased gently.

"You remembered that part, too?" Embarrassment flooded her senses again, heating her core.

"Actually, that reminds me, I'm supposed to have you sign some papers affirming this is your house now, and you are who you say you are. Then I'll get out of your way," Brogan said, sweeping those green eyes over Emma's face, and added, "I bet you're exhausted from the trip."

She pressed her lips together at the polite excuse for the bags she knew underlined her eyes and the sallow state of her complexion. She was exhausted from much more than the travel, and as the adrenaline faded, the weight of those emotions settled across her shoulders again.

"Of course." She scanned the sheets of paper on the table as she picked up a pen. "Where do I sign?"

Brogan pointed to the first one. "Here, to state you found the place in good enough shape to accept. If you want to walk through the other rooms first, you can."

She didn't. From what she'd seen of the entryway, living room, and dining area, she didn't expect any more surprises tonight.

As she signed on the line, Brogan continued. "The second one says I met you with the keys and they are now your sole responsibility."

Glancing at the two identical key rings in the center of the table, she quickly autographed that form as well.

"And lastly, this form is for me, saying I made a reasonable attempt to confirm your identity, which I guess technically I haven't." Brogan ran her hand through her mop of wavy red hair again and grimaced a little. "Edmond's a bit of a stickler for following rules."

The comment suggested she didn't share that particular trait with her brother but wanted to honor his wishes anyway, which made Emma's heart constrict. "Let me find my passport."

She rummaged through her purse, then unzipped the front pouch of her carry-on suitcase, pulling out several manila folders, one of which held her travel documents. She dumped all three onto the table.

"Oh, where did I put the passport?" she muttered to herself. She'd had it when she'd come through customs in Dublin. "I thought I'd need it to get from Ireland to England, but I didn't have to go through customs in Newcastle."

Brogan stood quietly as Emma spoke more to herself than to anyone else.

"I would *not* have left my passport somewhere," she said more emphatically. "I would *not* have been that oblivious." The last word stuck in her throat, making it harder to breathe. The pain returned in a flash, and she placed a hand flat on the table to keep from doubling over. What did she know about what she would or wouldn't miss? She'd been oblivious about so much more. What reason did she really have to think she couldn't misplace a travel document?

"Miss Volant?" Brogan asked softly.

"I'm fine," she said, her head still angled toward the papers in hand so the tears in her eyes wouldn't show.

"Maybe you put it in a pocket or something."

She patted the back of her khakis, knowing the pockets weren't deep enough, but she couldn't stand still, not with the panic revving her pulse again. What if she'd lost her passport? She'd be stuck here. But she lived here. But without the passport, could she be deported? Her breath came short and quick. "What did I do?"

"Hey," Brogan said, her voice soothing and her accent thicker, "were you wearing something else earlier?"

The last thirty-two hours flashed through her mind in a blur. "My coat."

She looked up to see the concern etched across Brogan's furrowed brow.

"I put the passport in the inside pocket of my coat, and then put the coat in my big suitcase before I left the airport because I didn't want to lug it with me."

"There you go." Brogan's voice carried a modicum of the relief Emma felt.

"I can get it. Let me open the big suitcase." She dropped to her knees and tipped the mammoth piece of luggage onto its back.

"You know what? I think I'm actually good."

Emma stared up at her in disbelief.

"You're clearly Emma Volant. Like, I'm ninety percent sure I've seen your picture on a book or in a paper or something."

She didn't know if the statement was meant to be flattering, but it didn't quite get there.

"And you've obviously had a wicked-long day."

What had given the woman that idea? Her disheveled appearance, the glass-shattering scream on sight, or maybe the way she was thrashing through her luggage and talking to herself? The panic that consumed her gave way to embarrassment once again, and all she could manage was, "But you need to see my ID for your brother."

"He'll get over it."

"No," Emma said, "you shouldn't get in trouble because I'm a mess."

"You're not a mess." Brogan held out a hand to help her up. "You're lovely."

Her embarrassment butted up against whatever shred of her pride remained intact, and she shook her head. She wasn't helpless, or at least she didn't want to be anymore. Not here in her new place for her new start. She didn't want her first encounter in Amberwick to involve some unsuspecting local having to literally pick her up off the ground.

Apparently sensing her conflict, Brogan dropped her hand and looked helplessly around before latching onto one of the many documents Emma had dumped out of her manila folders. "Here, there's something with your name right on the top. Looks official enough to me."

Emma pushed herself to standing and picked up the stack of papers fastened together with a thick black clip. Sure enough, her name was right there on the top, right over Amalie's. The juxtaposition was the final shot in the war that had raged within her much longer than today. She couldn't hold herself together any longer. Her shoulders began to shake with silent sobs.

"What? What is it?" Brogan asked.

She shook her head and sniffled but couldn't speak yet.

Brogan stepped forward as though she might pull her close, then clasped her hands together nervously and stepped back again. "I am really sorry, again, and I don't know what that is, but—"

"My divorce papers," she finally squeaked out, though the words were punctuated with a little hiccup.

"Pardon me?"

She took a shuddering breath. "These are my divorce papers, so yes, they are official."

Brogan chewed her lips for a second before saying, "So, I think I'm done here then."

Emma nodded and turned back to the papers in her hand.

Out of the corner of her eye, she saw Brogan edge toward the door, pausing only briefly to ask, "Is there anything else you need?"

She shook her head, not even looking up when Brogan said, "Okay then, well, have a good night."

As the door clicked shut behind her, Emma knew that would not happen. New house, new town, new country, and yet this would be one more in the same string of very bad nights.

Chapter Two

"Aunt Brogan!" She heard the call, but she couldn't see the speaker over the edge of the bar she stood behind, so she knew which one of the kids it must be.

"What can I get for you, Padrig?"

"Crisps please, the mustard kind."

She leaned over the bar to see the top of his red head. "And will Uncle Charlie be paying for those?"

"Come on, Brogan," her youngest brother called from a few tables over. "I got all four of 'em till seven, and you know Ciara's not going to pay me enough for my own drinks, much less the kids'."

She couldn't argue with his premise, but she didn't see how that was her problem. Other than the fact that Padrig looked up at her with his little freckled nose and gap-tooth smile. "All right then, one for you. Then tell Eoin and your sisters they can each pick one, too. But that's all for Friday Club, so make it last until you get home with your mum."

The boy nodded seriously as he held out his little hands for the yellow bag, then turned toward the table where his siblings sat and shouted, "Eoin, Aoife, Reg, come and get your crisps 'cause it's all ya get till tea time."

Three other little redheads popped up and sprinted toward the bar, as people in their path grabbed hold of their pint glasses to keep them from getting jostled in the stampede.

"Geeze, Brogan, the least you can do is warn a chap before you summon the hounds," Tom grumbled.

"Now you hush." His wife, Diane, swatted his arm. "You were just complaining no young people are raising families in this town anymore. Don't go fussing at those who do."

"But he's not wrong," said another man, as he shed his wool coat and hung it on a hook near the door. "I just got back from Bamburgh, and the streets are full of people pushing prams. Our streets are deserted this time of year."

"It's because they're having the festival at the castle this weekend, Will," Diane said. We don't have a castle here, only a beach."

"And thank the good Lord for that," Tom huffed. "We want families, not more tourists."

"Right, 'cause tourists haven't got any relations," Charlie jabbed, as he sipped his ale.

Brogan handed Will the ale he hadn't even ordered yet.

"I know what you mean, Tom. I'm not sure there's a whole five full-time residents left within a mile of Bamburgh Castle. It's all holiday homes now."

"There you go." Tom nodded at the affirmation. "Towns are either dying out and falling apart, or getting overrun with city folks trying to escape to the country for their weekends."

"That's the truth of it," Esther said as she wandered in from the loo and took the seat opposite her sister. "No offence to you and yours, Brogan and Charlie, but if not for the McKay clan breeding like rabbits, there wouldn't be a single full-time resident under the age of fifty in this village."

Brogan took no offense at the statement. It wasn't the first time she'd heard it. She simply shrugged and set about wiping out a few of the glasses gathering dust behind the bar, but Charlie cut back in. "That's not true."

Will clasped a hand on his shoulder and nodded toward the kids, who were now wrestling over the last bag of bacon rasher crisps. "Maybe not rabbits, but you have to admit your clan reproduces at a rate that outstrips the rest of us."

Charlie rolled his green eyes. "I meant there's another full-time resident under fifty now. The new writer got in a couple nights ago."

"Emma Volant?" Diane and Esther squealed in unison.

"That's the one."

Brogan's chest tightened, and she focused on the glass in her hand as if attempting to polish it enough to check her own reflection.

"I didn't think she was here yet," Diane said. "I've asked around. No one's seen her or heard a peep from her place."

"And the whole town has been watching the cottage with binoculars," Tom added.

"She's there all right. Edmond told me they transferred the keys earlier this week." Charlie turned to Brogan. "He said you did it."

Brogan glanced behind her in some vain hope he might be addressing someone else. Then she closed her eyes for a second, but the only thing she saw behind her own lids was a vision of Emma on her knees, her shoulders shaking with shallow breaths, her eyes red-rimmed as she looked up helplessly. In an attempt to flush the memory from her mind, she focused on the people opposite the bar and managed to mumble, "Yeah, I saw her."

Everyone in the large corner booth stared at her with a mix of open mouths and raised eyebrows, as if waiting for something she couldn't or wouldn't give them. Despite only one short inter-action with the woman, something protective stirred in her, and she set her jaw against the instinct to fill the silence.

"Aye?" Diane finally did an exaggerated imitation of her low Geordie accent. "Out with it. What's she like?"

Sad was the first word that came to mind. Even before the woman had begun to cry, Brogan had seen something almost heart-wrenchingly sad in her blue eyes. Emma's panic had felt closer to that of a drowning woman than someone who'd simply misplaced her passport. The frail set of her shoulders, and the way she'd nearly folded over the divorce papers had made Bro-gan want to cradle her in her arms and hold her tightly, but she

13

couldn't hardly say so to folks drinking in the Raven on a Friday night. Doing so would feel like a betrayal of Emma, and it would likely earn her a solid round of ribbing, too. "She seems nice."

Both women frowned at the completely nondescript descriptor, but Tom's smile turned conspiratorial. "How nice?"

"Yeah." Charlie grinned. "Nice can mean a lot of things coming from you. Seems like that's how you described the Spanish tourist who took out Tom's holiday let last summer, and then I woke up to find her making coffee in our kitchen the next morning."

Everyone laughed, and even Brogan smiled at the diversion Maite had provided, both then and now.

"So, is she nice, or is she *nice?*" Tom asked.

She rolled her eyes, but couldn't deny Emma Volant would turn many heads around town. She was tall, and despite the sunken eyes that indicated she might have recently lost weight, her frame suggested she'd always been a bit willowy. Her long, amber hair and blue eyes capped off a classic combination. She didn't have the movie star polish many people associated with beautiful Americans, but she'd reminded Brogan a bit of a ballet dancer—strong, serious, graceful. She supposed she could have safely said the last part, but instead she went with a more mundane explanation. "She got in late. We were both tired. Honestly, we just signed our papers and went our separate ways."

"Mum says she's famous," Reg cut in from the kids' table. "She has, like, five of her books, and they are huge. She must be smart to write so much."

Brogan hadn't been aware Reg was listening, but she wasn't surprised. Of all her nieces and nephews, Reggie was the most likely to pay attention to the subtleties of what was going on around her. The girl wore jeans and a jumper Brogan suspected had been handed down from her older cousin James. Her red hair was cut in an unruly bob, but as usual Reg preferred to keep it under a cap. Brogan remembered feeling the same way at ten years old, always in between the boys and the girls, the kids and the adults, the insiders and the outsiders. Was that why Reg had

14

tuned into the others' talk of women? Did she sense the vague pull starting to stir, or was she merely inquisitive? Either way, Brogan would have to be more careful about stories like the one Charlie had just shared. She tried to redirect the conversation to more appropriate topics. "Ms. Volant probably is pretty smart. She also seemed to have kind of a sense of humor, even though she was tired."

"And she's young, too, right?" Charlie asked.

"I'd say mid-thirties," Brogan said, then internally added that she might have looked younger if she hadn't been so downtrodden. "Certainly young enough to qualify as an under-fifty resident."

"And she's rich," Tom added, raising his glass in some sort of salute. "Obscenely rich if she can buy a sea-view cottage without even seeing the place. Who does that?"

"Edmond said she's never even been in town. She chose it because her grandmother lived here as a child."

"I don't remember any Volants, and I've lived here my whole life," Will said with a frown.

"Lucky you, you're not as old as the woman's grandmother," Diane shot back.

"Could be a married name," Esther offered.

"I don't think she's married anymore," Diane said, causing Brogan to see the divorce papers in her mind once more, another detail she didn't feel comfortable sharing.

"Maybe it's a mother's name. Or maybe a pen name," Esther said.

"We'll have to ask when we see her out and about."

"If she ever goes out and about," Tom said.

"She's got to leave the house at some point," Diane said matter-of-factly. "She bought a house here for a reason. She has to have some sort of connection to the place. Who knows? Maybe having someone like her will bring other authors to the area."

"Wouldn't that be lovely?" Esther's voice had grown higher with excitement. "If we can get her involved with some of the local charities or the church, she would bring a lot of attention."

Brogan went back to scrubbing dirty glasses and trying not to picture Emma clutching her chest in the doorway to her new cottage.

"Artists and authors, now that's an idea I can get behind," Tom said, his usual grumble fading. "Artists would be nice. They're quiet. They're stable, respectable. They would bring some life to the town without all the transient qualities of tourists."

Brogan smiled down at the glass in her hand, wondering how many artists or authors Tom had even met in his life.

"Someone might even open a gallery or a little bookstore. Maybe we could have readings or salons." Esther added on to the fantasy.

"I've never been to an author's salon," Diane said, with a hint of awe.

"Maybe Emma will start one for all of us," Reg added, seeming happy to contribute to the web they were all building. "Do you think she'll come talk to my school about her books?"

The hope in her niece's voice was finally enough to break through Brogan's own inner musings. She didn't want to let them down. In a town the size of Amberwick, causes for excitement were few and far between. Who was she to begrudge the only people in the pub on Friday night a fun conversation? But she suspected that's all that would come from such flights of fancy. She didn't want to take any part in fostering false hopes, but she didn't see why she should have to be the one to tell them all that, from what she saw, Emma Volant didn't seem up for being a spokesperson for anything.

The sun seemed to shine from everywhere. It burned through the glass enclosing her sunroom and shimmered across the glittering waves below. Warmth played across her newly bare shoulders as she stripped off her sweater to reveal a white tank top. She hadn't packed many summer clothing items, noting that the temperatures in Amberwick rarely rose above seventy degrees even in August, but she hadn't counted on the glass enclosure acting like her own personal greenhouse. What had the agent called the space?

"Conservatory," she said softly, enjoying the unfamiliar word. It sounded so formal, so upper class. What would her father have said if she told him she had a conservatory overlooking the North Sea? What about her grandmother? Both of them would've been amused no doubt, but likely for different reasons.

She sat for several more minutes, thinking about her family and watching the waves fall mutely in the distance, until the rumbling of her own stomach shattered the silence. She'd have to address her most basic needs soon. The tranquility would carry her only so far now that she'd eaten the box of granola bars she'd brought with her and consumed the entire bowl of fruit the real estate agency had left on the kitchen counter as a housewarming present.

She made a muscle-twisting mix of a grimace and a smile at the memory of Brogan. How long had she been sitting in the cottage with that bowl of fruit? Hours most likely. And then Emma had scared the living daylights out of her, but she'd still responded first with humor, then with understanding as she'd watched the subsequent meltdown. Emma had been in that situation enough over the last few months to know most people responded with cheap platitudes or inappropriate questions when faced with those raw emotions, but Brogan had been patient and respectful, and she'd mercifully extracted them both from the awkwardness as quickly as possible. If only everyone in the world could be kind enough to stay out of her personal life and let her wallow in peace, maybe she wouldn't be in a strange place on the verge of starvation right now.

Her stomach growled again, and she sighed heavily at the reminder she'd soon have no choice but to trade her pajama bottoms for real pants and interact with a real person—at least long enough to stock her cabinets.

Wandering back through the house to her open suitcase, she gave herself a little pep talk as she pulled on a pair of jeans and a light blue sweater. "You can do this. You can go outside and buy food and maybe even say hello to someone."

Pulling on socks and a pair of sneakers, she added, "You used

17

to like people. Despite how you've acted lately, 'introvert' does not mean the same thing as 'hermit.'"

Well, at least she hadn't been a hermit before her entire life had been splashed across the front page. Her stomach roiled again, only this time not from hunger. She pushed herself off the bed and put in the undue effort it took to place one foot in front of the other. She didn't have a choice. She had to go out. Never mind that anyone she met would likely know about her shame and shortcomings, but maybe the English would be more polite than Americans. Once again, she thought of Brogan's quiet sympathy and quick exit. Maybe those traits were national hallmarks of Brits. With that thought and a weak smile, she summoned the strength to step outside.

The air was crisp and cool with a subtle hint of salt. In the distance she could make out the sounds of waves and the call of seagulls. Instantly her own bad memories were replaced with someone else's joy. Strolling down the crooked streets between rows of houses all connected to one another by stone and plaster, she could hear her grandmother's voice echo across the years. "It looked as if the whole town was one long house down one side, with only archways for people and carriages to pass into courtyards or gardens out back."

She'd been enthralled with the idea of such a communal approach to living then. Her own childhood subdivision of hastily constructed, boxy buildings, each one surrounded by a privacy fence, had felt woefully disjointed by comparison. She walked along one of the long row houses now, trying to picture them as they would've looked in the 1930s. Aside from the modern cars along the street, she doubted much would be different. The stone was the same, the window frames all painted in a simple whitewash, and on the other side of the street the sea would have still peeked out from the end of each offshoot and alleyway. Grandmother would likely still feel very much at home here. The thought and the immovability of her surroundings allowed some of the tension to slip from her muscles. Headlines, conflicts, even generations would come and fade from this place without so much as scarring the surface.

18

She felt lighter than she had in ages by the time she reached the end of the main street running through town, and she might have kept strolling all day if not for the fact that fresh air and movement also amplified her hunger. Looking back at the length of Amberwick, she'd passed a tea room, an Indian restaurant, a pub, a church, and several bed-and-breakfast type businesses, but no grocery store. Frowning, she glanced around her again, as if maybe she'd missed a turn, but with a solid row of houses to one side and the sea only a block to the other, there didn't seem to be many options left.

The tension returned in an instant. What was she doing here? She wasn't stepping into her grandmother's stories. She was a modern woman in a foreign country with nothing to eat, no working cell phone, and no one to ask for help.

"What do you need, dear?" a soothing voice asked in the most liltingly familiar accent.

Her breath caught as she whirled to see her grandmother approaching. Only it wasn't her grandmother as she'd last seen her. She was younger now, her silver hair longer, and her gait smoother as she easily covered the cobblestones up the side street, but her eyes were just as blue as Emma's own.

"Grandmother?" a young girl asked, pulling on the woman's long skirt. "Who's that?"

Emma blinked as if trying to process the new addition. Had she lost her grip on the present? Was she having a mental break? Did the child represent her younger self? If so, why did she have red hair?

"Who?" Another child appeared to sprout from behind the grandmother—no, two of them, in a mirror image, both carrot-topped little boys, and their appearance was enough to shatter the spell. The woman who sounded so much like home was merely a stranger with a striking resemblance to someone she'd loved, and her brain had worked hard to fill in details that didn't exist. The woman before her was fair and elegant. Her eyes bore the softness of love and laughter, but her skin was still too smooth and her body too fluid to have survived a depression a

19

world war. Still, the similarities were enough for Emma to forget her earlier reticence and extend her hand. "Hi, I'm Emma, and I'm new here."

"The writer. How lovely to meet you," the woman said cheerfully and accepted her hand into both of her own. "I'm Margaret McKay."

"I'm Ginny," the little girl added, unprompted, but the boys were too busy running in circles around them all to make their own introductions.

Emma smiled at the girl. "And are those your brothers?"

She wrinkled up her nose and shook her head. Emma wondered if that was the truth or simply wishful thinking.

"Her cousins, Wendell and Seamus," Margaret said, then with a smile added, "though I won't be able to tell you which is which until they slow down enough for me to get a good look at their faces."

"You've got your hands full."

Margaret laughed, the melodic sound stirring an almost painful nostalgia in Emma. "You really are new around here, aren't you? That explains the lost expression on your face when we walked up."

Emma frowned. She'd nearly forgotten about that. "I do seem a bit out of the loop on several counts. Chiefly, where's the grocery store?"

"The nearest proper grocer is in Newpeth," the woman said calmly, as the children continued to spin laps around them, "but we're on our way to the post office if you want to follow along."

The offer didn't seem like a reasonable response. She needed food, not stamps. "I'm afraid I don't have anything to mail."

Margaret tilted her head to the side, her eyebrows pulled close together with confusion before shooting up. "You're an American, of course. No, the post office here is different."

"My mum is the boss," one of the boys shouted.

"My mum is the boss," the other echoed.

"Both true," Margaret said, as she nudged them along Northland street back in the direction Emma had come from. As she followed along, Ginny tugged on her hand. Emma glanced down at her, noticing a faint spread of light freckles when the child looked up at her, holding up two fingers as if the dexterity to do so took a lot of concentration. "I'm this many."

"I'm three," the boys shouted in unison, though how they'd even been aware of their cousin's statement with their frolicking was beyond her.

"I'm going to be the big brother," one of them shouted, shoving his twin and sprinting off down the sidewalk.

"No, I am." The other chased after him.

Ginny sighed dramatically as she reached for her grand-mother's hand. "Arfur's my bruvver."

"He is," Margaret said sweetly, then for Emma's benefit added, "my daughter Nora is expecting again, and someone is feeling a little left out that she's not getting a younger sibling when every-one else seems to have one."

"I know how you feel," Emma said conspiratorially. "I don't have a little brother or sister either. Or any older ones for that matter."

"An only child?" Margaret asked, coming to a stop outside a door with a red sign overhead marking it as a post office. "All my children and grandchildren would find that downright exotic."

"All of them?" Emma asked, getting the sense the phrase might be a bit loaded.

"Eight of my own, and twelve grandchildren with at least two more on the way."

Emma put a hand out to steady herself against the brown stone of the building, but Margaret only laughed as she scooped Ginny into her arms. "Don't worry. We won't expect you to learn everyone's name right away, but if you see a shock of red hair about town, you've got a better-than-fifty-percent chance they're a McKay.

As if to illustrate her point, she swung open the door to the post office to reveal two more redheads. One of them appeared to be about eight months pregnant, and the other happened to be Brogan McKay."

Her smile was instant and broad. Emma couldn't help but return it, until she realized the expression hadn't been directed at her. Brogan's green eyes were focused on her mother and the little girl she held.

"Hey, there's two of the prettiest girls in town," Brogan said as Margaret stepped to the side, fully revealing Emma behind her.

Brogan's eyes widened, and her smile faltered but didn't disappear completely. "Now that's awkward. There are three women here."

"Four," the pregnant woman said. "I'm standing right here."

"Oh Brogan." Margaret chuckled and patted her cheek. "You have such a way with words and women. I take it you've met Miss Volant?"

Emma blushed at the memory of their meeting once more, but Brogan simply nodded. "Briefly."

They stood in the silence for a few seconds too many before the twins came crashing through the door. "Mum!"

The pregnant woman braced herself for impact, and Emma gasped, but inches before the boys reached her, Brogan and Margaret each stuck out an arm and caught a twin apiece, hoisting them up off the ground.

"Hello there, Wendell," Brogan said to the boy squirming to get away. At the sound of her voice, he immediately went limp and fell into fits of laughter. "I'm Seamus, Aunt Brogan."

"No, I'm Seamus," the boy in his grandmother's grasp called.

"I'm Seamus!" the other twin shouted, as if saying the same thing louder might actually make it more true.

"Mummy!" the other one yelled.

The pregnant woman sighed exhaustedly, then glanced at Emma. "Three-year-olds. Everyone complains about the terrible twos, but honestly, they're much worse now. If they'd behaved this way when they were two, I'd have never done this." She pointed to her enlarged stomach.

"It's a phase." Margaret put a hand lightly on her daughter's shoulder. "And they still have a lie-down, which is why I brought them here. I'll watch the store while they sleep, and you can have a lie-down, too."

"And you can get a break as well," Brogan said to her mother, "because I came over to man the till for a couple hours."

"I'm not an invalid," the pregnant woman said, a hint of stubbornness in the set of her jaw. "I'm Nora, by the way."

"I'm Emma."

"I'm Ginny." The little girl introduced herself again, unnecessarily.

"And I'm taking over." Brogan asserted herself once more. "I've got three hours before I have to be back at the pub. I suggest you all get out of here and get some sleep instead of fussing about."

Margaret didn't seem to need much convincing, but Nora at least opened her mouth as if intending to argue before Seamus-or-Wendell broke loose from his grandmother and bolted out the door shouting, "I'm free."

"Go," Brogan said firmly, setting his brother loose, and this time Nora followed without an argument.

Margaret smiled at her daughter and held her granddaughter a little closer before saying, "Your Aunt Brogan's a good girl, even when she pretends to be tough."

Brogan rolled her eyes. "You can be both, Ginny. Good girl and tough girl aren't opposites, and don't let anyone tell you otherwise."

"And on that note, we'll call our feminist class concluded for the day and go have a lie-down." Margaret turned to leave and nearly bumped into Emma. "Miss Volant, I'm sorry. I almost forgot I'd brought you in here to shop."

For the first time, Emma took a second to look past the people to the shelves lining the walls around them. Bread, crackers, canned soups and candy, there seemed to be a little bit of everything.

"Thank you," she said with a little more relief than she'd meant to reveal. "This is exactly what I needed."

Margaret smiled sympathetically. "Then I'll leave you to it. And if there's something missing, let Brogan know. She's fully capable of taking care of anything you need."

Brogan blushed at her mother's parting words. Margaret McKay wasn't a woman to deal in innuendo or double-entendres, but that didn't stop Brogan from hearing them. A quick glance at Emma, who'd found something interesting on the tissues shelf, suggested she'd caught the added meaning of the statement as well, or maybe she'd noticed Brogan's embarrassment. It wasn't the first time Emma had seen that emotion on her. A surge of guilt washed over her again about the hasty exit she'd made when they'd met. She'd spent several days wondering if she should have or could have done more to comfort Emma that night, but had yet to settle on any real answer. Instead she blurted out, "Do you need something?"

Emma perused the shelves some more. "Actually, I need everything, really."

"Oh?"

"That sounded bad, didn't it?" Emma tried to laugh off the comment, but the sound came out a little choked. "I mean my cupboards are completely bare. I have literally nothing."

Hearing the desperation creeping back into Emma's voice, Brogan's protective instincts reared up in her. She fought off her first impulse to hug Emma, and instead handed her a shopping basket from beside the counter. "If you've got nothing, anything is a step in the right direction."

Emma smiled weakly as she accepted the basket. "That's one way to see it."

"Let me give you the grand tour," Brogan offered, then, pointing to the wall behind Emma, said, "As for the breads, we've got your white and brown and some croissants that were not at all baked fresh this morning."

Turning a quarter way around the room, she continued. "There's a whole wall of sweets and chocolate biscuits. The ones in the brown wrappers are my own personal favorite."

Emma made a mental note, though she wasn't much of a sweets-eater herself.

"And behind me we have canned soups of the cream or vegetable variety and, of course, teas." She motioned for Emma to follow her through a doorway to an even smaller room with two walls of upright freezers and refrigerators. "In there we've got cheese, Cumberland sausages, milk, chicken goujons, and some frozen pizzas, while to the other side we've got some canned pasta sauces, mustard, ketchup, and a random assortment of beach and cleaning supplies." She turned back to Emma and shrugged. "It's not much."

"It's actually probably more than I need," Emma said, then with a half-smile added, "I'm not much of a cook."

"Then the post office is the perfect place for you."

"The post office," Emma repeated with a bit more amusement in her voice. "That means something different in America. If I told my friends I went there to get a pizza, they'd probably think me insane."

"To be fair, some of the foodies in England might judge you the same way, but they wouldn't assume you'd chosen postage stamps as a topping instead of pepperoni."

"Do you even have postage stamps?"

"Oh yes, we connect to the Royal Mail services. If you want to send a message back home, you certainly can."

Emma frowned slightly, the expression causing creases around her mouth that shouldn't have been there on someone so young. "I think I'll just look around for now."

Brogan nodded. "Of course."

She tried to busy herself behind the counter, but since she only ever filled in for Nora at the till, she didn't know a thing about stocking shelves or keeping ledgers, which mostly left her stealing glances at Emma as she inched her way along the wall, inspecting packets of noodles and tins of cream of chicken soup before putting them both in her basket.

Brogan would've expected a famous writer to have more expensive tastes. If what they'd said about her buying the cottage sight unseen was true, Emma could certainly afford steaks and fine wine. Why was she currently stocking up on Bolognese sauce in a jar? And if she was used to eating those sorts of foods, why didn't she weigh more? As her father would've said, a stiff Northern wind could blow Emma off her feet and out to sea. Not that she was unattractive. Brogan eyed her from behind. Her long, blond hair hung loose down to the middle of her back, and the slight curve of her waist was one a great many people would love to trace with their fingertips. Her linen pants hung off her hips, but if they'd fit her properly when she'd bought them, Brogan could imagine her cutting a truly alluring figure.

Emma turned around and caught her staring. Brogan looked down at the newspaper in front of her on the counter, only to find Nora had been reading celebrity gossip about the Duke's daughter throwing some lavish party. She wrinkled her nose and glanced back up to see Emma still watching her.

"I thought you were a property manager."

"Not me. My brother's an estate agent. I help him out sometimes."

"And your sister runs the post office, and you help her out sometimes, too?"

"Yes. I sort of have a big family."

"I've noticed."

Brogan grinned. "You haven't even seen the half of it. Literally."

"Do you help all your siblings?"

"Them, my parents, anyone else who needs an extra set of hands around town. I do a lot of jobs. It keeps me from getting too bored."

Emma's eyes narrowed slightly as she regarded Brogan more seriously. The inspection was mildly disconcerting, and Brogan shifted under her gaze. "What?"

"Nothing," Emma said with a slight shake of her head. "You just don't strike me as someone who'd be prone to boredom."

She didn't know whether to take the statement as a compliment or not, but before she had the chance to give it much thought, the door swung open.

"Brogan, I'd almost given up on finding you."

They both turned to see a woman, bringing with her a gust of wind that fanned a few newspapers across the counter. As the woman turned to shut the door against the chill, Brogan struggled to place the voice, not familiar enough to recognize right off, so not someone from town. The face triggered a memory, though, albeit a foggy one. And the smile the woman directed at her hinted at something more than a casual acquaintance.

"You're not an easy woman to pin down. When you weren't at the holiday let office, I went to the pub and the dock."

Brogan did the math: all tourist spots. A holiday home hopper. It wasn't hard to figure out their connection from there. How long would it take for Emma to draw the same conclusion?

"I should've known you'd be working somewhere," the woman continued. "At first I thought you were making excuses to get away last August, but then you kept coming back."

August, and coming back multiple times. The pieces fell into place. A long weekend, a little flat above the Raven, and Julia.

"How have you been, Julia?" Brogan asked, trying to keep her tone polite enough to be warm without giving too much away.

"I've been working hours like yours, only with a wicked commute into London. I survived the gray drudgery of winter only by promising myself I'd take a week away as soon as the first signs of spring struck."

"You picked the right place for some rest and relaxation."

"Hopefully not too much rest." Julia's laugh caused her brunette hair to fall forward across her shoulder. "If you know what I mean."

She did, and apparently now Emma did, too, as she stepped slowly away under the guise of inspecting some teas on the far wall.

"I rented the same place above the pub." Julia plowed on. "The room service was beyond the pale, and the food wasn't bad, either."

Brogan saw Emma's eyebrows go up at the brazen comment, and another flush of embarrassment warmed her skin. She opened her mouth, ready to cut the conversation off, when Julia's smile turned sweet, almost shy. "You will stop by, won't you?"

She looked from Emma, who'd turned her back fully on them now, back to Julia again, details of their nights together coming to the forefront. Sex had filled the majority of them, but there had also been a nice dinner, a movie, a walk on the beach late at night. She wasn't ashamed. If Emma hadn't been in the room, her predominant emotion at seeing Julia again out of the blue would've made her whole week. Why should the presence of a woman she barely knew change anything about the situation? Emma had no right to judge her, and even if she did, she wouldn't be the first or the most important person to do so.

"Of course." Brogan lifted her chin with a little bit of defiance. "I'll be working the bar at the pub tonight until ten."

Julia bit her lip enticingly as she nodded. "Maybe I'll see you there. If not, you'll see me later?"

"I look forward to catching up," Brogan said, and she did.

As Julia waved and walked away, Brogan felt a little twinge of anticipation deep in her stomach. She loved that feeling. It kept her going on long nights behind the bar or cold days on the dock. She liked believing something good, something exciting was right around the corner, and the fleeting nature of those sponta- neous flings gave them their edge. She didn't begrudge anyone their fairy-tale fantasies, but she contented herself with being content and left the happily-ever-afters to the fiction writers of the world.

The thought drew her attention back to watching Emma Volant walk around the store, picking up tins of vegetables or plastic-wrapped biscuits, and the twinge in her stomach transi- tioned from one of anticipation to something a little more wistful.

Emma stared at her tiny freezer jammed with food she didn't have any real desire to eat. She'd bought weeks' worth of meals at the post office in the hopes of not having to go back out again until she felt ready, whenever that would be. But days later, not a single one of her many options held any appeal. And yet she was hungry. Sort of. At least she'd come to recognize the hollow feeling in her stomach as hunger, over the last few months. It was her body's way of reminding her she needed fuel even if she didn't have any appetite to speak of.

She briefly considered walking back to the post office, but what was the use? She'd already basically bought one of everything they had, and she'd run the risk of having to be social again. Odds were good at least one of the McKay women would be working the register, and she'd have to make conversation, not that it had been painful last time. Margaret reminded her so much of her grandmother, the pleasure of those memories had far outweighed the pain of missing her. And seeing Brogan again hadn't brought back nearly as much embarrassment as she'd expected. Not that the two of them had shared the exuberant welcome offered by Julia.

Funny how the name had stuck in her mind though the two of them hadn't been formally introduced. Emma had met so many people over the last few years, and she'd never developed any reliable methodology for remembering their names. She never had any such trouble with her fictional characters. She could flesh them out with ease and memorize even the most trivial aspects of their pasts or family trees without so much as a character sketch, but when it came to publishers, lawyers, agents, cover artists, or even neighbors, she had to keep meticulous notes if she had any hope of telling them apart from strangers on the street. And yet, not only had she remembered the McKays, she suspected she'd never be able to unhear Julia saying, "The room service was beyond the pale, and the food wasn't bad, either."

Maybe it was just the brazenness of the comment that'd stuck with her. She'd never expressed her sexuality so easily, not even when things had been new and exciting with Amalie. Maybe that had been part of the problem, even from the beginning.

The thought tightened her chest with the sharpness of a screw splintering the wood it was supposed to hold in place. She brought the heel of her hand to her sternum as if she could somehow stanch the flow of emotions.

29

A knock at the door shook her from her pain, and she froze as if any movement might alert the person outside to her presence.

The knock sounded again, and this time she could barely make out the sound of voices. Plural.

Her heart beat faster. She did not want to see people. Not now. Not strangers. And they had to be strangers, because she didn't know anyone in town. Except for Brogan and Margaret, and sort of, Nora. Or the kids. Or Julia. But she didn't want to see Julia. Did she want to see the others? She certainly would've preferred Margaret or Brogan to sitting here thinking about how her previous relationship had probably been doomed from the start because she wasn't enough like some woman who'd clearly slept with Brogan.

The doorbell rang. She hadn't even known she had a doorbell. And from the voices growing louder outside, she could now tell there had to be more people on her doorstep than there were people she actually wanted to see. It sounded like hordes of them. Which, once again, made her think of the McKays. Did she really want to hide from them? And if so, would they know she was hiding? Or maybe they'd worry she'd died, since she hadn't gone outdoors in days. Had they come to check on her? Would they kick down the door?

Why did her mind always go to the worst place? Because she was a writer? Why couldn't she write a happier scenario for herself? Or at least something benign, which was more realistic than torch-wielding villagers kicking down doors. With a heavy sigh, she chided herself, both for the hiding and for the way she'd let her mind run away with her. Then in a mix of self-chastisement and rash judgment, she swung the door open.

The sight of four bodies hovering close together on the doorstep greeted her, and she took an involuntary step back, trying to process each person individually. Two of the women had strikingly similar short, gray hair and ruddy complexions, while the next woman was much younger, and if what Margaret had said was true, her red hair marked her as a McKay. Then her eyes fell on the youngest member of the group, a child, or maybe a preteen, wearing a pair of denim overalls and a floppy cap over a mop of red hair.

"Hello," Emma managed to say over the still-accelerated beat of her heart. "Can I help you?"

"Could you come to my school?" the young one asked, in a voice belonging to either a girl or a boy who hadn't yet hit puberty.

The redheaded woman nudged her in the side with an elbow. "She meant to say, 'Welcome to Amberwick.'"

The two older women held out a large platter filled with baked goods, as if making an offering. "We run the book club in town."

"Oh." Emma frowned. A book club. They knew who she was. Or who they thought she was. Her chest tightened at how far their expectations likely fell from her current reality. She briefly considered closing the door in their faces in an attempt to get their disappointment out of the way straight off, but then the aroma of freshly baked flour met her nose, and she gushed, "Those smell amazing."

All of the women seemed to relax at the pronouncement.

"I'm Ciara." The redhead said the name slowly, like *Key-rah.* "And this is my daughter, Regina."

The girl scrunched up her nose and mumbled, "Reggie."

"And this is Diane and Esther," Ciara continued. "We stopped by to share some scones and welcome you to town."

"How sweet of you," Emma said, not sure if it was the sentiment or the scones that had begun to loosen the tension in her shoulders. "Do you do this for every new resident?"

Ciara laughed. "I don't know. We haven't had any new full-time residents in so long it's hard to tell."

"And when we have got new people to town, they've always come because they had families to help them settle in and introduce them around," Diane, or maybe Esther, added. Then they all stared at her as if waiting for her to fill in the blanks. She wasn't so socially awkward that she didn't realize they were trying to pry as politely as they could. They wanted to know her story, especially the part about what had brought her here, but where would she even start? She wasn't hiding anything, but she never knew how much information was too much. Admitting she'd run away from home in shame and heartbreak would certainly be an overshare, so she went with, "I suppose I'm a bit of an anomaly."

A few slight frowns suggested that hadn't been nearly enough to satisfy her new neighbors, so she added, "I had family ties to the area once upon a time, and I guess I felt a pull to return to a place I'd never seen."

"You Americans are so romantic in your ties to where you've come from," Esther said almost dreamily.

"I suppose you all know you came from somewhere else, don't you?" Diane asked. "Whereas we all just assume our people have always lived here unless we have strong evidence otherwise."

"But we all have cousins who have gone to America or Australia or such. Maybe it works in reverse for us," Ciara said.

Even as the grandchild of immigrants, Emma had never given much thought to the traffic patterns across the Atlantic or the idea that she'd moved in the opposite direction of most people, at least historically speaking.

"We didn't mean to disrupt your day," Ciara said, "but if you've got any questions about the area or need a helping hand with anything, we wanted to let you know we've got a friendly community here."

"We all know each other, and most of us were born and raised in the area, so if there's anything you want while you're getting settled in, let us know," Diane or Esther added.

"That's very kind. I can't think of anything right now, but—" Her stomach growled loudly, betraying her most immediate need, and she clasped her hand over her midsection. Blushing, she said, "Well, maybe I would like to try one of those scones."

"Of course!" Esther exclaimed, thrusting the tray into her arms.

"And we didn't know if you had all the trimmings." Diane held up a tote bag. "So, we brought clotted cream and some jams."

"And some Earl Grey tea," Ciara said, nudging her daughter, who quickly produced a purple tin from the large front pouch of her overalls.

Emma looked from one of them to another, both arms already full to the brim, and her head feeling a little light, either from hunger or the delicious smell of the scones right under her nose. She couldn't carry everything, and she couldn't wait a minute longer, so her baser needs won out over her self-protective instincts, and she said, "Do you want to come in for a second?"

"We don't want to intrude," Ciara said quickly, cutting off the others. "Why don't we just help you get these things to your kitchen?"

And with that little bit of permission granted, they all flooded past her, inside.

Emma followed and watched like a guest in her own house as they laid out a spread on her dining-room table. There were little jars filled with brightly colored jams, as well as deep purple, red, orange, and ceramic bowls filled with something that looked like butter, but lighter and not as firm. And there was milk and a few teacups set next to the tin of Earl Grey.

Her mouth watered as she carefully placed the tray of scones in the center, and she might have shoved one in her mouth if Diane hadn't laid a hand on her arm. "You do have a kettle, don't you, love?"

"I do," Emma said hesitantly, "but it's electric. It came with the house, and I've no idea how to use it."

The older two women chuckled. "It's just the flip of a switch. Come along. I'll show you."

She allowed herself to be led into the kitchen, but she didn't have to do anything as Esther filled the kettle with water and set it back on the base, then lifted a small lever at the side. Nothing happened. Frowning, Esther traced the cord with her finger until she reached the wall outlet and flipped another switch, this one white and right next to the plug. The light on the kettle blinked on, and it was as if a light turned on in Emma's brain, too.

"Each outlet in the house has one of those switches on them, don't they?"

"Of course."

"That probably explains why half of my lamps work and the

33

other half don't. I've been searching for light switches at eye level, not outlet switches behind tables and chairs." Then, since she'd already shown her ineptitude, she added, "Would there perhaps be something similar for my hot water?"

"My goodness," Diane said from behind her. "Have you been without hot water since you got here?"

"My shower has a little box on the wall to heat the water," Emma said.

"A power shower, yes."

She nodded at the term she'd never heard until that moment. "But the hot water for the sink and the bathtub . . ." She waited, embarrassed to admit she'd gone through an unreasonable amount of soap trying to counteract the fact that she had no hot water for hand- or dishwashing.

"There's probably a switch for the water heater," Reggie said, hopping up and following the wall around the dining room to where it met the sliding-glass doors to the conservatory. "Here it is."

Emma peeked around the corner and, sure enough, to the edge of her curtains found a small white box on the wall with three switches that each had multiple settings, one for radiators, one for the water heater, and one for a timer.

"You can set your heat to come on at various times, or leave it running, and the same is true for the hot water," Ciara explained. "You can leave it boiling in the tank all the time, or turn it on and off when you need to do some washing or want to soak in a hot bath."

She let slip a small groan. Why hadn't she noticed these controls before? Probably because she hadn't known to look for them.

"You poor thing," Diane tutted. "You've had a time of it, haven't you?"

"Yes, what an ordeal, moving across an ocean by yourself to where you don't know a soul," Esther added.

"And to a house you've never seen," Ciara said without judgment, but it didn't matter.

34

Emma's panic began to rise again. They weren't saying anything she didn't know, but having someone else state those facts only brought home the absurdity of what she'd done. She looked from one of them to another, and then around the house. She had the essential pieces of furniture, but there wasn't a single picture on the wall, not a pillow or throw on the couch. Everything was a bland sort of beige, and she hadn't bothered to unpack any of the meager personal effects she'd brought from home. She didn't even know how to turn on the hot water.

What must they all think of her?

As if reading her mind, Reggie smiled broadly and said, "I think you're brave."

She shook her head, almost frantically, unable to speak around the knot of emotions in her throat.

"Yes, you are, dear," Esther said, as the kettle began to gurgle behind them. "You're quite the adventurer."

"Come on now," Diane urged quietly, placing a gentle hand on her shoulder and guiding her into a chair. "I can't even imagine the jet lag and the disorientation that come with a move like you've had. You must be exhausted."

She nodded. She was tired, but for so many more reasons than jet lag. Shame settled over her again. These women had no doubt come searching for a famous author, someone creative, glamorous, engaging. What she would've given to be that person, both for their benefit and her own. Instead, she'd revealed herself to be a barely functioning excuse for a bestseller. Now they were all making excuses for her out of kindness or embarrassment, which was more compassion than her wife, or rather ex-wife, had managed to do on her way out the door.

"Let's fetch you a cuppa and get out of your hair," Diane said, and Esther whisked one of the teacups they'd brought into the kitchen.

"Here." Reggie pushed the plate of scones toward her. "Put the clotted cream on first."

"No," Diane and Esther both called in unison, then laughed. "We put the jam on first, then the cream."

Reggie stood behind them, shaking her head in mock horror, and Emma smiled at her, a genuine smile that stretched her cheeks in unfamiliar ways.

"It doesn't matter how you do it," Ciara said lightly, then added with a grin, "so long as you judge people who do it differently."

"That's a true British hobby," Esther said, setting the tea in front of her, "which is why we won't stay around long enough to see how you take your tea. We wouldn't want to think less of you for using too much milk until we get to know you better."

With that she patted Emma's arm again and turned to go. The others all took the hint and moved toward the door.

"I left our phone numbers on a notepad on the kitchen counter in case you need help with anything else around the house," Diane said as she left.

Emma started to stand, but Ciara waved her off. "No need to get up. We managed to barge in on our own. We can find our way out. I'm sure we'll meet again when you're all rested."

"We all go to the Raven every Friday before tea," Reggie said. "You should come and talk about visiting my school."

"Reg," Ciara warned, as she wrapped an arm around her daughter's shoulder and directed her toward the door.

"Nice to meet you," Reggie called, and closed the door behind them.

"It was nice to meet you, too," Emma replied, though she doubted they could hear her now. Then again, she hadn't made the statement out of politeness, so much as her own surprise.

As she split a scone in half and reached for the red jam, she pondered the fact that she had enjoyed meeting them. She'd enjoyed having some life in her new home. Despite Diane's last comments about the tea, she hadn't felt judged at all. She spread some clotted cream on one half of the scone then put the jam on top, before turning to the other half of the scone and assembling it in reverse order. Surveying them both, she smiled remembering the horror on Reggie's face and picked up the one with cream on the bottom first.

As she bit into the scone, all other thoughts vanished from her mind, no memories, no comparisons, no words. Closing her eyes and tilting her face toward the light streaming in from the conservatory, she basked in the glory of her scone. It melted in her mouth, the flavors mingling—creamy, buttery, sweet, and soft. Maybe soft wasn't exactly a flavor, but the scone made her certain it should be.

She shoved the entire half in her mouth in a series of near ravenous bites, then greedily reached for the other. She tried to slow down enough to notice the variations between the jam and clotted cream layering, but she could tell no difference once the scone passed her lips. She didn't know which version she preferred. All she could process in the moment of complete food abandon was that no matter how she applied the topping, the scone tasted amazing. Like, life-alteringly delicious. If her mouth hadn't been full, she might have laughed a little at the hyperbole, but nothing felt like an overstatement in that moment, because for the first time in over six months, she was taking pleasure in eating something.

Chapter Three

A hand snaked its way up Brogan's bare back and gave the tired muscles at her shoulder a tantalizing squeeze. She closed her eyes and leaned back into the touch.

"Are you sure you have to work tonight?"

She sighed, knowing the answer was yes, but she didn't want to say the word any more than Julia wanted to hear it.

"We could call down for room service and watch a movie . . . or not."

Mostly it had been a whole lot of "or not" for the last week, though they had watched a banal superhero movie and shared breakfast in bed on more than one occasion. Most of all she'd enjoyed the rare occurrence of waking up with the same person more than two mornings in a row, but their time together was coming to an end. Julia would go back to London the next morning, and Brogan would miss her. Or at least she'd miss having someone around to do things with, other than work. She and Julia didn't seem to share any real interests other than sex and food, but that was something. And she wasn't likely to have that again for at least a month when tourist traffic began to pick up for the season. Of course, when the tourist traffic picked up, so would her many jobs.

And still, none of those facts changed the reality that she had to go downstairs, both to tend bar and to keep herself from getting too comfortable in the bed of a woman who'd be gone tomorrow. "It's Friday, which means Friday Club at the pub for locals."

Julia lay back on the bed. "Sounds thrilling."

Brogan smiled and pulled on her jeans, knowing Julia wouldn't find the village tradition enjoyable in the least. All the inside jokes and small-town gossip would be lost on her, and even if she could follow along, she'd find the inner dealings of their lives to be trite and tedious. In a way that made everything easier because it meant Brogan didn't have to feel guilty about not inviting her.

Grabbing her white Oxford shirt off the floor, she turned the sleeves right side out as she searched for her bra.

"What time do you get off?" Julia asked, then snorted and sat up. "Off work, I mean."

"Pub closes at ten, but I'll start cleaning up a little earlier if no one's in after we stop serving food around eight. With any luck I'll be able to turn the key in the lock and sprint right upstairs."

"And what if I order room service before then?" Julia asked, her voice coy. "Would you bring it up to me?"

"Maybe, depends on how busy the bar is."

"And what if I promised to be naked when I open the door?"

"Then I'll be sure to send Charlie and tell him it's an early birthday present," Brogan teased, then laughed as she located her bra under the duvet they'd kicked off the bed. "Really, though, don't make any assumptions about room service tonight. I can't make any promises."

Julia fell back to the pillows. "No promises beyond coming back here for one more night, right?"

Brogan checked her reflection in the mirror by the door before stepping back to kiss her once more. "Aye, I can promise that one if you can."

Julia gave her a little shove. "I suppose we'll both take what we can get while we can get it."

The sentiment was still echoing through Brogan's ears as she checked the taps of real ale behind the bar. Taking and getting were fluid concepts in her life, as fluid as the tides in the estuary and as seasonal as the company she kept. She rarely gave the pat-

39

terns much more thought than she'd give her work calendar, but hearing Julia put things so bluntly on the eve of her departure tweaked something inside her she couldn't quite place.

"Hey, stranger." Ciara pushed through the door to the pub, and a slew of children huddled in behind her. "Where's Charlie?"

Brogan shrugged. "Haven't seen him today, but I'm sure he'll be along any minute. Not like he's got anything better to do on a Friday night."

"Especially when I owe him for babysitting two weeks in a row," Ciara said with a smile. She turned to the kids. "You lot can grab some crisps and go down to the park if you want."

A cheer went up from the three younger ones, who didn't even shed their coats before taking their snacks and freedom on the run, but Reg hung around.

"You getting too big for the park?" Brogan asked.

Reggie shook her head. "I'm going to wait for Lily and James to get here."

"If they're counting on their dad to drive them, you might be waiting awhile. Archie's never shown up at a reasonable time for anything in his life."

"You'd think he lived in London instead of five miles up the road," Ciara said, shedding her coat. "I haven't seen him in over a month."

Brogan rolled her eyes and put on an air of false importance. "You know his work's important. You know he's very busy."

Ciara snorted. "You know he thinks he's the Duke himself instead of one of his employees."

The door to the pub swung open again, stopping them short like a pair of girls afraid their older brother might have heard them having a go at him, but it was only Diane and Esther bustling in ahead of Tom.

"Good evening," Brogan called and moved to the tap, pouring an ale for Tom and two ciders for the women.

"What's the good word?" Brogan asked, leaning on the bar as she passed the pint glasses to the regulars in the corner booth.

"The same two words over and over again for three days," Tom groused. "Emma Volant."

40

Brogan's heart gave an involuntary jump she didn't want to examine. "Oh?"

"They bombarded her earlier in the week."

"We didn't bombard," Ciara said calmly. "We went over to welcome her to town."

"And good thing we did," Esther added. "The poor darling might have sat there in the dark and cold, half-starved for weeks."

"Half-starved?" Brogan asked, remembering the sacks of food Emma had purchased.

"Have you seen her? She's wasting away," Diane said, "and her stomach growled so loud I thought she had a dog behind her."

"What do you expect?" Reg jumped in. "She can't work a kettle or a hot water tank or her light switches."

"Wait, how many of you went over there?" Brogan asked. A picture began to form in her mind of half the town barging in on Emma. She didn't know the woman well, but from their limited encounters, she didn't seem like the kind of person who'd enjoy impromptu visitors.

"Just the four of us," Ciara said, "and don't you start in on us, too. Between our spouses and our mother, we've heard enough about not overwhelming our new famous neighbor. But you weren't there. You didn't see her. She's already overwhelmed. We'd offer the same help to any new person in town."

"Exactly what I told Tom," Diane said. "I know we aren't supposed to treat her like she's special because she's rich and famous, but I'm not going to treat her any worse because of those things, either."

"You told her you ran the local book club," Tom said. "Did you mention the book club didn't exist until she moved to town?"

Brogan laughed.

"Look, I'm as game as anybody about getting her to stay and bring us a little bit of notoriety beyond beachcombers and property flippers," he said, laying both his hands on the dark

41

oak table, "but let's not pretend we're vying for sainthood here."

"Not sainthood." Esther clucked. "Basic human decency. I'm telling you, rich or not, that girl is lost. She's scared. She's got big, wounded eyes, and a smile too tentative for someone so pretty and talented."

"And young," Diane added. "No one her age should look so bone-tired."

Brogan couldn't argue with the hint of protectiveness she heard in their voices. In fact, she felt a wave of relief at knowing she wasn't the only one experiencing a surge in those instincts when it came to Emma. Maybe she inspired them in everyone she met.

Just then Charlie walked in, his jacket open at the front and his hair tousled from the wind.

"What'd I miss?" he asked. He turned to Ciara. "Aside from two weeks' worth of babysitting money."

"It's good to see you too, baby brother." Ciara pulled a few bills from her purse and handed them to Brogan instead. "Take whatever you need to cover his tab, and then pass the rest over to him."

"Ha ha," Charlie said sarcastically, and snatched the bills from Brogan. "I paid the tab last Friday, and I picked up some groundskeeping work in Newpeth on Monday, so I've been eating all of Archie's food all week."

"Ah, good on ya, Charles," Brogan said, with a smile and the hope that her fridge wouldn't be empty by the time she got home tomorrow.

"Wait." Ciara held up her hand. "Why didn't you know that?"

"Huh?"

"You haven't seen Charlie all week? You live together."

"Busted." Charlie laughed and pulled a stool toward the corner of the bar closest to them. "You want to try to dance your way out of this, or should I spill?"

Brogan gave a pointed glance at Reggie, and Ciara got the hint. "Regina, please go check on your sister and brothers."

Reg knew better than to object when her mother used her full

42

name, but that didn't stop her from scowling on her way out the door. All the adults sat quietly until the kid was out of earshot, but Tom raised his eyebrows suggestively as he asked, "Did tourist season start early this year?"

"Come off it. A friend of mine is up from London. We've been catching up is all."

"Not catching up on sleep, if those red rings around your eyes are any indication," Esther said, causing her to look away, and everyone else to laugh.

"All week, Brogan?" Ciara asked with a mix of disbelief and amusement. "Where do you find the stamina?"

"Says the woman with four kids."

"Runs in the family, eh?" Tom asked, turning to Charlie.

He shook his head. "They must've used up all the suave parts of the gene pool before I came along. Brogan has more luck with women than I can even dream of."

"Aw." Esther patted his cheek. "You've got a good face, Charlie. Brogan, why don't you help your brother out?"

"He's beyond help."

Charlie laughed. "Come on, Brogan. Tell us your secrets. Who's the girl? How'd you win her over? What can you possibly do to keep women hopping trains all the way from London to spend a whole week in the Raven?"

"Yeah," Diane said. "I actually want to know the answer to that question, too. Help us live vicariously through you."

Desperate to dodge having to answer, Brogan made a giant leap for a redirect. "I thought you were living vicariously through Emma Volant. What happened to helping her find herself and save the town from oblivion and holiday let agents?"

"Nice try," Ciara said. She sipped her cider.

"Actually." Tom drew out the word. "She might be onto something. If the Volant woman is as sad as you say, and we want to get her out and about, but not so out and about that she leaves, why not find her a local fella to lift her spirits and put down some roots?"

Diane and Esther both smiled at each other, then at Charlie, but Ciara held up her hand. "Don't even think about it, Charlie. I read some articles about Ms. Volant before we went over there. Not to snoop, mind you, just for conversation starters, and she's very recently divorced . . . from a woman."

Everyone sat back in their chairs for a few seconds as the same idea seemed to dawn on them simultaneously, and then one by one they slowly turned to smile at Brogan.

Her chest tightened, and her face flamed as the implication of the conspiratorially hopeful gazes settled over her. Finally, she spit out the only word she could manage. "No."

"She's pretty," Diane said.

"And talented," Esther added.

"I think she's probably very sweet." Ciara's tone made it clear that was a more important criteria for a big sister.

"Who cares?" Tom laughed. "She's rich."

Brogan shook her head. Not that she could argue with any of their reasoning. In less than ten minutes together, she knew Emma Volant was everything they said, and likely much more, which meant this was one fantasy she wouldn't entertain. "No thanks."

"Why not?" Diane whined. "You're the only lesbian in the village. You're attractive enough. You come from a local family. Sure, you've got a history of flighty women, but they obviously like whatever you do with them well enough to make them want to spend time with a small-town bartender and whatnot."

Diane's lukewarm description of her didn't exactly bolster her confidence. Emma was pretty, talented, and rich, while Brogan's most outstanding feature was being the only out lesbian in a five-mile radius.

"Come on," Tom prodded. "You can woo the woman. It's not like you've got anything better going on."

"Thanks for the ringing endorsement," Brogan mumbled, then shaking off the sting that always accompanied such backhanded compliments, she added more clearly, "I'm not in the market for a serious relationship, and I'm pretty sure Emma Volant isn't either."

Everyone laughed, and Tom let out a low whistle.

"What?"

"Famous last words," Diane said with a shake of her head. "Famous last words."

Emma's laptop was open. That was something. She hadn't written in months. She wasn't writing now, either, but at least she'd had the intention of doing so, which constituted a step forward in some sense. She'd gone as far as opening a blank document so she could write something immediately if an idea struck her, and just because it hadn't happened immediately didn't mean it never would. Or that's what she told herself to try to hold the panic at bay as she walked through her yard.

"Garden." She corrected her thoughts aloud. Like the sunroom was a conservatory, the "yard" should now be called a "garden." And in the case at hand, the new vocabulary shouldn't be hard, because her garden was unlike any yard she'd ever had. A little stone path led from her back door to a small patio decked out with a wrought-iron table and chairs. From there the stones skimmed along some low ground cover and toward a set of paver-topped stairs that ran down the center of three terraced levels until it formed a *T* at a long row of high hedges constituting a bushy privacy barrier.

As she stepped down onto the lowest level, a throaty little click and croak sounded to her right, nearly startling her out of her skin. She clutched her chest and bit her lip to hold back a scream as a huge pheasant took flight. Its large wings flapped close enough for the breeze they created to rustle her hair, and the bird came to rest atop a small maroon shed Emma had barely taken note of before. The pheasant was bigger than any bird she'd ever seen in the wild, its body as big around as a bowling ball, and its brown and black mottled wings probably two feet across when fully spread. The camouflage and the serious glint in the bird's eye made Emma suspect she'd disturbed a female in a nest.

"I'm not going to hurt you," she whispered. "It's only, you're on top of my shed. And now that I've seen it, I sort of want to peek inside."

The hen cocked her head to the side but didn't shift on her perch as Emma inched closer. Opening the door slowly, she glanced in, then back up at the bird. "See, there's room for both of us."

As her eyes adjusted to the dim light, she could make out a few, mostly barren, shelves along the rough-hewn walls. The shed was barely tall enough for her to stand upright in, and if she positioned herself in the exact center, she'd be able to touch each wall. There were a few cans of paint stacked on the floor, and a handful of garden tools in one corner. She moved the shovel and a rake aside to grab a set of hedge clippers, then exited the shed to the great displeasure of the pheasant, who took one look at the long blades in her hand and croaked loudly as it flew off in a huff.

"These weren't for you. I only wanted to trim the hedges," Emma called fruitlessly, then shook her head. Why was she trying to convince a bird of her banal intentions? Probably because that was the longest conversation she'd had in nearly a week? Sighing heavily at what her life had become, she set to work snipping errant branches off the tall hedges at the back of her property.

It started with small clips, but the more she cleared away, the deeper the branches went. She found something therapeutic in slowly peeling back layers of twigs to reveal their source. Along the way, she scooped aside some clumps of dead leaves with her hand, and at one point she cut away a particularly stubborn branch to find it completely wrapped in a withered vine. She tugged and pulled like a magician emptying his pocket of never-ending handkerchiefs until finally the last of the vine broke free, bringing with it a ball of sticks and leaves that must have been acting as a kind of plug, because once she popped it loose, a great beam of sun came streaming through the hedge and illuminated her feet.

She peeked inside tentatively, as if spying on her neighbors, but instead of other houses and gardens, she saw only a small clearing, bordered on every side by hedgerows as tall as her own. And there in the center sat a child, frozen and startled, holding an open book in her lap.

"Reggie?"

The girl nodded slowly, then swallowed hard before saying, "I'm sorry."

Emma frowned. "Why?"

"For being in your garden."

"Is that my garden?"

"I don't know." Reggie shrugged and stood. "You're the only other person who I've ever seen here."

"Oh, well . . ." Emma didn't think the land belonged to her, but she hadn't paid much attention to the property survey she got when she bought the house. "I'm not sure it's mine, but if it is, I'm glad someone's put it to good use."

"Really?" Reggie asked suspiciously.

"Of course. What would be better than a secret reading garden?"

The girl finally smiled. "I bet you read a lot."

"Not as much as I used to as a kid," she admitted almost wistfully. "But maybe now that I know I have such a wonderful place to hide, I'll make more of an effort."

"Why would you want to hide?"

Emma shifted her feet awkwardly while keeping her face steady enough to maintain eye contact through the hedge. "I suppose I didn't mean hide in the physical sense as much as in the . . ." What was she supposed to say to a child to explain the concepts of hiding in an emotional sense? "Well, possibly for the same reasons you do."

"You have too many brothers and sisters?"

She laughed, then caught herself at the look of confusion on the girl's face. "No, maybe not the exact same reason."

"The little kids bug me all the time," Reggie offered, "and the bigger boys like Liam and Callum don't want to let me play rugby with them because I'm too small to hit hard. And the girls never want to play in the estuary or climb the big hills."

Emma nodded. She understood. She may not have had the

same experiences while growing up, but she did know how it felt to feel out of place and isolated, even in a crowd.

"And if I lie around at the house, my mum always gives me chores."

"That's more along the lines of what I'd hide from," Emma said honestly. "I have lots of work I'm supposed to do, but I can't seem to make myself do it, and if I stay inside, I feel guilty for not doing it."

"Then you should come outside and read sometime," Reggie said excitedly. "No one even knows where you are, so they can't tell you to do something else."

The thought appealed to her more than it probably should have. "And what should I read?"

"There are so many good books!" Reggie beamed. "Have you read *Harry Potter*?"

"Absolutely," Emma enthused. "Hermione is my favorite."

"I like Ron," Reg said. "Sometimes when people are trying to be mean they call my family the Weasleys, you know, 'cause of our red hair and there are a lot of us, but I don't mind. I like the Weasleys."

Emma's heart gave a little jump of affection for a child's ability to find strength in something others tried to treat as a weakness.

"But if you like Hermione, you have to like Annabeth Chase. She's in the Percy Jackson books. Did you read those?"

"No. I think they might have been after my time."

"You should catch up on them. They are exciting, and there are demigods, which is sort of like magic. Hey, do you have any magic in your books?"

"Hmm, not magic, exactly," Emma explained, "but I do have a series with some time travel."

"Like Dr. Who?"

She smiled. "With women, and without the TARDIS, but they aren't really for kids."

"Yeah, that's what my mum said. I mean, I know a lot of big words, though."

"I don't doubt it," Emma agreed. "You'd probably just be a little bored. They have a lot of history and a lot of mushy love parts."

Reg wrinkled her nose as if she found the idea distasteful, and at this point in her life, Emma had to agree, which was probably why she was out here talking to a child rather than writing her next book.

"I like adventure stories," Reggie continued. "Aunt Brogan got me this one. It's called *Hatchet*, and it's about a boy who gets plane-wrecked in the woods and has to learn how to survive. Aunt Brogan could do that, and she said she could teach me."

Emma smiled again at the adoration in the child's voice as she spoke of Brogan.

"She promised when the weather gets warmer she will take me camping on the beach so we can make our own fire, or maybe we can sleep on a sailboat and catch our own fish for dinner. Aunt Brogan has done all that before, 'cause she's good at, like, everything."

Emma had no inclination to argue. She'd seen nothing to suggest Brogan wasn't everything her niece thought her to be. The memories of Julia throwing herself at Brogan hinted at skills Emma only hoped Reggie couldn't imagine. Then again, as she surveyed the girl's oversized overalls and canvas cap, she wondered if someday Reg would find even more in common with her aunt. The thought that Reggie would soon find her place in the world, and that when she did she'd have someone like Brogan to show her that was okay, made Emma happy. Her own family had been supportive enough when she'd come out, but they'd all been a little baffled. Even she'd been confused when her newfound community had so many rules and labels and social norms she always tripped over. With someone like Brogan as a role model, hopefully Reggie could be more comfortable in her own skin from an earlier age.

"So, what are you doing out here?" Reggie asked, making Emma suspect she'd zoned out a little bit.

She held up the clippers. "I'm gardening. Or I'm trying to

garden anyway, but I don't seem very good at it. I managed only to chop a hole in my hedge."

"I can help. I'm good at outdoors stuff."

"I don't know. I mean, I don't even know what most of these plants are, much less what I want to do with them all."

"I know a lot of them. Brogan used to tend this garden when it was for holiday renters. I came with her a few times. She told me the names of things. I know I can do a good job."

Emma's chest tightened uncomfortably. She liked Reggie, she really did, and she understood her loneliness and her eagerness to please. Maybe that's also why she didn't want to get too attached. Plus, she'd have to supervise Reggie, and then she'd feel responsible for her, and she wasn't sure she had the emotional energy for that these days.

As if reading her mind, Reggie's exuberance faded. "I won't be a bother."

Emma sighed at the sadness she heard there and the earnestness she saw in the big green eyes staring up at her. "I suppose you might be able to help with a few of the smaller jobs, like weeding or clearing things out, until I decide what I want to do with the big picture."

Reggie's wide smile returned, but her voice remained serious as she pledged, "I promise I won't mess up."

"I believe you," Emma said with equal solemnity. She only wished she could make the same promise.

Chapter Four

Brogan jumped back from the shelves she'd been straightening as a ball of energy wrapped in denim exploded through the front door of the post office. Several rolls of paper towels toppled to the floor. "Whoa."

"Aunt Brogan!" Reggie exclaimed. "What kind of roses did you plant in Emma Volant's garden?"

She stared at the child blankly. While she understood all the words individually, she couldn't manage to put them together in the context of the moment or the speaker. "What?"

"The roses you planted for Emma Volant."

She shook her head. Had Reggie somehow got pulled into some village plan to play collective matchmaker? "Sorry, kiddo. I never gave that woman any roses. Or any other woman I can recall."

Reggie rolled her eyes. "I was with you. When I was like, seven, and we planted rosebushes along the little wooden fence things by the shed."

"The trellises," Brogan offered. "Geeze, how do you remember things like that?"

"Because I *have* to," Reggie said, rummaging through a rucksack. "I'm going to be her gardener now. She said I could. She doesn't know how, so I got a book from the library on how to take care of plants, but some of them have different rules. I need to know what kind she has."

For emphasis, Reggie produced a large gardening book and slapped it on the shelf left empty by the cascading paper towels. "You have to show me what you planted in Emma's garden."

Brogan bit the inside of her cheek to keep from laughing. Of course Reggie had got a book on gardening to help Emma. It wouldn't even occur to her that doing so was odd for a ten-year-old. She was smart and curious with a strong desire to please. Brogan wanted to affirm her for all those good qualities by telling her she'd do fine, but that kind of enthusiasm could also lead to Emma's garden getting hacked to bits while the poor woman had to babysit an inquisitive child.

Rubbing her chin for dramatic effect, she said, "You know, I'm not sure I remember everything we did over there, but if I saw the plants, I could probably figure it out. Why don't I walk down there with you to refresh my memory?"

"You won't do the work, though, will you? I can do it."

"I wouldn't dream of it."

Reggie nodded, then grabbed her hand. "Then let's go."

"Hold up. Aunt Nora's in the storeroom. Let me tell her I'm heading out."

"I'll meet you down there."

Before Brogan could stop her, Reggie sprinted off again. Laughing, she shook her head and went quickly to inform Nora she'd see her tomorrow, but in the forty seconds it took her to get out the door, Reggie had disappeared down the street and likely into Emma's garden.

Hopefully the kid wouldn't be too excited to remember to mention Brogan was joining her. She certainly didn't want a replay of the last time she'd surprised Emma at her house. Thankfully when she strolled up the front pavement to the Volant cottage, Emma met her at the door. Maybe it was the lack of fright, or perhaps the jet lag had finally faded, but Emma appeared more put-together than Brogan had ever seen her. Which didn't mean formal, as she leaned up against the door jamb in gray sweatpants and a cream-colored Aran jumper that hung loosely from her frame, but her hands were steady as she cupped a mug of tea, and her blue eyes had lost both their dull sheen and the dark rings encircling them.

"Reggie said you'd be joining us," Emma stated.

"I don't want to intrude, but I thought it wouldn't hurt to keep an eye on what she's doing," Brogan said. "I promise we'll keep out of your way."

"She's no bother," Emma said with a hint of hopefulness in her voice that might have been forced. "I'm the one who should stay out of your way. I've had only about a handful of plants in my whole life, and none of them lived what anyone could call a long or healthy life."

Brogan smiled. "Everyone's got to start somewhere."

"Brogan!" Reggie called from somewhere behind the house. "We have work to do."

Emma lifted the tea to her pale lips, but Brogan saw them curl up a little behind the mug.

"I'd better get to it."

Emma stepped aside, and Brogan caught the scent of soap— clean, fresh, simple—as she passed, and the idea of someone as rich as Emma forgoing expensive perfumes made her stomach feel warm.

"I brought some paper and a pencil," Reggie called before Brogan had even made it through the conservatory. "I want to make a map of the garden and write in the names of all the plants so I can know which ones I need to learn about."

She nodded, once again impressed by the thought Reggie had put into her plan. "Okay then, let's divide the rectangle into three, to represent the three levels of terrace, then draw a line down the middle for the stairs."

Reggie leaned on a little wrought-iron table, causing Brogan to notice the open laptop beside her. The screen was dark, but for how long? Was Emma working? Writing? If so, their intrusion seemed even less advisable.

She turned back to the woman standing in the full light of the conservatory now. "We're not interrupting, are we?"

"Not at all." Emma gestured dismissively toward the computer.

"Sadly, there's nothing there to interrupt. Go about your map-making. It'll do me good to hear something other than my own thoughts for a while."

The statement raised more questions than answers for Brogan, but even if she'd had the inclination to give them voice, she didn't have the time, as Reggie straightened up, pointed to the nearest ground cover, and said, "That one's first. What kind of grass is it?"

"Chives," Brogan said, falling back on something she knew for sure. "Wild chives. They've spread a little farther than they were meant to. We could cut them back a bit, and then we'd all smell like sour cream and chive crisps for days."

Reggie was too studious to appreciate the joke. "And what's next to it?"

"Lavender," Brogan said, then cheekily added, "the English variety, which means stronger and heartier than the French kind. I think it smells better, too."

"Really?" Emma asked, stepping forward, the first hint of genuine interest Brogan had ever heard in her voice.

"I might be biased. My last name isn't as French-sounding as *Volant*, but I love our version of lavender." Reaching down, she stripped a few of the dry buds from the dark sprigs and held her hand out toward Emma. "The stems are woodier and stronger in order to survive the winters up here, but that gives the smell of the lavender a little strength too. It's not as floral, a little earthier, but I find the combination more soothing."

Emma leaned close, closed her eyes, and took a slow, deep inhale. The subtle creases in her brow smoothed out, and a slight pink of pleasure gave color to the normal pallor of her cheeks. Also, the temperature went up a notch outside, or maybe just inside Brogan.

Reggie must have noticed the transformation, too, but didn't seem nearly as transfixed as she blurted out, "If you like lavender, we could plant some more, maybe where Aunt Brogan said to cut back the chives."

"I would love more lavender," Emma said sincerely. "Actually, if you could . . . Never mind."

"What?" Brogan asked.

"Nothing. I got a little carried away in my mind. It happens a lot, sort of runs away with me."

"Nothing wrong with that. It's your garden. This is your space to let ideas run as wild as you want."

Emma's blue eyes held hers for a few seconds before she looked back toward the ground, but the connection was long enough for Brogan to glimpse something alluring behind the blankness at their forefront. Something was stirring inside the woman before her, and she found herself almost wishing it wasn't simply a desire to garden.

"Could we do a row of lavender all along the patio here? Then every time I step out my back door or write at my little table, I can be surrounded by something soothing."

"Sure we can!" Reggie said with renewed enthusiasm, then turned to Brogan. "We can, right?"

She nodded thoughtfully. "Actually, it's about the perfect time of year for replanting lavender. A week, maybe two, will put us in the heart of spring soil temperatures. We might even be able to work from the shoots you already have. Clipping them back should help them to grow stronger and spread out. Counterintuitive, I know, but sometimes when you make a living organism feel threatened, they dig deeper and reach farther than they would if they felt comfortable."

Emma's lips parted slightly, and her chest rose slowly as if she were trying to take in more air.

"Great." Reggie scribbled some notes. "Let's go down another level."

Brogan followed along. What else could she do? She was there to keep an eye on Reggie. She was there as a gardener. She wasn't friends with Emma. She didn't have any right to pry, not about what made her so sad, and not about what Brogan could possibly do to bring back the smile she longed to see.

£ £ £

Brogan followed Reggie around the garden calmly and patiently, explaining what each plant was along with when and how it could be trimmed or transplanted safely. The extent of her knowledge impressed Emma, even if it didn't exactly surprise her. Much like Reggie, Brogan seemed to notice things, not that they'd had much of a chance for her to test the theory, but the way Brogan's green eyes swept over a room or a person simply gave Emma the sense she saw more than someone else might. She sometimes found that suspicion mildly unsettling, but never quite unpleasant. And now, in the sunshine, amid stems that might someday bear roses, she felt a warmth of gratitude for the McKay women who spoke of the coming spring with such certainty she almost believed them.

"Okay, that's all," Reggie declared as they reached the bottom back corner of the garden. "I have a complete map of the garden exactly how it is now."

"Perfect," Brogan said, clasping her on the shoulder. "All done for today."

"For you maybe," Reggie said stiffly.

Both Brogan and Emma raised their eyebrows at her.

"Now I need to make a map of how we want the garden to look when we're done."

"Right, but can't you do that another day or from home?"

"It won't be the same," Reggie said matter-of-factly, "but I can do this part on my own. You can leave."

Brogan folded her arms across her chest and cocked her chin to the side. "Dismissed. I see how it is. And what if I don't want to leave? What if I want to stay and watch a great landscape artist at work?"

Reggie sighed heavily, causing a strand of copper hair to flutter under the bill of her cap. "You're trying to babysit me."

"What? I'm wounded." Brogan clutched at her heart and laid on a thick Irish brogue. "My favorite niece, my own spitting image, the lass I taught to hold a cricket bat and spit off the river bridge like the boys accuses me of ulterior motives."

Reggie's eyes narrowed at Brogan as if she was ninety percent sure she was teasing, but not certain enough to laugh. She then turned to Emma with the same green eyes Brogan had used to examine her earlier, and Emma couldn't bear it.

"I think you're off to a marvelous start," she gushed, then noting the surprise on Brogan's face, added, "I don't think you need any supervision at all, but I do have a few things I want to ask Brogan about the house. Would you mind if we popped into the conservatory and had a chat while you work?"

"No," Reggie said, her shoulders a little straighter. "I don't mind."

Brogan gave the bill of her cap a little tug as she turned to go. "The student becomes the master."

Emma followed her as she headed in through the conservatory and out of Reggie's hearing range. "Would you like a cup of tea?"

"Why don't I take a look at whatever you need help with around the house first."

Emma shook her head. "Sorry, I don't have a list. I merely made an excuse to let you stay without hurting Reggie's pride."

Brogan smiled warmly. "I suspected as much, but then I remembered hearing something about you not knowing how to use your hot water tank and didn't want to take anything for granted."

Emma's face flushed. "Does the whole town know?"

"Only a few locals with a strong desire to be helpful," Brogan said casually. "None of them as helpful as Reggie, though. She's a great kid—lots of passion, and a real instinct to be useful, but she's also a bit like a puppy. If you throw the ball, she'll keep coming back with it for more."

She liked the cute analogy, and the gentle affection with which Brogan made the comparison. "I don't mind having her over. I mean, maybe if I were on a deadline or a writing binge, but neither of those things seem on my horizon unless some of her youthful energy rubs off on me."

"You like kids?"

"I don't have much experience with them. They've never found me very interesting, I suppose, and maybe they've never held much interest for me, but then again I've never met a ten-year-old with a passion for reading and gardening."

Brogan's shoulders relaxed, and her smile took on a hint of pride. "I love all my nieces and nephews. Every one of them has a personality all their own and is special in some way, but I've got a soft spot for Reg. She's always been a bit out of the box. She wants to break things down, figure out what makes them work, and once she starts, she doesn't stop until she's got a solid grasp. I want to protect that instinct, make sure she gets a chance to explore until she finds what she's looking for."

Some of the tension that always knotted Emma's chest loosened. "I guess we both see bits of ourselves in her in different ways. I wonder if that's how parents feel every day."

"My parents had enough kids to see themselves somewhere in the lot of us. I don't know if they found the likeness comforting, though."

"I've never even considered how terrifying and affirming that must be. I'm an only child."

"Lucky you." Brogan's laugh clearly indicated she'd made the comment in jest, but Emma didn't laugh along. As she glanced out of the conservatory windows to watch Reg work, she ruminated on the fact that while the girl might second-guess herself or her place in the world at times, she'd never have to doubt the love of the wide support system, that was put in place before she was ever born. She and Brogan would never have to face anything alone.

"Did I say something wrong?" Brogan asked softly.

"No. I'm sorry. I was thinking about the way your family all help each other. I've been here only a few weeks, and I've already seen you in the act of supporting each other at least three times."

"It's what families do."

"When you have them. I'm the only child of two only children. Not that I went unloved as a child. My grandmother especially doted on me, but she's gone now, and so is my father. I don't have much family left. There's no built-in safety net there."

"Family doesn't have to be based on blood. It can be something you build with people who love you, who cheer for you, who celebrate the ups and downs."

The knot not only returned to her chest, but worked its way up into her throat. Once upon a time, she'd shared Brogan's idealist views on family of choice. She'd even thought she'd built exactly the type of bonds Brogan spoke of. She'd been wrong on at least the latter count, which made her suspect she'd been mistaken on the former as well.

"Hey," Brogan whispered. "It's going to be okay."

Emma blinked away the haze and searched those green eyes. "What is?"

"Whatever is making you so sad right now," Brogan said softly.

Emma was slammed with simultaneous instincts to argue with her and to throw herself into her arms, begging Brogan to show her how. Both impulses were likely inappropriate to act on, and before she'd found some middle ground, Reggie trotted up to the back door, waving her new map.

"I've got it." She beamed proudly. "See?"

Emma accepted the paper she had thrust at her and scanned the pencil drawing of boxes and circles filled with the names of plants. Lavender around the top, an array of shrubs that would flower at different times through the middle, and varieties of roses around the perimeter, which would add flashes of color to the hedgerows. She could almost visualize the bright vista against the ocean backdrop as it reflected the summer sun. She could sit out at the table and listen to the waves, smelling the lavender, and . . . the ice in her core melted noticeably at the thought. Summer. Ten minutes ago, she hadn't even been sure of a spring, and now she was already making plans for the summer.

"Do you like it?" Reggie asked, her hope laced with an uncertainty Emma hadn't heard in her before.

"I love it." She held the drawing close to her chest. "Can I keep it?"

Reggie lifted her little chin and squared her shoulders. "Sure. I mean, I made it for you."

"And how much should I pay you for your work?"

"Nothing." Brogan cut in quickly. "We don't help our neighbors for money."

"No, I wouldn't expect you to, but if you'd come here in your official capacity as a landscaper, I would've paid you."

Brogan opened her mouth as if to argue, but Emma held up her hand. "Besides, I'm an artist. I value creative work. I firmly believe artists need to support other artists, and this map is a kind of artwork that will be the blueprint for a different type of art, which will hopefully inspire my own art. That's worth something to me."

Brogan nodded and took a small step back, then turned to Reggie, whose cheeks had gone a bright shade of pink.

"What do you think would be a fair price?" Emma asked gently.

Reggie looked at the ground and shuffled her feet along the concrete shyly before finally saying, "I don't want any money."

Emma was about to reiterate her argument, but then Reggie whispered, "I would really like it if you came to my school on book report day, though."

Emma's breath caught at the simplicity of the request, and her heart raced at the complexities of accepting. She hadn't made a public appearance in well over six months. She hadn't written since then or done a single interview. She'd barely even spoken to the people she knew, much less strangers. And she'd achieved some sense of distance from the life she'd had before. She'd just moments earlier begun to hope for a time of peace and serenity. Would stepping back into the persona that had led to all her pain undercut her progress, or even kill the forward momentum completely? The risk seemed unreasonable to take when she was still in such a precarious position emotionally.

And yet, there were Reggie's green eyes peeking out from under the bill of her black cap, as if almost afraid to look at her directly. The pleading there was too much for her, and the pulse of panic pounded through her ears. Turning toward Brogan for help, she was hit once again with the same green gaze, only deeper, with a sympathy that both heartened and amplified the silent request not to let them all down.

Her heart gave a sharp twist as she blew out a shaky breath. "Yes."

Chapter Five

"Brogan!" several little voices shouted as she walked through the door of her parents' home. Immediately a ball of energy and elbows crashed into her thighs, followed by two more of slightly varying heights.

"Hello there . . ." She placed a hand atop each red head, one at a time, and tilted them back until she could see their faces. "Wendell, Seamus, and Arthur."

"And me." One more tiny person came careening around the corner on a collision course with the bodies still entangling her legs, and in the last second before impact, Brogan scooped her up and slung her over one shoulder. "Wow, I caught a Ginny, too. What a lucky day. Think I've got enough to make McKay stew with lots of little carrot tops."

The boys shrieked and giggled, then took off running through the house again, leaving Brogan clutching only Ginny, who squirmed and laughed as she stomped through the entryway to the big, warm living room.

"Mummy," Ginny wailed between gasps and giggled. "Daddy, she's going to eat me."

"Good catch," Neville said, as he rose from beside the fire he'd been stoking. "Fire's on. Let's ask Mum for a pot, probably a midsized one. She's not too big yet, not much meat for stew."

"Arthur's bigger. Eat him," Ginny yelled, throwing her brother quickly under the bus.

Both Brogan and Neville froze, stared at each other, then burst out laughing. Brogan doubled over and set Ginny on her feet. Then the girl took off running.

"She takes after her dad, the squirmy little rat."

Neville shrugged amiably. "Learning to undercut your older siblings is a survival skill for younger children in a big family. Don't tell me you didn't blame Archie every time you did something wrong."

"I didn't have to," Brogan said. "Nora used to beat me to the punch."

"Used to?" Archie came in from the kitchen with a bottle of cider in one hand and the other one clasped on his daughter Lily's shoulder.

"Wow. The prodigal son made it to a family dinner?"

He rolled his eyes. "I've been here more times than not, and I was even at Friday Club last week. Can we knock off the absent child routine? Or better yet, direct it at Siobhán?"

"As much as I enjoy taking potshots at the firstborn heir to the throne, she lives in Belfast," Neville said.

"And whose fault is that?" Brogan asked. "How's she supposed to protect her long-standing rule over us from fecking Northern Ireland?"

"She's not," Archie said. "Titles and power pass through the male line in this country. All authority falls to me."

"Dad!" Lily huffed. "Sexist."

"Yeah, Dad." Brogan gave her niece a wink. "You really going to leave everything to James even though Lily's older and obviously got both her brains and her looks from her mother?"

He smiled down at his daughter, who, despite having inherited his copper top, had her mother's eyes, nose and, from the expression on her face, also her steely resolve. Brogan enjoyed watching her older brother's will buckle when faced with even the slightest resistance from either one of the women in his life.

"Of course it's sexist. And therefore, when I am king, I will change the law."

"Not if Grandpa beats him to it," Liam McKay said, as he

stuck his head through the living-room door. "I'm still chieftain of this clan, and I say my ungrateful children need to help their mother set the table."

There was a flurry of activity Brogan had often mused would be overwhelming to outsiders. Even people who'd been around awhile, like her brothers- and sisters-in-law, still stood back on the peripheries when the McKay clan rushed to the table, a mix of hands and platters and clinking silverware amid the clamorous voices and scraping chairs. Everyone had their places, though those places were more hierarchical than static. The order usually preferred spouses in precedence, followed by siblings, alternating sides in accordance to age. Leaves had been added to the table over the years, and then kids' tables popped up along outer walls. A pair of high chairs rotated next to the sets of parents with the most pressing needs, but none of this was ever discussed as much as intuited, and always assembled quickly.

Within minutes of Liam's decree, the entire family sat shoulder to shoulder and hand in hand around the table, with heads bowed as their patriarch's baritone washed over the silence. "Bless us, oh Lord, and these thy gifts, which we are about to receive from thy bounty through Christ our Lord, Amen."

"Amens" echoed around the table as her dad added a hasty, "Tuck in."

Again, conversations erupted in every corner of the room.

"Can you pass me the Yorkshire puddings?" Nora asked, straining in vain to reach even halfway across the table, with her big baby-belly holding her back.

"Here, take two," Brogan said, tossing them onto her sister's plate. "You sure it's not twins again?"

Nora's narrowed eyes and flared nostrils clearly expressed how unfunny she found the joke.

Edmond blew out a low whistle from across the table. "You're either brave or stupid, talking like that to a pregnant woman."

"Why's that?" his own heavily pregnant wife asked, shooting him a similar look.

Brogan laughed. "Yeah, no experience there."

"Yet," Neville corrected, as he cut a slab of roast beef for Ginny, who was sitting on his knee. "I still hold out hope your day will come."

"If the town has their way, it'll come sooner rather than later," Charlie said, then shoved a forkful of Yorkshire pudding into his mouth before going on. "They all want to hook her up with Emma Volant."

"Did you hear she's coming to my school?" Reggie called from her place at the kids' table.

"Yeah." Ciara frowned. "I've been meaning to ask you about how she talked Emma into going to Book Day. Please tell me she didn't badger the poor woman to death."

"Mum." The exasperation in Reggie's tone suggested this wasn't the first time Ciara had broached the subject. "I already told you."

"She didn't do anything wrong," Brogan defended quickly. "In fact, she turned down money even though Emma said she should name her price. Emma got off pretty easy, just having to say hello to a few kids instead of cutting a big, fat check."

"I don't know," Ciara muttered, as she covered the majority of her plate in brown gravy. "She's got plenty of money to toss around, but last time I saw her, she didn't seem up for public appearances."

"I think she's getting her feet under her now," Brogan said, then chewed on a piece of beef to give herself a little time to choose her words. She didn't want to overstate anything. Emma had still certainly revealed moments of deep sadness, but she'd also smiled a few times, and in the sunlight, her hair had a little more luster and her skin a bit more color. Brogan couldn't say anything to that extent with her merciless siblings gathered 'round, though. "She seemed happy in the garden."

"Wait," Archie said. "You were hanging out with Emma Volant in her garden?"

"We weren't hanging out. I went over there to help Reggie with a few landscaping questions."

"But I did the work," Reggie said proudly. "Emma and Brogan went inside and talked."

Brogan stifled a groan as her brothers' smiles all widened in unison.

"Well, well, well," Neville said, as he lifted his pint of ale off the table. "Let me raise a toast to my new favorite, and hopefully richest, sister."

"Here, here," Charlie echoed. "May your streak of never failing with women not desert you now."

"She may have a perfect record," Edmond cut in, "but Emma Volant is no bored tourist in for a weekend romp."

Brogan's teeth ground at the blunt assessment of the type of women who generally found her attractive.

"I think he challenged you," Archie said with a grin.

"Come off it," Brogan said, trying to stem the blush creeping into her face.

"Are you really interested in her?" Liam asked.

"Dad, they're just taking the piss."

"That's not what I asked. I wanted to know what you thought of her."

"She's nice. Very kind, and generous, and good with Reggie."

"So, you're interested in dating her?" he pressed.

"No," she said flatly. "I'm not."

"Is she ugly?"

She shook her head, but before she could get a word out, both Ciara and Nora began to talk at once.

"She could be pretty."

"She could use some sun, though."

"A bit of rest, too."

"And she's too skinny."

"Way too skinny."

Everyone's head swiveled from side to side as if watching a verbal tennis match while her sisters launched volley after volley, and the muscles in Brogan's neck tightened with each lob.

"She's certainly not ugly, though," Ciara said.

"A little plain."

"And worn."

"And—"

"And nothing," Brogan finally cut in, and smiled in a way she hoped covered how agitated she felt. Turning to her dad, she said, "Emma's very pretty, actually. Just under a lot of strain. She'd probably rather make some friends instead of having the whole town try to marry her off or treat her like a tourist attraction, though."

Everyone stared at her now, eyes wide, some of their mouths open.

"Mummy!" Seamus kicked the table. "Wendell took my tay-toes. He put his hand in them and took them."

"Wendell," Nora sighed, "did you steal your brother's potatoes and eat them with your hands?"

"You didn't give me any!" Wendell wailed. "I wanted tay-toes."

"You can have mine." Ginny palmed one of her own roasted potatoes and tossed it over Nora so it landed with a clatter on Wendell's plate.

"Ginny," Neville scolded with a strong hint of laughter in his voice, "good little girls don't throw food."

"Yes, Ginny," Charlie said, tossing a quarter of a potato over to his nephew. "That's a job for uncles."

"Charlie." Nora rolled her eyes, but Wendell gave a little laugh, and Seamus joined in. Before any more parents could scold anyone else, everyone was chuckling, and Brogan was off the hook.

As her breathing and heart rate returned to normal, she sat back in her chair and tried not to unpack all the feelings the topic of Emma had stirred in her. Why had she made such an outburst? She wasn't the woman's keeper, and nothing they'd said about her being rich or famous was untrue. And Edmond might have been joking in his insinuation that someone like Emma would never fall for someone like her, but he wasn't exactly wrong, either. Emma was clearly smart and talented, and Brogan had seen a glimpse of passion in her when she'd spoken to Reggie about artists and inspirations. She might be in a dark place at the moment, but that spark would once again grow into a flame, and when it did, Emma would undoubtedly outshine anything Brogan could offer. Not that she wanted to offer her anything. It was only some silly town scheme to get them together. Why was she even indulging their half-baked fantasies?

She pushed back from the table and scraped clean a pile of plates before walking to the kitchen sink. She flipped on the water and stared out the back window at the blue expanse of sea rolling relentlessly toward the sandy shore. She must have stayed there longer than she'd intended, because when a hand reached around her to slap off the tap, she glanced down at a basin nearly overflowing with suds.

"Sorry," she mumbled.

"No worries," her mum said, giving her a little squeeze. "You've always been a daydreamer. It's one of the things I love about you."

She smiled. "One of many, right?"

"Absolutely." Her mum pulled a towel from the counter and tossed it to her, then set about washing the first load of dishes. "You're a good person, smart, hardworking, kind, and helpful. You always have so much to give to the people around you, and you give it freely."

That was laying it on a little thick, even by mum standards. She rolled her eyes and began to dry the pot her mum had rinsed. "You're not trying to fix me up with Emma, too, are you?"

Margaret chuckled and stared out the window.

"What's funny?"

"I'd merely been thinking of you," Margaret said gently, "but I do find it interesting that *you* were thinking of Emma."

"You came!" Reggie exclaimed as Emma entered the large multi-purpose room at the Duke of Northland Primary school, flanked by the head of the PTA and the principal. Or not the principal, because they called them something else here. How had the woman introduced herself? How was she supposed to remember how to thank her properly if she couldn't remember her title . . . or her name? *Oh, good Lord, I've forgotten the woman's name, too.*

This was why she didn't like to do these kinds of events, especially without an agent or a manager of some kind to help her. The publishing house would've sent someone up from London if she'd asked. They would've been ecstatic to do anything to help her get out more. No event would be too small for them, which, of course, was why she hadn't called them. No event was too small for them to make a big deal out of. If she'd told them she intended to make a public appearance, Reggie's book report day would've become a three-ring media circus.

So here she was, facing a room full of young readers. Alone, except for two adults whose names and titles she couldn't remember.

At least Reggie was beaming at her from the front row. Emma gave her a little wave, while silently praying she wouldn't let the kid down. What if she tripped? What if she forgot how to speak? What if she had a panic attack and passed out and knocked herself unconscious, and—

"Ms. Volant," the not-principal said, "if you'll have a seat on the stage, we're still waiting on one more guest. Then I'll make some announcements, and the kids will ask a few questions before you have a chance to walk around and view their projects."

She smiled and nodded like a fool as she took her seat on the low riser and clasped her hands in her lap before anyone could see how they trembled. Thankfully no one seemed interested in her as a flurry of activity occurred around the door. A woman carrying a clipboard pushed through the crowds, accompanied by a man holding a camera lens large enough to overcompensate for something, since it certainly wasn't warranted by the size of the room. Finally, a young woman strode in, wearing jeans, a charcoal turtleneck sweater, and a brown corduroy vest. She'd pulled her long blond hair into a messy bun, which added a touch of librarian appeal to the hipster chic ensemble.

The woman nimbly bounced up the stairs without so much as a glance around for directions, and taking the seat next to Emma, extended her hand. "Hello, I'm Vic."

A bit blown back by the wash of charisma, Emma managed to shake her hand lightly and say, "Emma."

"Wonderful to meet you. My mother is a big fan of your books."

"I do well with the mother market," she managed.

Vic laughed. "I wish I did a little better with them if we're honest."

Emma was about to ask if Vic was a fellow writer, but before she could, the woman clasped a hand on her arm. "What's the head teacher's name? I've forgotten again."

"I have, too," Emma admitted, feeling less guilty now. "Honestly, I'm glad you remembered to call her a head teacher. I knew 'principal' wasn't right."

"Ah, yes, an American. I suppose we could refer to her as the headmistress in our opening remarks."

Emma's heart hammered. "Were we supposed to prepare opening remarks?"

"They always make me prepare opening remarks. I'm sure you'll be fine, though."

"They?" Emma asked suspiciously, but before Vic could answer, the head teacher ascended the riser steps, and the room fell silent.

"Children and guests, thank you for your attention. We are honored today to have not one, but two distinguished guests for our book report celebrations. I know some of you have prepared questions for them, and others are looking forward to showing off your hard work, but please go calmly to your projects after we dismiss and don't linger about the stage."

Emma saw Reg frown and suspected she'd planned to do just that.

"And please mind your manners at all times around our distinguished visitors," the head teacher continued. "We want to show them we're worthy of the name and crest that adorn our school."

What an odd remark to end on. Emma wasn't quite sure why any child's behavior would make her think less of some Duke or his crest, but before she could process any more, the head teacher said, "And now let me first introduce Lady Victoria Charlotte Algernon Penchant, eldest daughter to His Grace, the Duke of Northland."

If Emma had been drinking a glass of water, she would've sprayed it all over the floor, and she suspected she'd made a similar expression even though her mouth had gone completely dry.

Lady Victoria Charlotte something or other? And she'd been shooting the breeze like she ran into royalty every day? How was she supposed to speak to a lady? Should she have bowed or curtseyed, or at least gotten to her feet in some sort of acknowledgment? The panic engulfed her again. *What have I done? Why am I here?* What was she supposed to say to the kids, to the head teacher, to the eldest daughter of the Duke of Northland?

"Thank you, Lady Victoria." The headmistress's voice cut in, and the closest thing to royalty Emma had ever met flashed her a smile. Their knees practically rubbed together as the voice coming through the microphone said her name, and now all the children and teachers were applauding.

She used the context clues to ascertain she'd missed her own introduction, and rose. Thankfully her knees didn't give way in the three steps it took her to get to the podium, and she clutched either side for balance. "Thank you. You're very kind to have me here today."

About two hundred little faces stared up at her, eager with anticipation and interest. There was something calming about their open expressions, so different from the inquisitive stares and whispered judgments she'd come to expect from their elders. They had no expectations, and all appeared as if they believed her capable of anything in that moment, and she found the idea strangely liberating.

"And thank you to your head teacher, or indeed all your teachers for letting me come meet with you. I especially want to thank my friend Reggie." She waved to the girl in the front row, who puffed out her chest with pride. "She's the one who told me about this event and all the wonderful books you've been reading in preparation. I know your teachers have probably told you all I'm a writer, and that's true, but long before I published my own books, I learned to love stories by reading the ones written by others. I'm sure some of us have some of the same favorites, but mostly I'm here in the hopes that your book reports will give me some good ideas for what I should read next."

There. Short and sweet, and while she hadn't said anything overly powerful or inspiring, none of the kids had squirmed or yawned, and they all clapped again as she took her seat . . . next to the duke's daughter, which felt a little bit like surviving the frying pan only to hop into the fire.

"Well done," Lady Victoria said with a nod. "Now bring on the firing squad."

Emma looked at her blankly, then back out at the audience, and sure enough, a line of children had formed down the middle row where the parent-teacher liaison woman appeared with another microphone. "We've selected a student from each year-level to ask a question of our two visitors. First up is Arthur McKay from year one."

Emma's nerves were overridden by the smile, the name, and the shock that the bright red hair atop the little boy's head inspired. He held the mic tightly in both hands, leaned so close his little nose almost bopped the top, and said in a clear, sharp voice, "What's your favorite books from when you was little?"

Lady Victoria smiled back at him brightly and accepted the microphone from the head teacher. "Arthur, you may know this, or you may not, but I live in the big castle in Newpeth, and we have lots of lions. Not real lions, mind you, but lion statues at the front gate, and lions carved into the walls, and lion heads peering down from the tops of the towers, and to be honest, I was a little frightened of them until my mum read me a book called *The Lion, the Witch, and the Wardrobe*."

A little ripple of excitement went through the audience, and she paused to let them have their moment of connection. "There was a lion in that book called Aslan, and he was not a tame lion, but he was a good lion, and once I got to know him, I liked our own lions a lot more. From then on, when I'd walk through the castle grounds, I'd pretend those lions were Aslan, and I'll even let you in on a little secret, sometimes I still do."

The kids all laughed, and Emma joined them, marveling at Lady Victoria's open and easy way with them.

"So that's why *The Lion, The Witch, and The Wardrobe* was my favorite book." With that, she handed the mic to Emma.

"Wow," she said, unsure how she could possibly follow that. She started slowly. "I've loved so many books. And I did also adore the Chronicles of Narnia, though I've never lived in a castle, or even visited one. There aren't a lot of castles in America, I'm afraid. The very idea of them seemed purely magical, which might be one of the reasons I first fell in love with another castle, one by the name of Hogwarts."

A few cheers went up among the older schoolchildren, and she smiled to know she'd scored a few points.

"The wizarding world has always captivated me, with its mystical places, magical creatures, and all the epic adventures." She turned to Lady Victoria and added, "Much like you, I've refused to grow out of my firm belief that there are witches and wizards among us, and I still keep an eye out for them everywhere I go."

Lady Victoria accepted the mic back and said, "Good choice, and for what it's worth, I find it truly sad that you've never been to a castle. We've all been to the castle, haven't we, boys and girls?"

The children raised their hands and cheered once more.

"All of you?" Emma asked with great dramatic effect.

Lady Victoria nodded. "We hold a start-of-term picnic on the grounds every year."

"Maybe if I do a good job here today, you all will invite me along next year."

The kids clapped their approval of the idea, but Lady Victoria did them one better by saying, "I'll see what I can do about getting you an invitation long before then."

Chapter Six

Late April brought warmer temperatures and smoother seas along the northeast coast of England, and those two factors combined to bring the first groups of weekenders to the shores of Amberwick. More sun, more tourists, more work—thus was the cycle of the town, and Brogan in particular. Not that she'd reached the fever pitch of summer holidays, but the holiday hunters meant a few extra hours at the Raven, and Nora was due any day now, which meant more hours at the post office. And the return of the local flocks of puffins to their island sanctuaries just offshore meant more time on the water. The latter hardly counted as work most days, though, as sailing would always be pleasurable no matter how much she got paid.

She stripped off her woollen coat and tossed it into the cabin of the sloop to let the warmth of the sun soak into the navy wool of her jumper. Warmth was a relative term, as the temperatures were not what most Londoners would consider comfortable. Still, after months of days that never quite got cold enough to snow, but always brought a fog or a drizzle, any dry sunshine constituted weather worthy of removing an outer layer of clothing. With a little exertion, she might even be down to a long-sleeve T-shirt before she shoved off.

She set to work threading the sails that had been stowed all winter. Away from the damp and occasional icy morning, they'd fared well. As she ran the canvas through her fingertips, checking for tears or even brittle patches, she found none on either the mainsail or the foresail. Then, using a few fresh lengths of rope, she secured everything to the mast in rolls ready to unfurl when needed.

It had been low tide when she'd started the process, but the waves had rolled in, filling the estuary noticeably now. Her family's twin keel Macwester 27 was perfect for such a drastic tidal environment. The boat stood upright securely, even on dry land, but she could no longer make out the sandy bottom below when she leaned over the side. She would need the rowboat to get back and forth between the shore before long, and she needed at least one more run inland before she could sail. She made a mental list of things she needed to pick up. A quick peek inside the cabin confirmed Charlie hadn't packed the life preservers or the two-way radio when they'd launched yesterday. It had seemed to take everything in him not to drown when they'd hauled the boat from the yard into the estuary. He'd never taken to the water the way Brogan had, so it was her name Charlie had cursed when he slipped into the frigid river to the echoes of their father's thick laughter.

She smiled at the memory and hopped over the edge with a splash that didn't cover her thigh-high rubber boots, yet. The wellies did little to hide the cold, though, as she sloshed toward the boathouse with only slightly less speed than Charlie had the day before. Still laughing at the visual of her brother scrambling backward like a crab with his butt dragging the sand, she looked up in time to see a solitary figure come around a bend in the riverbank.

Even squinting against the sun, she instantly recognized the shape and set of Emma Volant's body. She was willowy and slender like the tall marsh grasses bending and bowing gracefully in the ocean breeze. The golden light of a Northland sun shimmered in waves across her fair hair, more luminous now than it'd ever appeared indoors. Brogan remembered defending her looks to a family full of good-intentioned gossipers. At the time their assessments had seemed unfair. Now they felt almost absurd.

Emma was beautiful as she strolled along the dirt path that skirted the seawall protecting the estuary.

Their eyes met as Emma glanced up from her feet and caught Brogan staring, standing knee deep in freezing water. Emma lifted her hand in a little wave.

"Hello," Brogan called, then instantly wished she'd thought of a better opening, but all she could think to add was the equally banal, "Beautiful day."

"Indeed," Emma said, walking closer. "I should be writing, but I couldn't stay inside with so much sun out here."

"Can't blame you. And plenty of other tourists will feel the same, come the weekend. You might as well make the most of the solitude while you've got it."

"Will the place turn into a raucous party beach before my eyes?"

She laughed. "Not hardly. Mostly families and retirees come for a day or two. Compared to other towns up and down the coast, we've got it easy." *Maybe too easy*, she mused, thinking about how low the preseason bookings at the Raven had been so far. "But you'll notice a difference. More traffic on the beach, fewer parking spaces to be found in the village."

"I don't suppose that will affect me much," Emma said amicably. "I'm not much of a sunbather, and I don't drive over here."

"Me either," Brogan said quickly. "I mean, I drive, but I've got my own parking space, and I don't do any sunbathing either."

"I imagine redheads burn about as badly as blondes do?" Emma asked, with a smile.

"Worse."

Emma gave a playful grimace, then glanced down at the water now rushing around Brogan's legs. "I hope you handle the cold better for it, though, because you're about to have some icy toes."

"Oh, yeah," Brogan said sheepishly, and bracing her hands on the stone wall in front of her, hauled her weight out of the water. "I came in here for something, but at the moment I can't remember what."

"In?"

She nodded over her shoulder. "From the boat."

Emma's eyes went wide as she surveyed the sloop, its blue hull now touching the water and its single mast glinting in the sun. "Yours?"

"Technically my father's, but he says he's getting too old for sailing, so I run most of the specialty tours, and he does the main puffin cruises on his motorboat." She pointed to a large gray and blue restored lifeboat with a small captain's cabin and a wide, flat deck that was anchored to a dock on the other side of the river.

"Puffin cruises," Emma repeated, as if she liked the sound of the words.

"There are plenty of companies who do them from various points along the North Sea, but I think the McKay clan's as good as any. Our boats aren't nearly as big as some of the others, but that allows us to get closer to the islands without disturbing the nests. Plus, we've all been exploring these waters since we were kids. No summer hire can learn in a season what I've spent decades navigating."

"I believe you," Emma said earnestly. "I bet you run a tip-top ship, Captain."

"Which reminds me, I came in to get some life jackets and a radio. Safety first."

She ducked into a nearby wooden hut and counted out eight bright-orange vests and tossed them out onto the grass before calling, "What about you? What have you been up to lately?"

"Not a whole lot, honestly. I'm afraid I lead a boring life."

"I don't believe you."

"It's true," Emma said sadly. "I think I'll be quite a disappointment to all the wonderful people who've been so nice to me. I fear they'd prefer their new neighbor to be more exciting or engaging, but I'm very much a bore."

"I hate to break it to you," Brogan said, as she exited the shed with a two-way radio in hand and began to toss the life vests into a rowboat bobbing just over the wall, "but Reggie's told everyone you were a total rock star at her school two weeks ago."

Emma blushed. "She's too generous. I barely muddled through. Those kids asked some tough questions. It started easily enough, but they got harder the older the kids got. By the time Reggie took the mic, I was half expecting her to grill me about Kafka or Proust."

"I wouldn't put it past her. She was so excited I think she probably did a fair bit of studying, but whatever bar she set for the event, you hurdled it. And thank you for that, by the way."

"For hurdling?"

"For agreeing to go in the first place. I know you probably didn't want to play guinea pig for a bunch of local school kids, but it meant a lot to her."

"I was sort of dreading it," Emma admitted, "but it wasn't nearly as terrible as I feared. I think it actually may have done me some good to share in the kids' excitement. It's fun to remember how much books mean to people at that age. They aren't commodities, they're portals to adventures."

Brogan liked the hint of color she saw rising in Emma's cheeks and the steadiness in her voice. "And what about you, Ms. Volant? Do you like adventures?"

She paled slightly at the question, her lips pressed tightly together, and Brogan rushed to fill the void spreading between them. "Nothing major mind you, but I was about to take the boat out for my first run of the season. Not far, maybe around Coquet Island, and I wouldn't mind some company or an extra set of hands."

Emma glanced out toward the island Brogan nodded to, then back at her with a grimace. Her heart sank. Was it the boat or her company that spurred such a response?

"I don't know." Emma hemmed. "I mean, you're taking the boat out into the ocean?"

Brogan looked around with a half-smile as if there was some other way to get to the island. "That's the general idea. But it'll be smooth sailing today, not much in the way of waves if you're worried about getting seasick."

"No, I don't get seasick. Or, I guess I shouldn't say that. I don't know if I get seasick, because I've never been out on the sea, or even in a sailboat."

Brogan laughed. "Then why the look of horror when I mentioned it? I hope it's not my company that inspires such terror."

"Oh no!" Emma said quickly, the hint of pink in her cheeks flushing crimson. "No, if I were to take a chance on the open water with anyone, it'd certainly be with someone like you. I don't know why my first inclination is always to think of all the reasons I shouldn't do something. I suppose to answer your earlier question, no, I don't normally go for adventures."

"I don't believe you," Brogan said again.

Emma's eyes filled with tears, but she managed to say, "It's true. Someone who knows me very well once told me, point blank, I have zero sense of adventure, and I think she was right."

Brogan despised that person. She didn't even know her, though she suspected she knew who she was, but apparently Brogan didn't have to meet someone for their existence to inspire a white-hot hate. She bit her tongue from saying so, though, as she strongly suspected Emma wasn't in an emotional state to hear it. Instead, she chose her words carefully. "That person must've known a different version of you, because the Emma I've met packed up her life and moved across an ocean to a place where she didn't know anyone. I can't imagine any greater adventure. Certainly no boat trip around an island full of birds could compare."

Emma snorted. "When you put it that way . . ."

Brogan could still hear the hesitancy in Emma's voice, but it was fading, or maybe being overtaken by something else, something lighter, something more hopeful, and the shift inspired something similar in Brogan, who nodded toward the blue rowboat floating mere meters away. "What do you say? Is a little bit of risk worth another adventure?"

Emma screwed up her shoulders, pursed her lips, and closed her eyes, then pushed out a rapid breath. "Yes, let's go."

£ £ £

Emma couldn't believe she'd said yes. She was not a "yes" kind of person. And yet here she was, sitting in a tiny shell of a rowboat as Brogan pulled on the oars and sent them gliding along the place near where the river met the sea. The water wasn't deep yet, maybe three feet, and she could still clearly see the top of slender grasses waving in the tide. A little minnow type of fish swam against the current underneath them, and she smiled at his efforts. What did she have to be worried about? She wasn't in the water, and she wasn't doing any work to keep them on course. Glancing up at Brogan, her smile only grew. Brogan was so steady and calm, Emma couldn't help but believe in her competence. As she steered them toward the sailboat with fluid strokes of the oars, a gentle breeze stirred her copper hair, giving a rugged and windswept appeal to her soft, green eyes and pale complexion. It was a look many woman would kill for, or kill to get close to. As close as Emma was sitting on the small bench opposite her. She could've reached out and brushed a strand of hair from where it had fallen across Brogan's forehead.

The thought warmed a part of her stomach she hadn't been able to fill even with her newfound love of scones. She didn't know what to make of that feeling, but she didn't hate it, and before she had a chance to overthink it, Brogan bumped the dinghy softly against the side of the sailboat. She dropped an anchor and tucked the oars along the sides of the rowboat.

"All aboard," she said, as she grabbed hold of a ladder extending off the back and pulled until the rowboat came flush with the sailboat.

Standing with only a slight wobble, Emma tightly gripped the handrails and quickly climbed the three rungs of the ladder. She was still steadying herself on the deck when Brogan practically vaulted up beside her, arms full of all the things she'd brought from shore. Emma blinked a few times, then stared down at the now empty rowboat. How had she done that?

"Can I help with anything?" she asked, more out of a sense of obligation than the sense she had anything to offer in this situation.

"You can stow these things in the cabin." Brogan handed her the stack of orange lifejackets. "I'll lift anchor and start the motor."

Emma took the two steps needed to duck into the cabin and saw two small tables and a single bunk piled high with rolled maps and coils of rope. Behind her, a gas engine rumbled to life.

"I thought this was a sailboat," she called, as she stacked the vests atop one of the tables.

"It is," Brogan said when Emma stepped back out into the sun, "but we keep a small outboard motor for turning around in the narrow confines of the estuary and in case of emergencies on the water. As soon as we clear the currents at the mouth of the river, we'll hoist sail."

We'll hoist sail. Not a phrase Emma ever thought she'd be included in. As Brogan brought the boat around to face the North Sea, Emma's heart beat faster. The North Sea. Wasn't this where Vikings sailed? She was no Viking. She was a suburban New Yorker who'd just gotten on a boat with a woman she barely knew. That wasn't adventurous so much as irresponsible and dangerous. Sure, Brogan seemed to know what she was doing, but honestly, Brogan could have told her this ship was made of dragon hide and ran on marshmallows, and Emma wouldn't have been able to authoritatively tell her otherwise. Honestly, she was equally versed in dragons and sailboats, which was to say she'd seen them both in pictures or movies.

"See the cross atop that hill to the right?" Brogan asked conversationally, as if her heart wasn't pounding in her rib cage, probably because it wasn't. "The first church in town was built up there by the monks based at the monastery in Lindisfarne. Then about a few hundred years later, a big storm came through and rerouted the river to run between the town and church. That's when they built the church the village still uses today."

"When was that?"

Brogan shrugged. "A couple hundred years ago."

"Is that all?" Emma asked, easing down on the bench seat opposite her. "It's a shame you all don't have much history to hold onto over here."

Brogan laughed and turned the boat until they angled out of the mouth of the river.

A few of the minor waves pushing toward the shore caused the bow of the boat to rise and fall several inches, and Emma clutched at the edge of her seat as if she might be thrown at any moment.

"It'll smooth out as soon as we pass this row of breakers," Brogan said genially.

"I'm fine," Emma admitted, both surprised by that fact and a little embarrassed she'd had to state it. Brogan, of course, was right. After a handful of small bumps, the water became little more than rippled glass.

She shouldn't have worried. She hated that she had. And yet Brogan hadn't poked fun or rolled her eyes at Emma's over-reaction. She'd merely modeled calmness and reassured her. She couldn't remember the last time someone had done either of those things for her.

No, she did remember. Her grandmother had been the picture of understanding. Her grandmother, who'd grown up on the very shore she was now sailing along. Emma let her eyes wander over the stunning landscape before her, the azure sea, the golden strip of beach rising in verdant dunes, and for the first time thoughts of her grandmother weren't accompanied by a wave of sadness. "It's beautiful out here."

Brogan nodded and looked over her shoulder. "Not a bad view of the village, is it?"

She took in the outline of stone buildings with red and brown roofs atop a rise, all peaks and angles with a church spire to keep watch over them all. "You have a gift for understatement."

"I'm sure you've been a lot more places than I have and seen a lot more amazing things."

"I have been able to travel a bit," she admitted. "My work has opened a lot of doors, but I'm not sure any of them has anything prettier than this."

Brogan looked down as if she'd found something important to do with the steering handle on the outboard motor, but

Emma liked the way the corners of her mouth twitched up with pleasure.

"My grandmother used to tell me stories about this place," Emma continued. "As a little girl, I thought it must be the most magical spot on earth, but as an adult, I'd started to wonder if she'd embellished her descriptions, either for my benefit or for her own."

"And?" Brogan asked, rising to fiddle with some ropes near the mast. "Did she?"

"Not a bit," Emma said, with a rush of affection, both for the place and the woman who'd loved it. "Not the views anyway. Or the colors, or the way the buildings stagger and stutter-step toward the sea."

Brogan finished loosening a knot, then turned to face her, green eyes flecked with hope and a hint of mischief. "What about the magic?"

The question lodged in her chest, or maybe it wasn't the words that made it hard to draw a full breath so much as the way in which they were delivered, or the person who delivered them. Either way, Emma couldn't find the air or the wherewithal to answer right away. Instead she looked out to sea, over the azure expanse, toward an island in the distance until the words came to her. "I thought I'd found some magic a long time ago, but I was wrong, or maybe I was unworthy, so I'm not sure I've even been looking for it lately."

"But you still believe it exists?" Brogan asked quietly.

Emma pondered the question, still watching the water, and the jagged point of gray rock jutting isolated and proud out of the vast, shimmering plane. "I think I have to believe in magic. I'm not sure I could trust myself if I didn't."

"Good," Brogan said, and with a sharp, strong pull on the rope in her hands the sail flew up the mast and caught hold of the breeze.

They were off, not at a breakneck speed, but a steady pace, gliding more than flying across the water, with a feeling of weightlessness Emma'd never experienced before. After months of carrying invisible weights on her shoulders, the sensation was gloriously freeing.

"Would you take the tiller, please?" Brogan asked.

She froze. "The what?"

"The tiller. The bar I was using to steer us," Brogan explained calmly, as she tied off the rope she'd used to hoist the sail.

"Take it where? How?"

"Steady us as I raise the jib."

She didn't want to. She didn't want to have any responsibility for their trajectory, or safety, but Brogan had already turned her back and walked toward the front deck. If Emma wasted precious seconds arguing, it might be too late for them. Sliding over, she willed her hand not to shake as she placed it on the smooth, wooden handle and noted the residual warmth of Brogan's grasp.

"Like this?" she called.

"Perfect," Brogan answered, as she unfastened another rope.

"You didn't even check to see what I'm doing."

"I don't have to," Brogan explained. "I can feel your movements. You're steady."

Emma snorted softly. She was not steady. She had been once upon a time, and it'd cost her too much. Now she wasn't steady anymore, and she might wreck them both. As with many things in her life, she never seemed to have what she needed when she needed it most.

Brogan gave a pull on the new rope and sent a second sail up the front of the mast. Emma tightened her already firm grip on the tiller, expecting the boat to list or lurch, but no sudden movements rocked their base. In fact, Emma didn't feel anything more than a slight tug while Brogan tied off her line and headed back toward her. She moved assuredly, her jacket open and a slight breeze pushing her hair off her forehead. She wasn't quite pirate-level rakish, but she played the part of seasoned sailor with ease. Emma's heart rate did a little two-step, as if she couldn't decide whether Brogan's approach should bring calm or something more thrilling. Ultimately, she settled on relief at being relieved of her steering duties. However, when Brogan hopped down from the cabin onto the lower deck, she didn't take the tiller again. Instead, she sat down on the bench to one side and extended her long legs.

Emma stared at her, waiting for something more, some action or task or explanation that never came.

"It's good to be out here again." Brogan angled her face toward the sun and closed her eyes.

Emma stared at her, willing Brogan to take the tiller again. She didn't trust herself nearly as much as she trusted this woman she barely knew. She had enough self-awareness to realize there were likely some issues with that, but open water wasn't the place to examine her inadequacies.

"So, your grandmother immigrated to America from here?" Brogan asked without even peeking at her.

"She, um . . ." Emma scanned the vast horizon, looking for danger, but seeing none, she considered the question she'd known the answer to since she was old enough to internalize stories. "She grew up here but fell in love with a French soldier when she was just a girl. He whisked her off to Paris on a grand adventure. She left home before they married. The way she told it, they were quite a scandal for the stodgy village residents, who were too old-fashioned for his libertine sensibilities."

Brogan snorted. "I bet."

"Her parents weren't pleased, but my grandmother was stubborn and in love. She never hesitated. Paris in the '30s was a world she couldn't have imagined, and then couldn't imagine ever wanting to leave. Then everything changed when World War II began. Heaven turned to hell, but Louis Volant was a solider. He couldn't leave when his country needed him most, and he couldn't let his young wife risk her life for his. He sent her back here to keep her safe with a promise that if he survived the war, he'd carry her across the sea to a place no one could ever threaten them again."

Brogan sat forward, interest etched in her features. "And did he?"

Emma smiled in spite of her lingering nerves. "He did. He lost his left leg from the knee down in the process, but he earned commendations with the French, British, and American troops he helped to navigate the French countryside, and he earned their passage to New York in 1946. My father was born in 1947, the first American Volant."

"Did your grandmother ever come back?"

She shook her head. "My grandfather was proud of what he'd done, but she said he was never quite the same after the war. He never wanted to go back. Paris was in ruins and full of ghosts, but the English countryside felt like a step back, a reminder of his failure to hold his family together on his own. America was new, unspoiled, something he'd given his family that made what he'd been through worthwhile. She never said so, but I think she worried that asking to go back would hurt his feelings. So, instead, she filled my childhood with stories of running barefoot along these beaches, or building bonfires on cool sand, or climbing the green hills overlooking the village. She talked of stone walls and pastures dotted with sheep, of fog rolling in from the sea to soak her skin, and warm kettles and open fires."

Brogan smiled. "She passed the memory of a place she loved to the person she loved."

Emma nodded and worried she'd been too sentimental, too soon. It wouldn't be the first time. "Does it seem silly to be homesick your whole life for someplace you've never seen?"

Brogan pondered the question for a minute. "I don't know. I've never had an occasion for homesickness, but I know what it's like to feel a kind of pull you can't explain. The way my bones ache to get on the water every spring. Or the way sometimes I wake too early in the morning and know I'll find my dad or a sibling walking on the beach. It's like there's something pulsing in our DNA that connects us to something we can't see. Sense memory, or the ghosts of our ancestors, or . . ."

"Magic," Emma whispered.

"Magic," Brogan echoed with a grin, and Emma didn't feel so silly anymore. She also didn't feel as nervous. The stories her grandmother had used to soothe her as a child served the same purpose now, and in asking her to tell them, Brogan had anchored her to something familiar in the midst of something new and frightening. The emotions associated with the former had overtaken the latter.

Exhaling slowly, she took in her surroundings again. The village seemed smaller from this far out, but the island that drew almost level to their right didn't feel nearly as lonely or distant. She could even make out little black dots bobbing in the waves near the rocks.

"Puffins," Brogan said, following her gaze. "They're kind of a big deal around here. Veer right and we'll get a little closer."

"Veer right?"

"Pull the tiller toward your body."

"Isn't that left?"

"Counterintuitive, I know," Brogan said evenly, "but it's sort of a mirror system. Pull the handle left to angle the boat to the right, and vice versa."

She waited for the panic to rise again, but when it didn't, she asked, "How far?"

"You'll know."

She did. As she pulled the tiller slowly toward her, the keel responded in micromovements. A few degrees at a time, their course shifted in a gentle arc, and the sails gave a few flaps in the breeze as the canvas adjusted to the new angle straining the seams.

"Nice," Brogan murmured. "You've got a light touch."

"Is that good?"

"Today it is."

"What about on other days?"

"You might need to move quicker or hold stronger, but the concept's the same. A good sailor knows doing something faster doesn't mean you're doing something different."

"But what if the wind turns against you? How do you fight it?"

"You don't. That's the secret. Sailing isn't about fighting the wind. It's about channeling it, literally. The wind doesn't work for you or against you. The wind goes about its own business. You can curse it, or you can adjust your sails. The choice is yours, but either way, the wind doesn't care."

There was a poetry to it all, and probably some life lessons, too, if she'd had the time or inclination to ponder them. Instead, she pulled the tiller a little closer to her side and tightened their arc around the island.

"There." Brogan pointed to the rocky incline around the back side of the island, and sure enough, they were now gliding close enough to see each crack and ledge crowded with the small black and white birds.

"They're adorable," she exclaimed in spite of herself, "like squat little penguins."

"They're playful, too," Brogan said as several of the birds hopped off the rocks and into the water. They popped up a few feet away and flapped their wings.

"Are we disturbing them?"

"No, they've just returned from their winter migration. They don't have much in the way of nests, and no eggs yet. Later in the season they'll puff themselves up to ward off any threats against the young, but right now they're mostly filling their bellies. Like that." She pointed to a tiny puffin who had surfaced with a fish in his curved, orange beak and flapped his wings to take flight away from the others who moved toward him mischievously.

Emma marveled as he managed to gulp and glide at the same time, his wings wide and graceful as he skimmed along the surface of the sea just to the front of their bow. Two of the other birds followed suit, and soon they swooped back around toward the island, never rising more than a foot above the gentle waves. "They're so smooth."

"I never get tired of watching them fly," Brogan admitted. "There's something joyful to it, like your heart can't help but soar a little bit with them."

Emma smiled at her.

"What? You don't think so?"

"No, I do. You described what I was feeling perfectly before I could form the words. Maybe *you're* better suited to being the writer."

Brogan laughed. "If so, then we'll have to switch roles entirely, because you're a natural sailor."

Emma shook her head. "Not at all. You've been very generous, but the highest form of mastery is being able to teach someone else. Anything I've done was under your instruction."

"Are you sure?" Brogan asked. "Because I haven't told you anything other than how to turn using a tiller, and somehow you've seamlessly carried us from the mouth of the river, around the island, and nearly made the turn back toward home."

Emma checked the horizon again to confirm they'd made a half circle, and the slanted roofs and spire of Amberwick stood sweet and proud directly ahead. Marveling at both the accomplishment and the pride she felt about achieving it without panicking, she whispered, "I did it."

Brogan flipped up the collar of her wool pea coat against the mist settling over the village. The sun hadn't quite got through enough to burn away the sea haar for today, and the chill clung to her skin like the gray that saturated the air. The weather wasn't unusual for this part of the country this time of year, but it felt particularly cruel after several days of sailing weather, as if the sunshine and fair winds earlier in the week were only meant to serve as reminders of what she wasn't quite entitled to expect yet.

She hunched slightly forward and lowered her eyes to the cobblestone-paved alleyway along the side of the Raven, which was why she saw their feet first, five pairs of them, all in well-worn boots or mud-splattered wellies that certainly didn't belong to tourists.

"Did I miss the memo on new bar hours?" she asked, as she fished the keys from her pocket.

"Hey, the customer's always right, and right now this customer needs a pint of cider," Tom groused as she pushed open the door.

"We've been standing out here for ten minutes in this haar getting soaked through."

"Well, why'd you do that?" Brogan asked, flipping on wall lamps that didn't do much to lighten the dark, wood interior of the pub. She headed straight for the bar since the others were already pulling chairs and stools down from the table tops and arranging them to their liking.

"You've had the women," he said, looking pointedly at his wife and sister-in-law, "in a right tizzy all week."

"Not a tizzy," Diane said. "You sparked our interest, and we didn't want to bombard you when you had customers, so we came in early to talk about the new developments before the cooped-up tourists mob the place. Come on, out with all the details."

There were so many things to question in the sentence, she didn't even know where to start except for they all apparently knew something she didn't, but the way they stared at her, she would've thought the situation reversed. "Me?"

"Yes, you," Esther huffed. "I've been waiting all week. You'd better make it good."

Brogan turned to Charlie, who was still standing by the doorway, arms across his chest, a big grin on his face.

"You took Emma Volant sailing," he said, "and apparently the whole village saw you."

Brogan rolled her eyes. "That was days ago. You're just now telling me?"

"I could say the same to you. Why did I have to hear it from Helen at the post office this morning?"

Brogan groaned at the idea of locals discussing her social life at the post office. "Because there's nothing to tell."

"No," both women said at once. "None of that. You took the most eligible lesbian in Amberwick on a private puffin tour."

"And Helen said you were awful cozy sitting close to one another on your way back into the estuary."

"I showed her how to work the throttle on the outboard motor."

90

Tom snorted. "Is that what they're calling it these days?"

"I'm here." Ciara pushed through the door, already unraveling her scarf from her neck. "Did you start without me?"

Brogan sighed. "Not you, too."

"Yes, me too, and don't try stalling. Also, gimme a glass of white wine, please. I had a pisser of a day. You can pour and talk at the same time, right?"

"No."

"Okay, pour, then talk."

Brogan ground her teeth together, but she used the momentary reprieve to gather herself. It didn't take much to figure out the entire town had been talking about her and Emma all week, and the story had likely got bigger every time it'd gone around. She wished she could laugh them off, but the knot in her stomach wouldn't let her, because she worried she'd done the same thing.

She'd spent an inordinate amount of time basking in the warmth of her memories from such a small number of minutes in the sun with Emma. At least she'd had the good sense to chide herself every time she'd caught her imagination starting to run wild, though. She wasn't full-on crushing on the woman. She enjoyed her company and found her attractive on multiple levels, but she hadn't had the urge to jump into bed with her or start naming their unborn children.

What drew her to Emma felt different from an infatuation or the lust-fueled electricity she was used to in her weekend rendezvous. The attraction went deeper than the mix of libido and boredom that usually drew her to women. And their time together had been different, too. Emma was more than someone to fill space or silences. When she talked, she offered more than the conversations about movies or sports Brogan had grown used to, and yet she got the sense there was much more beneath the surface. She loved to see the moods roll over Emma's features the way sunlight and shadows rolled over the hills between the clouds. That was probably the thing she'd thought about most since their time on the boat, the way it'd felt to watch the nerves and uncertainty give way first to reminiscence, and then contentedness, interest, and pride. She would've given anything to have kept Emma talking, to have kept her smiling, to have kept her present in that moment.

She shook her head at the thought. It scared her. She focused back to pulling a pint of Tom's favored ale from the tap. She'd already given too much mental time to Emma and the various things she'd like to show her, or ask her, in order to see her blue eyes shimmer with happiness. She didn't usually work that hard with the women she dated. She generally only invested her emotional energy in people who would be around for a long time, family or close friends.

Maybe that's it, she thought, as she passed glasses to the table of locals she'd known her whole life.

Friends.

Most of her friends from school had left the area, either for work or to get married and start families of their own. And as much as she loved her siblings, sometimes she could still get lonely, even at their big family dinners. Everyone had their own lives, their own priorities, their own jobs and relationships. Not to mention the fact that they all knew each other, so there wasn't much to be intrigued or surprised by anymore.

Emma had new stories to tell, and Brogan had new things to show her. They hadn't had any trouble making conversation. Emma had the makings of a good friend if Brogan could manage not to mess it up by letting herself even think about something more. Something like the way Emma's hand felt in her own when she'd steadied her in the rowboat, or the way Emma's eyes were the same color as the skies they'd sailed under. Just because she noticed those things didn't mean she had to let them dominate her thoughts, did it?

She supposed she could ask the people staring expectantly at her for advice, but she didn't trust them to offer unbiased answers.

"Come sit with us," Diane commanded, and patted the stool next to her for emphasis.

92

"I've got to get ready to open."

"You're open," Will said.

"I have to get ready for customers."

"What are we?" Esther asked. "We're paying for drinks and the attention of our favorite bartender."

"They aren't going to let up until you give them what they want," Tom said. "Trust me."

She suspected he'd been badgered into submission enough to know, so she sighed heavily and said, "You can ask me whatever you want, but I'm staying behind the bar."

"Fine," Ciara said, pointing at her with a wineglass in hand. "How'd Emma Volant end up on the boat with you?"

"She happened to walk by when I was getting ready to test the sails, and I mentioned I could use a hand."

"Did you phrase it like that?" Esther asked with a grimace.

"Basically."

"Did you at least show her a good time, or did you make her swab the deck?"

"I showed her the puffins," Brogan offered, "and how to use the tiller."

Ciara rolled her eyes, but Will smiled kindly. "It's a start."

"I'm not sure it was," Brogan said, "or maybe it was a start and an end in the same day. We made a round trip. We said goodbye, and I haven't seen her since."

"But you're going to, right?" Diane asked.

Brogan shook her head. "I don't have any plans to."

"You didn't have plans for your first outing," Esther said hopefully, "but you made the most of it. I bet a private sail on a pretty day makes for a lovely date."

"It wasn't a date," she said, frustration creeping into her voice now. "She's nice, and she's new here. We happened to be in the same place at a time when I was about to do something enjoyable, and I invited her to come along because that's the neighborly thing to do. If any of you had walked by, I'd have invited you to come along with me. That wouldn't mean I was accepting any responsibility for keeping you happy, or persuading

93

you to put down roots. I'm not going to do those things with her, either."

"Why?" Ciara practically whined.

Brogan's jaw twitched as the real answer almost jumped from her lips, but she couldn't tell them she wasn't good enough for a woman like Emma. Instead she said, "She's not my type."

"What's not your type?" Tom pushed. "She's a woman, and a lesbian."

Diane swatted his arm. "Even I know it takes more than that, you old dog."

"She's also rich," Tom offered.

"And talented," Ciara said.

"And pretty," Will added.

"And sweet," Esther piled on.

"And rich," Tom repeated, earning himself another swat.

Charlie laughed. "Maybe she's not her type because of all of those things. Maybe it's not Emma who's not ready to put down roots."

"Don't be silly. Brogan's already got her roots so deep in this village you couldn't pull them out with a lorry," Ciara said.

"But none of the women she's ever dated do."

They all turned to her.

"Is that it?" Ciara finally asked. "Are you really only interested in weekend romps?"

Her face flamed, both at the question and at the answer she wouldn't give.

"Oh my," Diane said. "I find that hard to believe, Brogan. All this time I thought you were waiting for the right woman to come along."

"I thought she hadn't applied herself," Esther confided, "the same way she keeps doing odd jobs instead of settling into a real one."

Brogan grimaced. Now they weren't just affirming her insecurities about Emma; they'd branched out to other parts of her life as well.

"Maybe she doesn't want a real job," Will said kindly. "Not everybody does. I suppose the same goes for relationships."

"Relationships are not the same as jobs," Diane said, and shot a serious look at her husband when he snorted.

"Maybe not," Will admitted, "but whatever the reason, she says she's not interested. And the last thing you want is to bully her into a halfhearted attempt at a short-term sort of thing that leaves Emma heartbroken."

Esther shook her head sadly. "No, that'd be the worst of all options, and probably the quickest way to run her off."

"True," Ciara said, "and to be honest, it was probably a long shot anyway. For all the inexplicable powers Brogan has over so many women, none of them have ever up and moved here."

Brogan's chest constricted at the blunt statement of the obvious. She knew her sister wasn't trying to be rude. None of them were. She should have been happy they were all letting her off the hook, regardless of the reason, but she wished their reasons weren't so sharply on point with her own. Somehow having other people confirm what she'd always suspected about herself made those realities feel all the more inescapable. Then again, maybe that was what she needed. At least with everyone else realizing she shouldn't even hope for anything more than friendship with Emma, her heart would start to listen to her brain.

Chapter Seven

"So, what's new and exciting in your life, Reggie?" Emma asked, as they planted cuttings of lavender in the cool soil while the sun soaked through the sweatshirts on their backs.

"I have a new cousin," Reggie said. "Aunt Nora and Uncle Marcus's, not Uncle Edmond and Aunt Joanne's. She's still huge."

Emma chuckled softly at how Aunt Joanne would probably appreciate the description, but it wasn't her place to correct Reggie's bluntness. There was actually something liberating about being around someone with no filter, after all the time she'd spent around people who always had a hidden agenda. She wished she could be a little more like her instead of always hemming and hawing or second-guessing.

"The baby is a girl," Reggie continued. "I think Aunt Nora really wanted a girl after twin boys."

"Probably," Emma said, "but now she's got to buy all new clothes."

"Nobody in our family gets all new clothes," Reggie said, without a hint of anger or resentment.

"Not even the oldest?"

Reggie shrugged. "Maybe my cousin Callum did when he was a baby, but now he gets some of my uncle Charlie's old stuff."

Emma cocked her head to the side, trying to conceptualize a family large enough to pass clothes between generations. It had never even occurred to her families like that still existed.

"But they live in Ireland, so I think they get some new stuff, too."

"Your uncle Charlie?"

"No, my cousins Callum and Little Liam. He's not little anymore. He's older than me, but we call him Little Liam because my granddad is Big Liam. But they don't live in the same place, so you don't really have to call them different things most of the time. I call my granddad 'Daideó,''cause he's Irish."

"Makes sense," Emma said, surprised that it did. It also explained Brogan's earlier comments about being Irish while having been born and raised in Amberwick.

"So anyway, I have a new cousin, and my mum is helping out a lot with the twins, and grandmother is helping out with the baby, so I get to play outside more."

"That works out in your favor."

Reggie nodded as she patted some dirt lightly around their last sprig of lavender. "But I can't play with Brogan as much because she's helping out at the post office."

"That reminds me, I need to get up there and get some more clotted cream before she closes."

"You better hurry." Reggie hopped up. "They are closing at five this week."

Emma glanced at her watch to see it was already four thirty, and also noticed her hands and knees were both coated in dirt. She could probably brush them off and be passable, but she wouldn't quite be presentable. Or she could wait until tomorrow. She'd lived her entire American life without clotted cream. Going one day without wouldn't kill her. Unless, of course, it wasn't just about the cream. The shopping hadn't entered her mind until Reggie'd mentioned Brogan.

She shook her head and rose to standing. She was merely overthinking again as she was prone to do. She wanted scones for dinner, she ate them with clotted cream, she'd run out of cream, and she needed to go to the store to get some more. A simple, logical chain of events would send her to the post office, and none of those events had anything to do with the fact that she hadn't seen Brogan since they'd gone sailing last week. As to washing her hands and running a quick comb through her hair, that was basic good hygiene. Her jeans and oversized T-shirt didn't exactly constitute dress-to-impress attire because she wasn't in any place to impress anyone, nor did she care about doing so, but then again, maybe her nice navy blue coat would spruce up the outfit a bit, while still being appropriate for the breeze that was picking up. And her sneakers had gotten wet in the garden, so it was only reasonable to trade them for her nicer boots.

By the time she walked to the post office, she'd cleaned up considerably, only in ways that made complete sense, but she'd also killed more time than she'd meant to. She reached the storefront as Brogan stepped out onto the sidewalk and turned the lock on the door.

"Oh, I'm too late," Emma said, her heart sinking as the cream suddenly felt more important than it had during the minutes she'd spent worrying about her attire.

Brogan smiled. "What did you need?"

"It's not important. You've locked up."

Brogan patted her pocket. "I've got the key right here."

"No, it can wait. You've turned off the register and everything. I was only after some clotted cream tonight."

Brogan eyed her suspiciously. "Are you living entirely on scones?"

Emma shifted from one foot to the other. "I like them, and I didn't get them for the first thirty-three years of my life."

"So you're making up for lost time?"

"Let's go with that," Emma said.

Instead of condemning her, Brogan laughed heartily. "As long as you're happy and you aren't doing it because you don't like any of the other food from our grocery stores."

Emma scrunched up her face. "I haven't exactly visited any of the grocery stores, other than this one."

"You've been here over a month. How can you live on the canned sauces and frozen pizza we sell to tourists?"

"And scones," Emma added. "Ladies bring me scones, like, once a week."

Brogan nodded sympathetically, and somehow her lack of judgement made Emma feel even more foolish. "I've been meaning to do a bigger shopping trip, but I don't know the bus system yet."

"There's one from here to Newpeth," Brogan said. "It runs at the half hour if it's on time."

"See, I could do that," Emma said, with forced cheerfulness. "I could take the bus to Newpeth, buy bags full of healthy foods, and then lug them all home on the bus again."

"Or you could ride with me," Brogan offered.

"What?"

"I wanted to pick up some things for Nora. She had the baby, so she's not up for a big shopping trip. Why not come along?"

Emma was closer to saying yes than she normally would have been. She did need to go, and taking Brogan up on her offer would be easier than learning how to use the bus, fitting her shopping into the bus schedule, and dragging all the groceries home with her. Still, she couldn't always depend on other people to cart her around, and Brogan had already done more than her fair share of babysitting. Plus, she wasn't at all certain Brogan wasn't just being nice about the whole preplanned shopping trip. "I don't want to impose. I really do need to be independent. Maybe I'll call a cab."

Brogan frowned slightly but didn't push. "Okay, well, there's only one of those in town."

"Great. I'll give them a call as soon as I find the number."

"I've got it." Brogan fished in her pocket and pulled out a wallet, then removed a black business card with red typeface advertising a coastal cab service. "You might want to dial them now, though, if you want to go tonight. Sometimes they get booked up."

"Okay," Emma said. "Thank you."

"No problem. I'm sure I'll see you again soon," Brogan said. Then with a little wave she crossed the street.

Emma's chest tightened as she watched her go, and the feeling unsettled her. To push it away, she pulled her phone from her coat pocket and dialed the number on the card. She might as well take the leap now, because if she went back home, she'd probably end up eating dry scones for dinner again.

She heard the phone ring in her hand, and then echo across the street. She had enough time to find the sound strange, but not long enough to process what it meant until a familiar voice answered, both close to her ear and only slightly farther away.

"Hello, you've reached Coastal Cab Shares and McKay Puffin tours. This is Brogan. How may I help you?"

She lowered the phone from her ear and glanced across the way where Brogan leaned against a car, smiling cheekily.

"You gave me your own number?"

"You asked for a cab," Brogan said with laughter in her voice. Then she hung up the phone and walked back across the street. "Just so happens my brother-in-law Marcus owns the cab company, and he's married to Nora, who had the baby, and—"

"You're helping him out." Emma gave Brogan a playful shove. "Is there anything you don't do?"

Brogan's cheeks grew flush with color that almost matched her hair, and Emma realized the comment could be taken as a double entendre. Her mind filled with myriad images of other things Brogan might be able to do, and too many of them came back to the conversation she'd overheard her having with Julia in the post office. The warmth spreading through her own cheeks suggested Brogan wasn't the only one blushing anymore.

She recovered as quickly as possible. "I mean, I suppose we're going to the store together."

Brogan nodded. "Unless you decide to drive yourself, I guess we are."

"Even if I could, I don't have a car."

"Luckily for us, I do." Brogan pointed to a blue Peugeot across the street. "Does now work for you?"

Emma wanted to say "no" out of instinct to avoid anything unplanned, but she also wanted to say "yes," and since logic also fell on the side of "yes," she nodded.

"Let's go," Brogan said in her usual amiable way, and off she went, leaving Emma to follow along.

"Why don't you have a car?" Brogan asked, as Emma fell into step beside her. "I mean, not to be rude or anything, but it seems like you could afford one, and you didn't seem keen on taking the bus, so it's not like you're a public transit aficionado."

"Not really," Emma agreed as she reached the car, and Brogan hit the unlock button on her key fob. The lights flashed, the locks clicked, and Emma pulled open her door handle to find herself staring at the steering wheel. Confused, she blinked a few times, then with a duh-style realization processed the fact that in England the driver sat opposite of where she was used to.

Emma felt a flash of frustration and embarrassment, but when she glanced up at Brogan biting her lip in an attempt to hide a smile, she couldn't help but laugh. "There. That's why I don't have a car. I would sit on the wrong side, and then I would drive on the wrong side, and then, well, someone would probably die."

"You'd learn," Brogan said, trading her places. "You're a smart, competent woman. I have complete faith in your ability to transfer your driving skills to the left side of the road."

"Thanks," Emma said, wanting to believe it could really be simple, but as soon as Brogan took a left turn into the left lane, she winced and instinctively reached for the dashboard.

Thankfully Brogan didn't take offense or even seem to notice the way she continued to flinch every time a car pulled out on the winding country roads ahead of them, and Emma had to admit, by the time they pulled into the parking lot of Aldi ten minutes later, her heart rate had all but returned to normal.

"You made it," Brogan said as she hopped out and grabbed a few reusable shopping bags from the boot of the car. "I think you've earned a treat. What will you choose?"

"Something fresh." Her excitement rose, as the first thing she saw when entering the store was a long row of fruits and vegetables. "Look, zucchini."

"Where?" Brogan asked, scanning the bins closest to them.

"There." Emma picked one up to show her.

"What did you call it?"

"Zucchini," Emma said, then faltered. "What do you call it?"

"Courgette."

"That makes them sound super fancy."

Brogan laughed. "But zucchini is much more fun to say. *Zucchini. Zucc-hini.* Say it again."

"Zucchini." Both Brogan's joy and the fact that she'd never given any thought to how fun "zucchini" was to say made her laugh along. She couldn't remember the last time that sound had escaped her own body, and over something so simple, something that could have easily been another frustration. "I wonder how many things in here I'd use the wrong word for."

"Not wrong, different. You're a writer. It's good to know different words for things. Besides, we get your TV shows and movies over here, so we can figure out most American words."

"I'm sad to say we don't get many of yours. It would've taken me a long time to figure out what you meant if you'd said 'courgette.' Maybe I should have studied British foods online before I came to the store."

"No," Brogan said quickly. "You should study them in the store, or in a kitchen, or at a table. Come on. I'll give you a quick tour."

And with that she went off down the vegetable aisle. "The foods here probably aren't much different, but they might be called different things. Like this is rocket."

Emma examined a bunch of greens she held up and said, "Arugula."

Brogan grinned. "Again, you win with the fun word."

"I don't know. Rockets are nothing to sniff at."

"Fair dues." Brogan moved along to grab a large purple bulb from another bin. "Aubergine."

"Eggplant," Emma said in American. "You win the fun points on this one."

"And this is a swede, unless you drive north about thirty miles. Then it's a neep."

"We call them turnips, so I think Scotland gets the points there."

"Agreed, but Ireland wins on potatoes," Brogan said, tossing a bag of them into her cart.

"We say potatoes, too."

"Yes, but you don't do them like the Irish. We have over a hundred varieties, and something like ninety different words to describe them."

"We?" Emma asked, as she perused the last of the vegetables and moved on to the fruits.

"My father's from Cork. He was adamant we grew up thinking of ourselves as binational, hence all the girls being given names like Siobhán, Ciara, Brogan, and Nora."

"The girls?" Emma asked, putting some plump grapes in her basket.

"My mum wasn't going to roll over and raise a brood of Gaelic-infused redheads, so she got the boys, Archie, Nevil, Edmond, and Charles."

"A matching set of his and hers kids."

"Exactly. I don't know what they'd have done if either of them had been particularly religious. We'd probably have been carted to two churches every Sunday. As it was, we spent regular Sundays in the Church of England, and Christmas and Easter holidays at the Catholic church since we were usually visiting family in Ireland."

"Did it get confusing?"

"Not at all. It's just the way things were, or are, actually." Brogan picked out a beef roast and a few steaks. "We didn't know any different until we got to school and found out not everybody cussed in Gaelic, or wore jumpers knit by their Irish aunts."

"Did the other kids at school find those things odd?"

"Of course. They treated us like walking stereotypes," Brogan said, then pointed to some refrigerated pastries. "Have you had any meat pies yet?"

Emma blinked at the non sequitur. "No."

Brogan grabbed two packages. "Then you need these. They won't be as good as homemade, but you'll get the idea. The steak and ale is more traditional, but the chicken curry is brilliant."

"Brilliant," Emma repeated, accepting both packages.

"What about a Cornish pastie?"

She shook her head, and Brogan snatched another plastic-wrapped hunk of what appeared to be a half moon of puff pastry, then paused.

"Do you like mushrooms?"

"Yes."

"Good. Chicken, bacon, and mushrooms make a good mix."

"Indeed." Her stomach gave a low growl as if expressing agreement, and she realized she actually did want to eat the things Brogan had dropped into her basket. She smiled broadly and pushed aside the questions about whether the foods or the person suggesting them had sparked the change.

"Hey, have you had Yorkshire pudding?"

She shook her head.

"It's not a full English roast without one, but you're not to get them from Aldi. Some Sunday you have to come by the Raven when I'm working, and I'll fix you up. Same with spotted dick; you're not to eat it out of a freezer case."

"I'm not sure I want to eat spotted dick under any circumstances."

"Right, probably not the way you Americans would use the term, but over here the spots are currants."

"It wasn't the spotted part that killed the dish for me so much as the other word."

Brogan laughed so loudly a couple of people turned to look at them. "I'm glad to hear you say so, and under any other circumstances I'd agree one hundred percent, but I'm talking about puddings here, or rather, what do you call them? Desserts?"

"Yes."

"In this case, I'm talking about desserts, and that's the one place I'll make an exception."

"Okay," Emma said, a smile stretching her cheeks. "Your scones are pretty different from ours, even though we use basically the same word, and your words can be very different from ours even when we use the same foods. If you say your spotted dick is different from any I've encountered before, which admittedly is zero, I guess I'd be willing to trust you."

They each left the store with several large bags of groceries, and Brogan's face was a little sore from all the smiling, but also trying not to smile so much she looked loopy. Which was actually how she felt with Emma hanging on her every word. She'd never had to work particularly hard to entertain people, but listing the names of fresh veg and various biscuits was a low bar, even for her. And when she'd explained that British supermarkets were required to charge for bags, which meant most people bought and reused their own, Emma was so thrilled by the idea Brogan felt like she should have got both a commission on the five freezer-grade bags Emma purchased as well as some sort of environmentalist prize for relaying the idea to her.

And yet when they reached her car, Emma happily walked right up to the driver's side, peeked in the window, and frowned before her face turned a flustered shade of pink.

"I did it again," she said sheepishly.

"No worries. You've got into cars the other way 'round for decades. You can't undo conditioning like that in two rides. You have to give yourself time."

"Time," Emma echoed sadly, "that's what everyone tells me."

The words, combined with the desolation flooding her voice, made it obvious they weren't talking about cars anymore.

"I keep trying to make these baby steps forward, and I even start to feel proud of myself when I do. Really enjoying the scones was a big deal for me, but then I realized I've basically eaten nothing but scones for two weeks, and the thing I was so proud of actually feels totally pathetic." The words seemed to burst out of Emma before she'd given them permission, and as soon as they did, she clasped her hands over her mouth. "I'm sorry."

"Why?" Brogan asked, more confused by the abrupt turn-around than the information that sparked it.

"For saying those things aloud."

"As opposed to in your head?"

Emma frowned. "Actually, yes."

"Do you normally run those monologues internally?"

She nodded, and Brogan's heart broke. "I'm no expert on . . . anything, but I'd suspect those kinds of thoughts are better let out than held in."

"You're too kind." Emma paused and stared across the hood with big, wounded eyes. "Honestly, I'm not sure why you've been so kind to me. I haven't given you any reason to be."

"I'm sorry you believe you have to give someone a reason to be kind. I think kindness should be a sort of default position, and someone should have to give you a pretty compelling reason not to be."

Emma's eyes shimmered, but she took a deep breath and pushed it out in a hurry. "I hope you're right, and I wish more people agreed, but I shouldn't repay your kindness by dumping all my depressing insecurities on you. You signed up for a taxi ride and shopping trip, not a therapy session."

Brogan smiled. "I'm a taxi driver and a bartender. I'm used to therapy sessions."

Emma's mouth twitched upward. "Really? Then what, in your double professional opinion, do you recommend for someone who eats only scones and can't get into a car without falling to pieces?"

Brogan thought for a moment, the best she could with her heart pounding out a desire to see that little curl at the edge of Emma's pink lips grow into a full-fledged smile. Then she nodded toward the passenger door and said, "Hop in."

Emma was either too down or embarrassed to argue, but she clearly didn't understand the answer. Brogan didn't really, either, if she were being truly honest. It had been only a half-formed idea, but the way Emma gasped as they pulled out of the parking lot and onto a busier road sort of cemented her direction. They'd come too far to go back now, and if Brogan let Emma withdraw after they'd had such a wonderfully open hour together, she knew that's what would happen. Emma would go back into her shell, into her fear and self-doubt and whatever else kept her locked in that little cottage alone, and Brogan would go back to doubting she'd ever had the right to try to draw her out in the first place.

Of course, if this little trip went awry in any of the multiple ways it could, they'd end up considerably worse off than where they'd started the evening, but as Emma winced again at the last intersection before the edge of town, she decided the gamble had more upside than down, except for maybe death. That would be a worse downside, but she really didn't think of it as a serious possibility as much as an outlier.

With that happy thought, she pulled the car over to the side of a country road and killed the ignition.

"What happened?" Emma asked, her voice barely containing a hint of panic.

"Nothing. It's just you asked me what we should do about someone who's afraid of the car, and"—she held out the keys—"the answer is driving lessons."

Emma's already pale face went ghostly white. "No."

"The quickest way out is straight through."

"Brogan, I can't."

"You don't know that."

"I do. I know me. I will kill us both."

"Can you drive a stick shift?" Brogan asked calmly.

"In America."

"Same concept." She tapped the pedals lightly with her foot. "Clutch, brake, accelerator."

"They're in the same places," Emma said softly as she watched Brogan's feet. "Not opposite."

"See, nothing to worry about."

"Except the dying."

"We'll go slow, and this is an old sheep-herder's road. We aren't likely to meet any other cars, but if we do, you can pull over and let them pass."

"What if I kill the engine?"

"You probably will," Brogan said honestly. "It happens. Sometimes it even happens to me if I'm not paying attention and have to slam on the brakes, but it's not the end of the world."

"Not the end of the world," Emma repeated, as if the phrase resonated with her.

"You can do this," Brogan said softly. "I'll help."

Emma's mouth pressed into a flat line, and for a second Brogan feared she'd set her resolve to fight her, but then with one curt nod, she unfastened her seatbelt and got out of the car.

Brogan gave a little fist pump and then scrambled to get out of her way. She didn't want to do anything to jeopardize their momentum, so she silently passed Emma the keys and jogged around to the passenger side.

Emma had a steely glint in her blue eyes as she adjusted the driver's seat and gave her seatbelt an extra tug, as if she needed to make sure she'd gotten it as secure as possible. "Okay, clutch, brake, accelerator."

"Put the clutch in and turn the key," Brogan said. "No need to worry about anything else yet."

"One step at a time," Emma murmured, then, putting her left foot on the clutch, she switched on the ignition and the car rumbled to life.

"Good," Brogan said. "Take your time, get your bearings, but remember, you know how to drive."

"On the right side," Emma shot back, but her voice trembled in a way that suggested she was more scared than mad.

"Then drive on the right side," Brogan offered as calmly as she could. She wasn't nearly as worried about wrecking as she was about Emma freaking out.

"What?"

"It's basically a one-lane road. All the locals take their half out of the middle anyway, and it's not like there's anyone around," she reasoned. "Go ahead and start on the right side of the road until you're comfortable with the car, and then we'll move over."

Emma opened her mouth as if she intended to argue, then

glanced in her mirrors and sighed. "Okay. You're right. I have time. I have space. I can do this."

Brogan smiled. "I know you can."

Emma's breath shuddered as she exhaled slowly, and her knuckles went white on the steering wheel, but then she released her right hand, reached down and grabbed the door handle as if she intended to shift with it. She clutched it tightly, her eyes wide, and then her body went slack as the car sputtered to silence.

"Oh my God," Emma said, closing her eyes. "I tried to shift with my door."

"It's okay," Brogan whispered.

"I tried to shift with my door," Emma repeated, louder, "with my right hand, because my door is on my right-hand side, and the stick shift is on the left-hand side. I've never shifted with my left hand in my life."

Emma's panic started to pick at Brogan's, and she fought to keep her voice steady. She did not want Emma to melt down. Even more, she didn't want to be the cause of her meltdown. She didn't think she could live with herself if she ended up making Emma feel worse than she already did. Fighting to keep her own voice level, she said, "It's the same concept, only the hand has changed. The gears are in the same spot. The mechanics work the same way, just with your left hand."

"But I'm right-handed."

"So am I," Brogan assured her. "Come on."

"I killed the car."

"Come on." Brogan pleaded with her now. "You knew you'd make mistakes. Everyone does. It doesn't define you. It doesn't mean you won't get better."

Emma's eyes shimmered again. "You really believe I can do this, don't you?"

"It's never occurred to me that you can't," Brogan said, honestly. "The only question is whether or not you will."

Emma nodded. "I will."

Air and lightness exploded in Brogan's chest, and she smiled broadly. "Of course you will. Go ahead and put the clutch in again."

Emma did as instructed and turned the key, bringing the motor to life once more.

"When you're ready, use your left hand to find the gear shift, and put it in first gear, keeping your foot on the brake."

Emma nodded as she dropped her left hand onto the stick. "Left hand, everything else is the same."

"Ease up on the clutch and give it some revs."

And she did. Within seconds they were rolling slowly along the right side of the road.

Brogan fought the urge to cheer, but she couldn't resist a little fist pump at her side, and she said, "Good. Well done. You're doing it."

"Not really," Emma said. "I'm still on the right side in first gear."

"No worries. One step at a time. Which of those things do you want to address first?"

"Um"—the car gave a little stutter—"first gear."

"Good choice," Brogan said, even though neither one of them would've been a bad choice. "Ease in the clutch, and use your left hand to pull down into second."

Emma executed both those moves but didn't accelerate enough, and the car immediately began to sputter.

"More revs," Brogan said calmly, then quickly repeated, "more revs, now."

At the last second Emma pushed down the accelerator, and they lurched forward into the middle of the road.

"Great," Brogan said with forced cheerfulness as she dug her nails into the side of the seat Emma couldn't see. "You did it. And you moved over. Two birds, one stone."

Emma shook her head. "I almost killed it again."

"But you didn't. You're driving!"

Emma let the words sink in as her eyes darted quickly around before returning to dead forward. "I'm driving."

"In England, in a stick shift, and on the left side, sort of."

Emma's mouth curled up slightly, and with the smallest motion she eased them barely onto the left half of the road.

"How does that feel?" Brogan asked.

"Weird."

"But not terrible?"

Emma thought for a moment, as if double-checking to make sure she wasn't about to pass out or cry. "Not terrible."

"Want to take it up to third?"

"Isn't that pushing it?" Emma asked, then shook her head. "Actually, I don't know why I said that. I do want to take it up to third."

"Left hand," Brogan reminded gently. "You got this."

And she did. This time the car didn't so much as whine when she made the transition. Brogan silently thanked whatever saint guarded manual transmissions. "Perfect, you're doing everything right now."

"What about when we have to turn?"

"We've got a good three miles before we have to worry," Brogan said, certain her own relief was evident. "Let's bask in this accomplishment for a moment."

And they did. Neither of them spoke as the Northland countryside rolled by in gentle swells and verdant valleys dotted with white sheep. As long as they were going straight and slow, Brogan could almost convince herself they were out for a scenic drive. Still, as the next turn crept ever closer, she knew that wasn't the case. Emma had another challenge ahead, and Brogan wasn't naive enough to think she'd fly through it. Her own palms pricked with sweat at the prospect, so she could only imagine how Emma felt. She wished she could take the trouble for her, and she certainly could take the keys back to save her the frustration, but that would defeat the purpose, so she bit her lip as a stop sign came into view.

"Oh no," Emma muttered. "Left side, left side, left side."

To her credit, she heeded her own warning as she decelerated to a stop; only in her worries about lanes and the brake, she'd completely forgotten the clutch, and the engine shook, then clunked to a dead stop several meters shy of the actual crossing.

Emma groaned. "I killed it again."

"Yup," Brogan said cheerfully. "I'm not bothered. No one else saw. Fire her up again, and we're all good."

"Then I have to turn."

Brogan exaggerated her movements as she looked right, left, and right again. "I don't see anyone coming."

Emma took the hint and revved the car again. Staying in first gear, she eased slowly into the intersection.

Brogan opened her mouth to remind her to stay left, but the words never had to leave her lips. Emma executed the turn perfectly and then without encouragement quickly shifted into second gear.

"You did it," Brogan said, hearing the awe in her own voice.

"I did." Emma grinned.

"You didn't panic."

"No."

"You didn't get overwhelmed when you stopped."

"Neither did you."

"I didn't even have to tell you how," Brogan said. "That one was all you."

"You kept me calm," Emma said, eyes still pinned to the road.

"But you did the work."

Emma's grin grew, and Brogan's heart swelled at the return of the expression she'd longed to see.

"Where to next?" Emma asked, hope balancing out some of the fear in her voice.

"Take your next right."

"But stay left," Emma warned herself. And she did, followed by another left, and then a bigger hill that required her to downshift.

Brogan encouraged her with a few reminders of "more revs," but little else. Soon they were practically zipping through the countryside, from one farm road to another, and as Emma soared over each new hill, Brogan's heart soared along with her. She felt an inordinate amount of pride, but not in her own teaching, or even in Emma's driving. She'd meant what she'd said. She'd never doubted Emma's practical capabilities, but she had had more than a solid dose of fear about her emotional fortitude. She shouldn't have. Emma faced her fears, and with very little encouragement she'd conquered them. Now that she knew she could do it in this area, what other doors would she see as open for herself?

Chapter Eight

"We're coming up on a town," Emma said as she saw the sign for some place called Warkworth.

"We are. It's a small one."

"I'm not sure I'm ready for a town of any size." She'd done better than she'd expected, infinitely so, but her shoulders were getting sore from the tension of keeping a death grip on the steering wheel and the mental fatigue from concentrating harder than she had in months. Driving for fifteen minutes on country lanes might not have been much to most people, but it had taken a lot out of her and given her a lot to process in return. Still, she worried for a second Brogan might protest or think less of her for not charging into the nearest village.

Instead she said, "No need to go into Warkworth in a car. I always park on a side street before we get to the bridge into town."

"Why?" Emma asked.

"It's a nice walk across the river and through the gates of the old town wall."

She shook her head, trying not to get distracted by such a pretty image or the foreign concepts of town walls and gates. "I mean, why are we getting out in Warkworth?"

"It's tea time, plus you've earned a treat," Brogan said casually. "And I know the perfect place."

"We have a car full of groceries."

"I didn't exactly plan the outing. We're being spontaneous, but you sprang for the good cooler bags, so I can't imagine anything will spoil in an hour. Unless you don't want to try the best scones in all of the English borders."

Emma's stomach growled its response, and she smiled weakly. She hadn't planned on a dinner out. She still had bits of dirt on the knees of her jeans, and her coat was covering a baggy, long-sleeved T-shirt, but Brogan had been so nice to her, and she did feel a little bit like celebrating her accomplishment. Plus, scones. So, feeling a little bit like a puppy whose handler had said "treat," she eased the car to the side of the road where Brogan indicated, and let the engine clatter from second gear to dead. "Oops."

"No 'oops,'" Brogan said cheerfully. "You're done, and you did brilliant."

She smiled as she exited the car in spite of her suspicion Brogan was overstating her enthusiasm, but before she could get too down on herself, they walked around a bank of trees and found themselves standing at a river's edge. Across the water, a stone wall encircled thickly packed houses and shops huddled close in the shadow of an ancient castle. "Wow."

"See," Brogan said, as she started across the bridge, "not a bad stroll."

Emma was too busy taking in the sights to comment again on Brogan's gift for understatement. They crossed a stone bridge and entered the town through an archway in the outer wall. She glanced up, half expecting to see archers standing guard overhead, or at least the spikes of an iron gate that could slam down at any moment. She found neither, but she didn't mind, as her imagination had already painted a vivid picture of what the entrance would've looked like a thousand years earlier. She could hear the mewls of animals on their way to market, and the crunch of wooden wheels against dirty cobblestones. She felt the press of bodies, the brush of skirts, the jostle of carts squeezing through narrow streets with two-story stone houses lining every side.

"Here's the tea house," Brogan said, and Emma had to blink a few times in order to see her pointing to a doorway in the row house to their right. Brogan eyed her curiously, her expression bemused, as Emma continued the disorienting mental return to their modern reality. "Unless, of course, you'd rather go somewhere else."

"No." Emma shook her head, unable to admit she had no interest in another place, so much as another time. Could she explain that without seeming crazy? Plus, Amalie had always gotten so annoyed with her daydreams. She didn't want to offend Brogan by admitting she'd forgotten she was even there for a moment. "This is fine."

A hostess met them at the door and took their coats, leaving Emma a little self-conscious about her attire, but as they entered the main dining room, she found it more similar to a large living room than a formal restaurant. Distressed wooden tables were pushed to the sides to make use of long, low benches along the wall. Every seat was stacked high with an array of throw pillows, and a large stone and cast-iron fireplace radiated warmth all the way across the room. "When I said 'fine,' I had no idea it was actually perfect."

Brogan beamed. "I was worried you'd expect a tea room to be more posh."

"I did," Emma admitted, "which is why I hesitated. If you'd told me we were going to drink tea in my grandmother's living room, I would've begged you to take me there immediately."

"Can I bring you some menus?" a waitress asked.

"I want the scones," Emma blurted, then covered her mouth, causing Brogan to laugh.

"Just scones or a full afternoon tea?" the waitress asked.

"Two afternoon teas." Brogan took charge. "One fruit scone, one cheese scone."

"And your sponges?"

"Lemon courgette and a Victoria, please."

The waitress nodded.

"And can you bring us a mix for the sandwiches?" Brogan asked.

"Of course," the waitress said with a nod and turned to go.

"That sounds like a lot of food," Emma whispered.

"It is," Brogan agreed, taking a chair from a small table and arranging the cushions to her liking.

Emma did the same, ensconcing herself in the corner of a church pew-style bench. Her voice low, she added, "I don't eat a lot of food."

"It's okay. I do."

Emma smiled, not surprised by the fact or the amiable way Brogan put her at ease.

The tea came in individual pots with plain white cups and saucers, accompanied by tiny pitchers of milk and lidded cups full of sugar cubes. The entire setup reminded her of playing tea as a girl, only this time she didn't have to wear a dress or a bonnet or sit up straight and cross her legs at the ankles.

"Are you comfortable?" Brogan asked.

"Yes." The answer was perhaps too simple. What she should've said but didn't, for fear of gushing, was the pillows, the tea, the warmth of the crackling fire, and most of all the company all combined to make her more comfortable than she'd been in ages. "You've got a talent for that."

"What?"

"Making people comfortable."

Brogan shook her head. "I'm not sure you would've said so half an hour ago when I made you drive the car."

Emma laughed, really laughed, for at least the second time in as many hours.

"Or when I dragged you out on the boat and made you take the tiller."

"No," she admitted. "I felt a certain amount of discomfort with assuming that task."

"And let's not forget the night we met and made each other scream like schoolchildren in a haunted house."

"Well, all right then." Tears sprang to Emma's eyes, from laughter now. She'd shed so many of them over the last few months, and yet never for this reason. "You're right. You make me terribly uncomfortable on a regular basis. I must be a glutton for punishment. Otherwise, I wouldn't keep coming back for more."

Brogan smiled and glanced over her shoulder at the waitress approaching with two contraptions Emma couldn't quite process until they were set on the table in front of her. Each one consisted of a silver frame holding three plates stacked at equal intervals to create a self-supporting tower of food. The lower level held finger sandwiches sliced into strips with the crusts cut off. The middle tier supported a generous slice of sponge cake with a layer of thick red jam and decadent cream icing. On top of the whole thing sat a plate of her beloved scones next to a dish overflowing with clotted cream and an individual jar of jam.

Emma's jaw dropped, but her mouth also started to water, and she worried she might actually drool on the table if she didn't pull herself together immediately, so she said the only words she could manage in the moment. "Thank you."

Brogan chuckled and shook her head, but Emma reached across the table to squeeze her hand. "I mean it. Thank you for the driving, and the sailing, and shopping, and for this three-story tower of heaven. I don't think I've done anything to deserve any—"

"Hey," Brogan whispered, her voice a little raspy, "you need to let go of this 'deserving' notion."

She shook her head. "I know. You're a nice person, but it's rare for me to meet someone who doesn't want something from me."

"Then I'm glad you moved across an ocean to get away from them all." The bite was back in Brogan's voice, accompanied by storm clouds in her green eyes. "I know it took a lot of bravery to—"

"It didn't."

"What?" Brogan sat back, breaking the connection between them and letting the coldness seep into Emma again.

"I'm not brave."

"But you—"

Emma held up her hand. "—moved to a place where I didn't know anyone, yes. People keep pointing that out as some sort of example of my fortitude, but it couldn't be further from the truth. I didn't immigrate in search of adventure. I ran away from home because I was scared and lost and ashamed. I crossed an ocean to escape my humiliation and the fear that even after being made a fool of by the person I trusted most, if given the chance, I might fall on my knees and beg her to lie to me a little longer."

Brogan stared at her, eyes wide, cheeks flushed, probably with embarrassment at the outburst.

"Oh, and I hid." She didn't see the point in holding back now. Might as well be out with the whole truth. "I went to a place where I didn't know a soul because I wanted to hide from human contact and become a hermit, alone with my writing and a set of memories that belonged to someone else in a different time."

They stared at each other until Emma couldn't take it anymore, and she turned her attention back to the food, which didn't quite have the same appeal as before. Still, she didn't know what else to do, so she snatched a scone from her food tower and took a bite without even adding the cream. It melted in her mouth, warm and soft with a hint of . . . cheddar?

"Is there cheese in this scone?" she asked, her mouth still half full.

Brogan laughed a little harder than the question warranted, or maybe it was the absurd non sequitur, or perhaps her vast relief at being let off the hook from the social awkwardness sparked by Emma's wildly emotional outburst simply came out in the form of laughter. Either way, they were back on neutral ground, and Emma had found out cheese scones were a thing, so she couldn't feel any great regret in the moment.

Brogan couldn't believe they'd rebounded. Fifteen minutes ago, she'd absolutely frozen with the fear that she'd inadvertently driven a knife into Emma's only partially healed heart. The horror and guilt felt like some sort of stake to her own chest, almost as though she'd committed a conversational murder-suicide. And now, Emma sat across from her, calmly polishing off her second salmon-and-cream-cheese finger sandwich.

Brogan wasn't sure her ticker could take any more ups and downs of that magnitude. She tried to remind herself this was why she didn't bring up serious topics with the women she dated. Not that she and Emma were on a date, but apparently similar principles applied. Movies, shopping, the weather, local attractions, careers, or services rendered, either in the personal or business sense, were all safe topics. Families, religion, money, exes, secret heartbreak, hidden fears, and darkest yearnings were on the long list of things she couldn't handle. And it wasn't like she didn't want to. In the moment when Emma's beautiful face had contorted with pain and her voice had cracked on the word "humiliation," Brogan would've gladly stuck her hand into the nearby fire to make her smile again. She might have sold a kidney to be the one to soothe those insecurities, or committed murder—not the conversational kind, but the actual cold-blooded variety—if she'd been within a continent of the person who'd hurt Emma.

And yet, she did nothing. She was not prepared. She was not capable of doing anything but silently gaping at her until Emma soothed herself with a garden-variety cheese scone. If pressed, she'd have to admit the vast swing left her questioning Emma's emotional stability for a moment, but as the woman across from her regained her composure, Brogan suspected she'd simply learned a great deal of self-control over many months of hiding the extent of her pain from others. If hurt like that simmered constantly beneath the surface, no wonder Emma had lost so much weight. She likely spent a great deal of energy trying to function under the weight of it all.

Brogan didn't have that kind of strength. Another reason to steer clear of serious relationships. She didn't share Emma's grace or poise or fortitude. She was a baby every time she got a cold or missed a meal. How would she be able to stomach complete devastation at the hands of someone she loved?

No, it was much better to stick to scones.

"This cake is amazing," Emma said, some of the color returning to her cheeks as she took another large bite.

"It's called a Victoria sponge," Brogan explained.

"After Queen Victoria?"

"I'm not sure she invented it personally, but yes, probably dates back to her reign, which I like to think of as a mix of subjecting foreign nations to colonial rule and creating new confectionary delights."

"So, a real mixed bag, then. Probably all comes out in the wash."

Brogan snorted and watched Emma manage to shove a rather large cut of sponge into her delicate frame. If she continued to add baked goods to the growing repertoire of foods she could stomach, she might not have such a slender frame much longer, though she had a long way to go before she'd get to anything approaching thick. Her jeans still hung a bit too loosely, and hints of collarbones still showed through her long-sleeved T-shirt, but her face wasn't as wan as it'd been weeks ago. Her eyes, still the palest of blues, weren't encircled in dark shadows anymore, either, and her high cheekbones were not quite as pronounced.

"I haven't eaten like this since," she sighed, "I don't know when."

"I can't say that I eat like this often," Brogan admitted.

"You mean British folks don't stuff themselves with cake towers and tea every night?"

"Sadly, no. This is likely more stereotypically British than I've been in a year."

"I'm honored to share the moment. I've mostly been forcing down the occasional bowl of soup from a can."

Brogan grimaced. "Because you've had no appetite, or because Americans really do rely on processed food?"

"Both," Emma said, without a hint of defensiveness. "I mean, I don't want to throw all Americans under the bus. There's been a resurgence of farm-to-table foods, but sadly you have to be able to cook in order to take part, and as a child of the '80s, I never learned to do much more than microwave or reheat. As an adult, I've traveled a lot and eaten out too often to make the effort feel worthwhile."

"I'd be happy to teach you a few basics, but in the meantime,

I work at the pub several nights a week. I can see to it you get a decent meal."

"Do you cook there?"

"Most nights I'm behind the bar, but if we're slow or short-staffed, I pop into the kitchen. I can do a steak with roasted potatoes or bangers and mash as well as the next person. They aren't complicated."

"That's a relative assessment. I wouldn't be likely to undertake either. Where did you learn?"

"My mum," Brogan said, a hint of pride seeping in. "She can cook anything, and in quantities to feed an army."

"With eight kids, I suppose she'd have to."

"Right?" Brogan laughed. "Cooking was likely a skill born out of necessity for her, and I know it was for me. When you're a middle child with four more that come after, you have to learn to help get the food on the table or learn to wait your turn. I was never much good at patience, so I got put to work earlier than some of the others."

"What's the age difference between you all?"

"Siobhán's the oldest. She's six years ahead of me and a full sixteen ahead of Charlie, who's the baby."

"I don't think I've met either of them."

"You'll not likely see Siobhán. She lives outside Belfast, and she's got two teenage boys with busy lives, but Charlie's been home from uni for almost two years. He lives with me and doesn't find much to do during the winters with his fancy degree in recreation sciences or something like that. I'm sure you'll run into him eventually."

"Let me guess," Emma said playfully. "He'll have red hair and some beautiful shade of green eyes, and he'll be working an odd job at some business owned or run by another McKay?"

"If you added, 'or on the cricket pitch claiming to coach the children as an excuse for getting a go at their game,' you'd have about summed him up."

Emma smiled. "Then I think I'll like Charlie quite a bit."

Brogan's chest warmed at what she took as a sort of reflected compliment, seeing as how Emma's assumptions about Charlie fit her as well as they did him.

"I love how your family helps each other so much, and I love how much a part of the village they are. It would be nice to stay in one place long enough to leave the mark of multiple generations on it."

"You moved around a lot as a kid?"

"Not in the exciting sense," Emma said, "mostly from suburb to suburb. We were always within commuting distance to New York City, and we always vacationed in the Catskills or the Adirondacks, but the places themselves were all blandly interchangeable."

"I don't know," Brogan said, sitting back and nudging the remaining cucumber sandwiches inconspicuously toward Emma. "New York City sounds pretty exciting to me."

"It is," Emma agreed. "I didn't go in much as a child, though. My parents both worked a lot and didn't want to make the commute again with their time off, but I went to college at Columbia, and I got my fill of the Big Apple then."

"You didn't like it?"

"I didn't dislike it. The arts scene was fantastic, with endless amounts of creative outlets, but with so many to choose from, I found it hard to focus my attention on any one of them. I always wrote best at all the little retreats in the mountains."

"Did you get to them a lot?"

Emma nodded, her eyes lowered, and Brogan watched, spellbound, as her chest rose and fell noticeably. There it was again, the subtle war for control. What had she said to spark it? What could she possibly say to sway the battle?

In the end, though, she didn't have to say a thing, as Emma forced a joyless smile and carried on. "My wi—ex-wife, she ran them. She was an accomplished writer in her own right, Amalie Max."

Brogan shook her head at the name. "I've never heard of her."

Emma winced, then, placing both hands on the edge of the table as if to steady herself, continued. "Few people have, except for avant-garde literary critics. Since she didn't have the commercial appeal to make a living, she went around the northeast running retreat-style workshops for budding writers."

"You were one of her students?" Brogan asked, then tightened up as she realized she'd once again asked a dangerous question.

"Just for a weekend, but we took off from there. I traveled with her a lot, and when she'd teach, I'd write. The balance was always unfair. She deserved the freedom I had. She's a much better writer. It's terrible for the market to reward me instead of her."

Brogan shook her head. "I don't know that it's an either/or equation. It's not as though you held up her book in one hand and yours in another and told all the world they could only read one. You simply managed to write books more people wanted to read."

Emma smiled sadly. "And I suppose if that's not unfair, it's at least ironic. I would've been content to spend my life in mountain retreats. Instead, I ended up with the fame and money and power and everything that goes with them."

"Like what?"

"Responsibility. A platform. Obligations to agents and publishers and readers. Bicoastal book launches followed by endless interviews. And then, even when I'd escape with Amalie to her retreats, I'd get mobbed by aspiring authors who no longer saw me as one of them."

"They saw you as what they wanted to become," Brogan finished, "and they wanted you to lead them there."

Emma nodded slowly. "Amalie, who actually knew how to get them there, who had the skills and talent and ambition, she couldn't . . ."

Brogan silently filled in the words Emma still cared too much to say, about a woman who clearly didn't deserve her protection, someone who'd let jealousy and pride overtake her. She couldn't have taken well to the role reversal.

"Eventually I bought a small house in the Catskills, not far from one of my writer friends, Talia, but even that got complicated because she'd signed a big movie deal, and soon there were actresses and musicians and designers around all the time. Reporters linked my place with hers and started acting like we had this powerhouse artists' collective, when all we really wanted to be was two introverts in separate cabins."

Brogan laughed in spite of the sadness underlying the comment. "Best-laid plans of mice and men."

"When the producers saw the success of adapting Talia's book into a movie, all they had to do was glance down the road to find their next target."

"They offered you a film deal? Like, Hollywood and big budget movie stars?" Brogan asked, unable to keep the awe out of her voice. If she hadn't known she was out of her league already, the topic certainly drove home the point.

"A full treatment."

Brogan didn't know what that meant, so she shook her head. She wished she could ask some sort of enlightened question or make an interesting point, anything to add to the conversation in a meaningful way. She only managed to blurt out, "What happened?"

"My life fell apart," Emma said bluntly, "and I ran away."

Brogan stared at her, unblinking. Here they were again, right on the cliff, and she feared if she breathed the wrong way, the shelf would give out beneath them again. Still, she had to say something, didn't she? She couldn't leave Emma hanging there alone, but the last time she'd waded into these topics, she'd hurt more than she'd helped. In the end, she merely offered a vague, "Wow."

"Yup," Emma said, then pressed her lips in a thin line for a second before meeting her eyes once more. "That's my pathetic story. Now please have mercy on me and tell me something about you, so I don't feel like I've ruined such a lovely afternoon by depressing us both again."

"No," Brogan said. "I'm not, I mean, not that I won't tell you, but you didn't ruin anything."

"I monopolized every topic," Emma said. "You've hardly told me anything about you, other than odd jobs and siblings."

She sighed. "That's really all there is to tell."

"You're holding out on me."

"No. Honestly, I'm an open book, just a boring one."

"You've lived in Amberwick your whole life?"

"Yes."

"What about school?"

"All local. I did *A* levels, but I didn't see the point in going away to uni. I had steady work in the village without it, and no real desire to do anything outside of the village."

"What about hobbies?"

Brogan shrugged. "I like to sail, but you've seen that. I enjoy spending time with my nieces and nephews. I help my family whenever possible, and I work."

"A lot," Emma added. "You work a lot."

Brogan frowned at the truth. She liked most of her jobs, or at least, she didn't dislike them. She felt productive and useful and social, but none of that compared to what Emma had done with her life. She felt aimless by comparison.

"And what about, well . . ." Emma's cheeks flushed, and she hid behind her cup of tea.

"What?"

"I didn't mean to pry, but I was going to ask about relationships."

Brogan's heart gave a dull thud. "None to speak of."

"At the moment?"

"Ever." She shrugged. "I mean, I started dating in secondary school, but things never got serious before my first girlfriend left for uni. Then there was another local woman for half a year, but she couldn't get work up here and moved to London. Same story a couple times over, but there's not much of a stable pool to choose from around here."

"A *stable* pool?" Emma asked, emphasizing the word Brogan hadn't wanted to focus on.

She shifted slightly in her seat. "There are tourists from time to time."

Emma smiled politely, but didn't respond, leaving Brogan to wonder why she felt so uncomfortable in the silence. She was an adult. She'd never made any secret of the fact that she enjoyed the company of other lesbians when she could get it. The whole town had a rather high opinion of her imagined skill set, and she'd never done anything to try to persuade them otherwise. Why now, sitting across from Emma, did those occurrences feel as bland and aimless as the rest of her story?

Brogan shook her head slightly. She didn't like those internal questions, and she suspected she'd like the answers even less. Glancing out the window, she noticed night had fallen, and the darkness confirmed she'd stayed longer than she'd intended. "I didn't realize it had got so late."

Emma followed her line of sight, but didn't seem nearly as shaken by the glow of a lone street lamp. "Did I keep you too long?"

The comment hit her in the chest with the full force of all its possible meanings. Brogan's first impulse was to say, "Not nearly long enough," but thankfully her voice caught in her throat, and she had to take a swig of her now tepid tea, which gave her time to remember they were not on a date. They were friends, maybe, and she couldn't let a flash of silliness risk that, so she pushed back from the table and said, "Not at all, but you've had a big day. I think I've taken up enough of your time."

Emma folded her napkin neatly and placed it on the table. "I'm not going anywhere anytime soon."

Brogan forced a smile, but she couldn't force her heart to believe those words. Emma was too strong, too talented, too beautiful, and had too many opportunities at her feet. She would rebound and go back to doing great things. Brogan, on the other hand, was the one who wasn't likely to go anywhere from here.

Chapter Nine

Emma swung open the door to the post office with so much enthusiasm it nearly took off with her. She barely pulled it back before it slammed into the shelves of bread lining the wall, and in doing so nearly got jerked off her feet.

"Whew," she said, aware she'd bumbled a rather mundane action into a fit of awkwardness. She glanced up, expecting to see Brogan smiling at her from behind the counter and was already anticipating another joke about lack of grace around each other, but instead she met the blue eyes of Margaret McKay.

"Are you all right, dear?"

Her face flushed. Somehow, tripping in front of Brogan would've been funny, but coming across as a doofus who didn't know how to work a door in front of the McKay matriarch sparked a lot more embarrassment. "Yes, I just stumbled, and I was sort of expecting someone else."

"Sorry to disappoint," Margaret said, her smile growing slightly.

"No, not at all." She kicked herself for being rude, especially to the woman who looked remarkably like her grandmother. "It's lovely to see you again."

"It's all right," Margaret said kindly. "I'm used to my children's friends stopping by asking for them."

Emma frowned. Is that what she'd done? She hadn't thought so. She'd had an excuse for stopping by. She even had an envelope in her jacket pocket to mail to her agent, but somehow Mar-

128

garet's simple statement of fact made it impossible to deny that part of her had come in with the hopes of seeing Brogan.

"She's been tremendously kind to me," Emma said softly.

Margaret's smile rose again, this time with pride. "I like to think I raised eight good kids, but Brogan was always more of a helper than the others. Like her father in that way. Liam can't sit still when there's something to be fixed or explored or improved."

Emma nodded. The description fit. Every time she'd had a problem, Brogan had been there to help, either by offering a solution, or not. Sometimes she sat still and calm while Emma composed herself. Everyone always rushed to fill the silence with empty platitudes or some blatant redirect. Brogan never did. Still, Emma didn't feel comfortable expressing something so personal to Brogan's mother. Instead, she said, "She taught me how to drive. And she took me sailing. And she actually helped Reggie plan my garden remodel, too."

"All things she's good at," Margaret said, but the flush of pink in her cheeks suggested she took the comments as a sort of compliment.

"Actually, saying all that out loud makes me feel like I haven't done nearly enough to thank her." She'd paid for their tea last week, but Brogan wouldn't let her pay for her cab services, saying she'd had to run to the store anyway. But still, paying for a ride wouldn't have been nearly enough. It might have actually been reductive, because Brogan had done much more than chauffeur her around. "I wish I knew more about her interests or tastes, so I could do something nice for her, but I'm afraid I wouldn't know what to get her for the boat, or camping, or her own garden, if she even has one."

Margaret nodded. "She does, but she's more likely to put the effort into someone else's."

Emma glanced around the store, racking her brain for anything else she could offer, as the need to offer something grew stronger. Finally, her eyes fell on the biscuit display, and a memory worked to the forefront of her mind. "I know she likes the cookies in the brown wrapper the best."

Margaret's smile actually faded at the comment, and Emma worried she'd gotten the wrong answer and questioned the assertion. "Or did I remember wrong?"

"No," Margaret said quickly. "Those have always been her favorites. I used to find them stashed in her dresser drawer, so her siblings wouldn't find them and eat them before she had the chance. They were the only things she ever hoarded."

Emma smiled and picked up a package. Maybe she'd give Brogan the cookies along with a little thank you note. She looked up to see Margaret watching her with some new emotion in her eyes, so blue, so reminiscent of her own grandmother's, and her breath caught. What did she see there? Affection? Sympathy? Did she find the gesture sad? An inadequate overreach? "It doesn't seem like much, does it?"

Margaret shook her head. "Not at all. It's probably too much. Brogan's not much for people fussing over her. Never thinks she deserves it. Most women love getting flowers at work or shiny jewelry to show off."

"I know the type," Emma said, even as she fought to hold back images of Amalie from her mind.

"Brogan's not one of them."

Emma nodded. She'd known that, but now the question remained: what would she appreciate? What would make her feel as seen and appreciated as she'd made Emma feel? Once again, she didn't feel comfortable asking such questions of Brogan's mother, so she merely paid for the biscuits and mailed her letter, but she was still wondering as she walked back along Northland street and into her little cottage.

Her musings, however, were interrupted by an unfamiliar ring. Confused, she followed the sound until she found its source in her cell phone, buzzing in the seat of an armchair she didn't use. How strange. No one ever called her. Few people even had the number. Her agent knew she preferred email, one or two friends from New York only texted, and her mother wouldn't call unless there was an emergency. Oh Lord, was there an emergency? She snatched up the phone and practically shouted, "Hello?"

"Good afternoon. This is Lady Victoria Penchant calling for Ms. Emma Volant."

Emma held the phone away from her ear and stared at it as if the device itself had spoken those strange words.

"We met at the school, Book Report Day," the voice on the phone continued, sounding slightly less certain now.

Emma couldn't process how a member of British nobility could be casually dialing up her private number.

"I invited you to visit my ..." She laughed nervously. "My castle."

Silence. Awkwardness. She had to say something, but honestly what did one even say when a literal lady mentions her castle? Finally, she blurted the only thing she could focus on. "How did you get my number?"

"Oh, well, that." Lady Victoria sounded almost embarrassed. "I'm guessing by my assistant's frustration it wasn't an easy task. I didn't ask too many questions, but I don't think she had to pull in MI5 or Scotland Yard. She's very resourceful, though. I probably don't pay her enough. Still, it never occurred to me you might not want me to call you, which actually when you think about it was quite presumptuous, and perhaps a bit pretentious, which is not the impression I wanted to give despite the whole castle thing. I wanted to come across as normal, because I am, which is why I'm rambling now, instead of being the graceful model of upper-class manners and poise."

Emma laughed in spite of her lingering confusion. "We've got that in common, as I have no idea how one's supposed to accept a call from a member of the ruling class, but I assume 'how did you get this number' isn't the traditional response."

"Here are two tips for you. One, stop thinking of me as a member of the ruling class, because I have virtually no power to command anyone to do anything. And two, treat me like anyone else who called you up out of the blue." Victoria paused, then with a bit more humor added, "Unless of course you would hang up on random, but friendly, callers, in which case, remember you are but a peasant, and I am descended from Eleanor of Aquitaine."

131

Emma laughed again. "In that case, how can I help you, Lady Victoria?"

"I'm calling to follow up on my offer to have you up to my family's home."

"And by 'home,' you mean 'castle'?" she asked as sweat pricked her palms.

"In the strictest sense . . . yes."

"That's very nice of you, and honestly, I'm honored," Emma started, then stalled. How did one politely tell a lady she didn't want to see her ancient and undoubtedly impressive estate? Nothing in her suburban upbringing had prepared her for this conversation, which she took as further evidence she had even fewer tools at her disposal for accepting such an invitation.

"But?"

"You really don't have to do that."

"Actually, I sort of do. My family is having a reception for local artists, and it will be terribly boring and frumpy, and I'll have such a hard time staying awake unless someone interesting comes along to keep me entertained."

"Then I know you have the wrong number," Emma said, not sure she liked the sound of a formal invitation to a group event any more than she liked the idea of a private tour. "I'm always the least interesting person at any given event. I'd probably find the quietest corner and stare at pictures or books on the shelves until I could sneak out."

"But you wouldn't here," Victoria said confidently, "because after I made my obligatory opening speech and a quick walk around the other guests, I'd whisk you away on a tour of the castle, and I'd take you to see our extensive library."

"What makes you think a library is enough to make an avowed introvert willingly attend a reception full of strangers?"

"I've seen *Beauty and the Beast*."

Emma's resolve started to waver. Victoria was funny, and not at all as stuffy as she might expect from someone of her title. Still . . . strangers, and small talk, and finding a dress to wear, because surely women wore dresses to these things, didn't they? She had no idea, which was another strong vote for declining.

"It's a big library." Victoria pushed.

"I use a lot of ebooks these days."

"Do your ebooks have those rolling ladders up the shelves?"

"I have always wanted to use one of those," Emma admitted.

"Come on over then, a week from Friday. There'll also be an open bar, for the sole purpose of getting people sloshed so they'll open their pocketbooks and give generously to local arts initiatives."

"There's the rub. I'm actually quite familiar with that genre of party."

"I bet you are," Victoria said, a little cheekily.

"You should've led with that, and I would've offered to send a check without your having to get me drunk."

"That's all the work and none of the fun."

Emma grimaced as the sentiment sparked memories of Amalie, holding court in a New York gallery with a cosmo in one hand and the other on the waist of one of her workshop protégés. "Actually, being able to write checks to charities is the only enjoyable part for me. I don't find the drinking or the socializing fun."

"I wasn't implying those were the fun parts for you," Victoria said smoothly. "I was referring to fun for me, in getting to hang out with you again, and I don't get that if you mail in your donation."

Emma's face flushed slightly at the flattery, and the war within her started again. "I don't know."

"Listen," Victoria said, "I'm an accomplished negotiator. I do this sort of thing a lot, and I usually do it pretty well, so I know you're at least curious about the castle and the library."

"True."

"And you've already offered to make a donation, so it's not the money holding you back."

"Right."

"And for my own pride, I'm going to assume your hesitation isn't because you've developed some aversion to me personally."

"Not at all," Emma said quickly. "I really am just firmly entrenched in my introversion."

"So, you don't want to make small talk with people you don't know, even for the half hour it takes for me to make my rounds," Victoria concluded.

"Exactly."

"Then you'll bring a friend. I'll make sure there's a plus one on your invitation. You won't have to even make eye contact with anyone you don't know."

She opened her mouth to argue, but before she could formulate the response, she remembered Brogan, her soft smile, the sea reflecting in her eyes, her hair stirring slightly on the breeze off the water. She glanced over at the small package of cookies on the table and thought about how much more substantial the gift would seem if it came with an invitation to a castle. They could make an evening of it.

"Ms. Volant?" Victoria asked, "is this the sound of your resistance crumbling?"

Emma smiled. The woman really was disarming. And she'd worked a lot harder than most would deem reasonable to get her to accept an already impressive invitation.

"Shall I take that as a resignation and have our invitation, plus one, sent by Royal Mail? Mind you, Royal Mail isn't a thing that's open just to lords and ladies here. It's what we call the regular post, open to even you commoners. No need to be impressed."

"All right, all right," Emma relented. "Please send your gracious offer by totally normal Royal Mail."

Victoria sighed as if she'd been holding her breath, or at least a bit of tension at her suspense. "Well done, us. I promise you won't regret it."

Emma couldn't quite bring herself to the same certainty yet, but as she thanked her politely and ended the call, she managed to feel at least hopeful about an outing for the first time in ages.

Brogan was locking the door at the post office when she turned to see Emma strolling up the pavement from her cottage. She raised her hand in greeting and was rewarded by one of those smiles she wished she could spark more often.

"Did you need something from the store?" Brogan called, as Emma got close enough to hear her.

"No. Actually, I was trying to catch you between your many jobs."

The answer made her heart tap an irregular rhythm, and her brain had to remind it there were a million logical and platonic explanations for why Emma would want to talk to her.

Emma held out a package of her favorite biscuits and said, "I got these for you. I know it's not much. And you work in the store where I bought them, so you can probably make way better things at home, but it's the only thing I could think of to buy for you to say thank you. I mean, I know it's not enough for everything, the garden and sailing and driving and tea and cakes, and"—she sighed—"listening."

"It's more than enough," Brogan said quickly, touched by the gesture and the fact that Emma had cared enough to remember her favorite snack.

"I would've made you dinner, but I value your life, so I set out with the intention of offering to buy you dinner, but I remembered you already work at the best restaurant in town. And you're probably headed there now. I won't keep you, but I—"

"I'm not."

"What?"

"I'm not going to the pub tonight," Brogan said. "It's Monday. We don't serve food on Mondays until summer holidays."

"Oh." Emma frowned. "I would offer to buy you dinner then, but I'm told the pub is closed tonight."

Brogan laughed at the completely endearing response. Her brain tried to remind her that thinking of Emma as endearing wasn't much better than thinking of her as attractive, though she was certainly that, too, with her fair hair pulled back loosely at the base of her graceful neck.

Brogan shook her head, refocusing on what Emma had actually said, and an idea occurred to her heart, then sprang from her mouth before her brain could comment. "I actually know a great place serving a very British special tonight, if you don't mind trying something a little smaller in scale."

Emma's blue eyes widened with interest. "Absolutely."

"I'm headed there now if you want to join me."

"I'm not dressed for anything formal." Emma indicated her jeans and cozy Aran sweater.

"It's a very casual place."

Emma looked over her shoulder as if expecting some objection to arise from behind, but she smiled as she shrugged. "Do you have a thing for spontaneous outings?"

Brogan grinned. "That depends. Do you have a problem with them?"

"To be honest," Emma said sheepishly, "I usually do, but you haven't steered me wrong yet."

Brogan tucked the compliment away happily as she led them across the street and under an archway cut into the row houses.

"I haven't been this way yet," Emma said, as she headed down a crooked alleyway.

"Not much need to," Brogan admitted, "unless you live down here or need an only slightly shorter path to the estuary."

"Not a prominent place for a restaurant," Emma mused, as they neared the end of the path and slowed outside a blue door in another bank of connected houses.

"No," Brogan admitted, "it doesn't do nearly enough paying business to make any money, but it's got its charms."

She pushed open the door, revealing a small living room with a pair of overstuffed chairs and a threadbare love seat.

"Brogan?" Emma asked from behind her. "I think you've stumbled into someone's home."

"I have," she said with a smile. "Thankfully, it's my own."

"What? Why? I mean it's lovely, but I thought—"

"That you were going to get the best Monday night meal in the village?"

Emma opened her mouth, then closed it so tightly her lips formed a thin line.

Brogan felt a flash of guilt, followed quickly by a bout of insecurity. Why would someone like Emma want to eat a home-cooked meal in her tiny kitchen when she was probably used to Michelin-starred restaurants? Sure, she'd eaten nothing but tinned soups and scones since she'd arrived in England, but if she was getting her appetite back, that was a sign she was coming back into her old self, a self that would probably want much more than Brogan could offer in the way of accommodations or company. "I guess I should've mentioned that the place serving a great, authentic, British meal was my place."

"Yeah, you sort of left that out when I said I wanted to buy you dinner."

"I'd already planned the meal when Charlie called and said he wouldn't be home until late, so I thought you might like his share, but I guess offering you my little brother's castoff home cooking might not have actually been up to your usual standards, because why would it be?"

"No," Emma said quickly, "I just worry I inadvertently invited myself to dinner . . . again."

"Not at all. I've wanted to try this meal for a while but had no desire to eat alone."

Brogan proceeded into the house with a little more confidence now she was sure Emma's hesitation stemmed from worries about being an imposition. She flipped on the oven and then turned to motion for Emma to join her in the kitchen. "Come on in. I've already prepped everything. I can throw everything together in no time."

She set to work quickly, both to prove her point and to give herself something to do that didn't involve watching Emma inspect her home.

She'd already cut the beef into single-serve portions and seared them before leaving for work so they'd be cool enough not to overcook in the oven. As Emma wandered around, taking in family photos and picking up books from end tables, Brogan began to sauté her pre-chopped mushrooms and garlic.

"That smells amazing," Emma said, peeking over her shoulder as soon as she dropped the mixture into a skillet on her gas hob.

"Can't go wrong with garlic," Brogan said, pulling a tray of mixed vegetables from the fridge and drizzling them with olive oil before popping them into the oven.

"Your place is cute."

"Thanks," Brogan said, aware of how small it was compared to what Emma was used to.

"It reminds me of my grandma's."

She gave the mushrooms a good stir before taking a sheet of puff pastry and a few thin slices of Parma ham from the refrigerator. "Um, thanks again?"

Emma laughed. "I didn't mean it was old-ladyish. I meant lived-in, comfortable, cozy."

"Okay, in that case I suppose it is pretty homely."

Emma froze and quirked an eyebrow. "Does *homely* mean something different over here?"

"I don't know. What does it mean in America?"

"Unattractive."

"Then yes," Brogan said. "Here it means what you described: cozy, lived-in."

"Whew, okay. Americans would call that *homey*, but *homely* means ugly. Good to know for future conversations. If anyone ever calls my place homely, I shouldn't get my feelings hurt."

"Not at all." She rolled out the puff pastry thinly on her cutting board.

"Not that anyone would call my place homely. I still have nothing but bare white walls and the same furniture the holiday renters used."

"You've got time," Brogan said, even as she pushed back a worry that Emma wasn't actually putting down roots as much as living a sort of extended holiday of her own.

"This looks involved," Emma said nervously, peeking over her shoulder once more. She was so close Brogan felt the heat from her body and caught the subtle scent of cocoa butter. Lotion? Shampoo? She closed her eyes, trying to isolate the smell over the aroma of the simmering food.

"You've gone above four ingredients." Emma's voice near her ear brought her back into the moment.

Brogan laughed nervously. "Is four the limit for casual food?"

"Two is usually my limit. The only time I approach four is when I make a grilled cheese to go with my canned soup."

"Butter, cheese, bread, and soup," Brogan counted, as she cut the puff pastry into eight equal rectangles and laid slices of the Parma ham on each one. "Yep, that's four. Do you at least use some posh cheese?"

"Never," Emma proclaimed. "I told you, I'm an American suburbanite at heart. I may love a fancy Brie or chévre with my wine, but I take a gooey American on a grilled cheese."

Brogan scrunched up her nose. "Isn't that stuff part plastic?"

"Indeed," Emma said, without a hint of defensiveness. "That's what makes it melt evenly."

Brogan shrugged. "To each their own."

"Are you sure I can't help with anything?" Emma asked, watching her top the ham with the individual cuts of beef.

"I'm about done with this part," she said, spooning mushrooms atop the meat, and wrapping each ensemble into a neat little parcel. "Actually, I'm quickly approaching the wine-drinking portion of the cooking process. You could choose a bottle from the rack on the back wall."

"I have to warn you, I don't know much about wine," Emma said as she perused the meager selection.

"Good, then you won't notice what shite wine Charlie and I drink. Mostly the five-quid variety from Aldi."

"Then we're well matched." Emma took a bottle of red off the rack as Brogan finished brushing a bit of melted butter on the pastry packs. "Where's the bottle opener?"

"Top drawer next to the sink."

Emma grabbed the corkscrew. "I may be without cooking

skills, but I at least learned to uncork a merlot in my last relationship."

Of course she did. Brogan snorted at the comment. That ex sounded like a real gem. Jealous, bitter, adulterous, and she had Emma pour her drinks for her along the way. Brogan had to force her clenched jaw to relax as she added the main course to the oven along with the roasting vegetables.

She straightened to see Emma extend a glass of wine in her direction and felt a twinge of guilt for enjoying the image so much. It had been a long time since she'd had a beautiful woman in her kitchen. Not that she wanted to keep her there, much less include her in any domestic labor. Brogan simply relished her company while she did her own cooking.

Emma poured and raised her own glass. "Cheers."

"Cheers to you," Brogan said with a little clink and a sip.

"You did all that in fifteen minutes." Emma sounded impressed.

"And now we've got fifteen more before we need to do anything else."

"Would it be rude to ask for a tour?" Emma asked.

"Not rude," Brogan said uneasily, "but I'm afraid there's not much to see."

"Show me anyway?"

Brogan nodded. Maybe she'd be better off to let Emma see everything right now. It might help cool some of the warmth spreading at her core.

"Well, we're in the kitchen." Brogan turned back toward the front door. "And you saw the living room when you came in."

"Yes, very cozy."

"And there's a laundry behind the stairs, which is nothing special," she said as she climbed up the stairs with Emma close behind her.

"Up here, we've got a loo." She pushed open a door when she reached the landing to reveal a small room with a big, clawfoot tub.

"Lovely," Emma said, her voice going a little higher. "I'm a sucker for a hot bubble bath."

Brogan swallowed and tried not to tuck the information away anywhere she might access it later. "Moving on, there's Charlie's room. Probably smells like old socks and stale crisps."

Emma laughed. "You make him sound like such a frat boy."

"He's not too bad, but he eats all my food."

"If you cook for him like you're cooking for me, I can't blame him."

"Fair enough." Brogan pushed open the only other door on this level. "And this one's mine."

"May I?" Emma asked with polite pleasure.

"Sure, but I didn't expect company today." She shifted a little nervously. "I didn't make the bed."

"Good. I would've thought less of you if you did," Emma said, sliding past her into the room. "No one should be perfect all the time."

"No worries there," Brogan mumbled, as she watched Emma turn from the double bed covered with a crumpled quilt her mother had made to a chest of drawers her father had finished, and a bedside table she'd built herself out of driftwood. Nothing was shabby, but neither was it chic, or even matched. Still, Emma smiled.

"I love all the personal touches. None of this is cookie cutter, and oh . . ." She stopped mid-sentence as her eyes fell on the large dormer window.

Brogan couldn't see the view Emma had caught sight of between the steep rise of the walls on either side, but she knew it well enough to be pleased by her reaction. This time of day, the estuary would be cast in the orange glow from the sun sinking low over the hilly rise in the distance. The water of the river would gleam sapphire and silver in the fading light as the grasses along the bank basked in the last warmth of the day.

Emma eased herself into the overstuffed armchair Brogan had angled into the nook, the dreamy haze of serenity across her beautiful features making her look like some sort of pensive painting. "Phenomenal."

"It's not the expansive sea view you have at your place."

"But, it's so perfectly . . . *here*." She shook her head. "Do you know what I mean? Your view right here, the stone buildings, the cascading roofs, the water sparkling as it snakes its way around the village. This window captures the essence of this place, like your room captures your essence."

Brogan couldn't speak. Whatever words a person could say in response to such a beautiful sentiment, she didn't know them. Instead, she stood transfixed in the doorway of her own bedroom trying to burn those words and the image of the woman who'd spoken them into her mind.

The silence must've grown awkward, because Emma rose, and blushing, said, "I'm sorry. I made myself at home in your bedroom."

Brogan tried to say "no problem," but only managed a little squeaking noise.

"Just like I made myself at home in your kitchen, and your car." Emma's cheeks were bright pink now. "I'm not normally like this. I mean, most people think I'm a total hermit, but somehow I keep barging in on you. All I wanted was to do something nice to thank you for all the other times, but I totally monopolized your time and energy, and you end up having to cook me dinner while I try to commandeer your personal space."

Brogan found her voice. "It's nothing."

"It's not nothing." Emma's tone neared panic level again. "I saw what you did down there in the kitchen. That dinner is not nothing. I think it's mini Beef Wellingtons."

"Well, yeah, it's definitely that, but I had the food anyway. It doesn't take anything to share it with someone I enjoy being around."

The last part seemed to pull Emma up short. "Really?"

"Yeah."

"I mean, not 'really the food' part. 'Really' as in the 'you enjoy being around me' part?"

"Yes," Brogan said more emphatically. "You're smart, and you have a quirky sense of humor, and I like your way with words. You paint pictures with them even when you're describing things I look right past every day."

Emma's shy smile returned. "Words are sort of my thing."

"Good, because they aren't mine, but I like it when you talk to me while I cook, or drive, or sail. It's nice."

"Nice." Emma mused, all the argument gone from her voice. "Okay."

"Okay?"

"Yes, I will stay and eat your food, and drink your wine, because, duh, and we'll call tonight even because of my serious talking skills, but you have to promise to let me take you out next time, to some place you don't work. Some place nice, and different."

"Yes, of course, because of . . . what did you say? 'Because, duh'?"

Emma grinned. "Totally logical explanation, duh."

"Same for me. Name the time and the place, and I'll let you take me there." The promise was out before both her heart and her brain had time to protest the open nature of the pledge in unison.

"The castle," Emma blurted.

"Which one?"

Emma scrunched up her face. "Oops, it never occurred to me there'd be more than one. Damn you, England, and your long, proud history. Um, the one where Lady Victoria lives?"

"Ah," Brogan said, her stomach sinking. "Penchant Castle. That is *the* castle around here, if you're looking for places people actually still live and function."

"Yes, function. I've been invited to a function there. A cocktail hour for artists, by personal invitation from Lady Victoria, at Penchant Castle." Emma said the words *castle* and *lady* as if they were exceedingly luxurious. "A week from Friday. It'll be my first trip to a castle."

Brogan's stomach clenched. It would not be her first trip to a castle, particularly *that* castle, but Emma seemed enamored of the idea, and proud to be able to offer an experience that must feel entirely impressive to her. Brogan couldn't possibly disappoint her, not after everything she'd overcome to reach this point of excitement.

"You will go with me, won't you?" Emma asked, her eyes hopeful.

"Of course." Brogan forced a smile. "I'd love to."

Emma bounced up to her and placed a quick kiss right on her cheek. "I'm so glad."

Glad was not exactly the feeling Brogan experienced as they headed back down the stairs. She wasn't sure what the feeling was, something akin to the sensations she associated with her sailboat cresting over a wave that was bigger than she'd expected, equal parts exhilaration and seasickness, but since Emma was probably the only person she knew who'd have a word to describe the sensation, she decided to simply leave it at "glad."

"That's one of the top five best meals of my entire life," Emma said, pushing back from the table so she wouldn't take a third Beef Wellington, but that didn't stop Brogan from trying to push another one onto her plate. She groaned, a mix of temptation and overstuffedness. "Mercy, please. If I eat any more, I'll explode. My stomach doesn't know what to do with all this solid food."

Brogan relented and put the pastry pocket back on the serving plate, but she did look awfully pleased with herself.

"If I didn't know better, I'd start to worry you were fattening me up for some weird Hansel and Gretel scheme."

"It's not like you have to watch your figure."

"I used to," Emma said earnestly, "and I will again if I keep eating your cooking. I have no idea how I'd fit into my pants if I ate this ravenously at every meal. As it is, I'm not sure how I'll manage to walk home tonight."

"There's no rush," Brogan said kindly.

"You say that now, but we'll see how you feel when you wake up to me still sitting at this table because I haven't yet managed to digest my first non-pastry-centric meal since before Christmas."

"If you're still here in the morning, I'll make you breakfast, too."

"Then you'd never be rid of me." Emma fought off a yawn as the words started to shift from teasing to wishful. She felt cozy

144

and sleepy and comfortable at Brogan's table with a full belly and a warmth at her core from more than the wine. "I could sleep right here, and then in the morning I could sit in the little nook upstairs and write a story about a woman from the past who sailed across the sea to escape a life that wasn't hers anymore. She'd brave the high seas until she couldn't take the turmoil any longer, and she'd sail up that little river to shelter from a storm . . ." Her voice trailed off and her eyes widened at the multiple implications of what had just happened.

Brogan watched her, eyes intent and curious.

"I'm sorry."

"I'm not," Brogan whispered. "Go on."

Emma bit her lip, unsure if she should, and yet unable to stop herself. "She'd meet a local fisherman who'd teach her the language and the water, and make her the most amazing foods she'd never had before."

Brogan smiled almost sadly. "But you wouldn't want her to lose herself."

"No," Emma said seriously. "She'd have to find herself before she could commit to someone else."

"How would she do that?" Brogan asked softly, as if she didn't want to press too hard but did genuinely want to know the answer.

Emma shook her head. "I don't know. I never know the answers when I start writing. I only have the questions."

"You don't know the endings to your own books?"

Emma smiled. "That would ruin the adventure. Who wants to know the end before they begin?"

"What if she gets lost? What if she gets homesick? What if she gets her heart broken?"

"She will," Emma said emphatically. "She has to. It's all part of the process. How will she know how strong she is if she's not tested? No one wants a book where the character is the same person at the end as she was on the first page."

"You understand a lot about how these things have to work."

"You do, too," Emma said, marveling at the truth of the statement. "You went right there with me."

"I don't know anything about writing books." Brogan shook her head, and a strand of red hair fell across her pale forehead.

Emma fought the urge to reach across the table. She wanted to push it back, to run her fingers through that copper mop.

"All I did was ask questions," Brogan continued, oblivious to where Emma's mind had wandered.

"That's all writing really is, asking questions," she explained. "What if? Who would? How could? Why not? Then going in search of the answers."

"That's where you'd lose me. I don't know the answers."

"And that's beautiful. You didn't try to pretend you did, but you went there with me anyway. I said something silly, just the voice of a daydream, and you didn't skip a beat. You didn't blink or hesitate or poke fun. You were right there searching beside me." She didn't say that Amalie had hated those kinds of non sequiturs, that she hated Emma checking out in the middle of normal conversations, that she always found her adventure stories frivolous and resented the way they detracted from more serious discussion of depth and craft. Amalie wasn't here anymore. Brogan was. And Brogan was profoundly different. "You didn't try to rein me in."

"Of course not," Brogan said softly. "Why would I?"

Emma smiled and finished the last of her wine. "Another simple question that pushes me gently forward. Do you know I haven't written more than a few sentences since my . . . well, for a very long time?"

"Do you feel like you could now?"

Emma sat still for a moment, listening to herself, paying attention to the pressure stirring in her chest and picturing the lonely river curling around the village. "I think I might."

"Then you have to go," Brogan said, pushing back from the table.

"What? No," Emma said quickly. "I'm going to help you with the dishes."

"Don't be silly. You admitted you have the urge to do some

146

-thing important, something that matters to you, something you've missed for a long time. Where's the adventure in passing that up for dirty dishes? Your character will be so disappointed if she never gets to board her ship because you had house chores."

Emma's eyes filled with tears, suddenly overwhelmed by Brogan's easy, unassuming support, her faith in her, and complete acceptance that a woman who'd only minutes ago come into existence in Emma's mind deserved her chance to fly.

She rose slowly and met Brogan at the door, then, clasping her callused hand between both of her own, managed to say, "You have no idea what this conversation means to me."

Brogan smiled. "Someday you'll have to tell me."

Another perfect response. Emma didn't even have the inclination to question herself as she released Brogan's hand, and instead tenderly cupped her face. "Someday soon."

Then she leaned forward enough to press their lips together. It was a soft kiss, but as a single question could spark a character into existence, this kiss sparked something new and thrilling in her.

Brogan's lips were strikingly soft. Clearly surprised, she didn't immediately respond, but neither did she pull away, her breath warm and tinged with the remnants of red wine. She was tender, sweet, with the hint of potential for much more. Brogan did what she did so well in so many situations. She stood, steady and strong, neither pushing nor retreating. The kiss and the woman offered calm, steady assurance that whatever Emma needed was right and welcome. And when Emma stepped back, Brogan did, too.

Their eyelids fluttered open at the same time, and a hesitant smile tugged at Emma's lips as she watched a haze clear from Brogan's green eyes. Then, ignoring the questions forming there and in her own core, she made a silent decision to set them aside until later, to savor the perfect end to the perfect evening.

"Goodnight, Brogan."

"Goodnight, Emma."

"Thank you, again, for everything."

Brogan's smile returned with a hint of bemusement. "No. Thank you."

And with that Emma stepped out into ancient streets feeling almost completely new.

Chapter Ten

Brogan was still sitting at her dining-room table, a new bottle of wine half gone by the time Charlie came through the doorway where Emma had kissed her.

"Drinking alone? That's the sign of a problem," he said cheekily. "Thankfully I'm home now, so if we polish off the bottle together, we go from alcoholics to upper class."

She snorted and pushed the bottle across the table to him.

He picked up the other glass on the table, then stopped and held it up to the light, where they could both see a few drops of wine still in the bottom and the faint print of Emma's lips on the rim. The same lips that had recently pressed against her own, though Charlie didn't know that. Then again, judging by his slow smile, he was starting to have his suspicions. Still, he didn't know who the glass had belonged to, and he didn't hazard any guesses as he took a clean one from the cupboard before making himself a plate of the food she'd left out for him.

"That smells wicked good," he said, setting the plate on the table.

"You could heat it up."

He waved her off. "The tatties are still a bit warm, and I'm ready to tuck in."

She supposed that was his way of saying it was good enough for who it was for, which she supposed had also been true enough the first time around, given how the evening had ended.

She couldn't say she understood, even after over an hour of pondering the kiss, but she must have done something right.

Or wrong.

Her assessment wavered with each glass of wine.

"So," Charlie said, as he finished chewing his first bite of beef. "You got a friend in town for the weekend?"

She shook her head slowly, and he raised an eyebrow but wasn't curious enough to ask more before jamming a forkful of potatoes into his mouth. Her social life wasn't his top concern right now, and he was taking the piss out of her to entertain himself while he ate. If she told him to drop the subject, he'd likely tease her a bit without asking any more questions. Likewise, if she changed the subject, he'd roll with it. And yet she still chose to say, "Emma Volant came over for dinner."

That got his attention, and he swallowed before he'd finished chewing. With a little cough, he managed to sputter, "What?"

"You heard me."

"Yeah." He wiped his mouth on his sleeve. "But you said, I mean, you told everyone you weren't interested in her."

"I wasn't. I mean, I'm not. I didn't ask her out, not really."

"She just showed up and demanded you make her Beef Wellington? Damn, those Americans are a pushy lot."

"Little bit." She smiled faintly. "No, she brought me biscuits to thank me for teaching her to drive last week and taking her to tea in Warkworth, and since I had the food out already, I invited her to stay. Friendly though, no expectations."

Charlie nodded. "Right, totally casual, like how you slipped in the part about driving lessons and taking her out to a super posh afternoon tea. Got it."

She rolled her eyes. "Both those things were also unplanned outings."

He sipped his wine. "Right. Sometime you'll have to explain to me how you end up on all these unplanned dates with beautiful millionaires you're not interested in, but for now, carry on."

"No, that's it. She stayed for dinner, we chatted about the village a bit and writing, and then she went home."

He nodded but didn't speak, even after he'd swallowed his last potato. He kept staring at her.

"What?" Brogan asked, shifting in her chair.

"I'm waiting for you to finish the last part of the story."

"What makes you think there's more to the story?"

"I don't know, just something about my sister sitting in a dark kitchen polishing off a bottle of wine alone. It's a bit too maudlin for a Monday night dinner with a friend. What gives?"

"Nothing."

"Right, you're super not *bovvered*," he said with sarcasm dripping from his voice. "Are you in a funk over this woman who wants to be friends?"

"No."

"It's all right. I've been there before, lots of times, the friend zone. It's not the end of the world."

"That's not quite it."

"You wanted to convert tonight and got shot down?" he asked. "'Cause I've been there, too."

"Nope."

He rolled his eyes. "She give you the brush off? Say she can't see you anymore? 'Cause once again, I've got experience."

"She kissed me," Brogan finally said.

Both his eyebrows shot up. "Say again?"

"She kissed me. We had this totally platonic evening and seriously just talked about her job when she up and tells me I can't know what it means to her, and then she kissed me. Not like a full-on snog, but a real kiss, on the mouth, and it lasted longer than a three-count for sure."

"And then what?"

"She said goodnight."

"What did you say?"

"Goodnight."

"That's it?"

She nodded. "Well, earlier in the evening I'd agreed to be her plus one at a reception Lady Victoria is hosting for local artists up at the castle."

151

He sat back. "Are you fecking joking?"

She shook her head.

"I went to uni for years. I did internships and shadowed football coaches in Sunderland, but I'm up at the castle mowing those people's grass all day and tilling up their flower beds and coming home covered in their dirt. You cook one dinner and get invited into the state rooms for drinks with Lady Victoria?"

"Not me," she corrected. "Lady Victoria didn't invite *me* anywhere. Not even to do her landscaping or tend her bar this time. She invited Emma, a totally talented, graceful, and famous author."

"Emma invited you, same difference."

"No," Brogan said quickly. "I'm the only person she knows, and she doesn't know any better yet."

"She knew enough to kiss you."

"Not really. She hardly knows anything about me."

"She knows your full name, your address, several of the places you work, a couple of your siblings, and that you're a lesbian, which is the big one if you ask me, though I've kissed a couple girls I haven't been sure about on that front."

She rolled her eyes, though if pressed, she'd have to admit to going further with women she knew less about, too.

"She knows you're hardworking and generous and a good cook," Charlie reasoned. "She's seen where you live and how you dress, so she knows you're not posh, but she's also seen you help people out, including her on more than one occasion."

"No more than anyone else around here would."

"Debatable," Charlie said, "but I guess that's the point, right? Why would you want to debate this? And you obviously do."

"I don't."

"I don't know how many women you've slept with in the last ten years. Seriously, please don't tell me, but I never got the sense any of them caused you much hesitation. I know for sure none of them left you brooding over a bottle of wine, or restless enough to confess even vague details to me. They all came and went without issue or comment."

She didn't argue with any of those facts.

"Why are you fighting this one so hard?"

"It's . . . she's . . . well." She sighed. "Emma's different."

"Yeah, I got that, but different in a good way, right?"

"Yes and no."

"Descriptive." He took a swig from his glass of wine and waited.

Brogan's cheeks burned under his patient scrutiny, until she finally blurted, "She's too good for me, okay?"

He laughed. "That's never stopped you before."

The words hit her in the chest, and she must have paled, because Charlie's face went white, too. "Shite, I didn't mean that. You know it's not true."

"It *is* true. We both know it."

"I don't. I thought you were being a numpty to get out of telling me the real reason."

"No, you were bang-on the first time," Brogan said, hoping her voice didn't sound as thick as her throat felt. "I'm always punching above my weight with the women who come through here. They all have real lives with jobs and homes and friends so far out of what I know or could ever feel comfortable with, and that's fine, because I'm never going to be part of any of those things. I'm a holiday fling, a good one, I think, but that's why it works. I know it. They know it. No one pretends I'm anything else. That's what I'm good for."

He shook his head. "Brogan, that's the biggest load of shite I've ever heard. If I'd known you believed that, I would've . . ."

"What?"

"I don't know, probably told Mum or Nora or someone useful, someone who'd do a better job of talking some sense into you, but honestly I don't know why I have to. You have women throwing themselves at you every summer."

"Yeah, every summer," Brogan said, "and then what? Do you see any of them trying to move up here? Any of them asking me to move down with them? Any of them wanting to have a go at a long-distance relationship?"

"Do you want that?"

She shook her head. "What's the use in wanting something you can't have? Why not learn to like what you've got?"

"Yeah, not a bad plan, but it seems to me like what you've got is Emma. She's here, she interested, she's—"

"She's hurting and lonely and coming off a breakup with a woman who didn't deserve her, but none of those things are going to last. She's on the equivalent of a long holiday." Brogan recited the speech she'd been giving herself for weeks.

"Fine," Charlie said. "What if you're right? What if Emma wants you for a while, and then she goes back to New York? You said yourself you've learned to want what you've got open to you. If you believe that, then why not enjoy more of the same with her?"

"Because she's not the same. She's special. She's full of contradictions. She's strong and fragile at the same time. Brave and afraid. Beautiful and broken. She's not in need of a break from her hectic schedule or tedious job. She needs time and space, and someone to believe in her. She needs a friend. And I'd like to be that for her."

"But you'd also like to be something more. Admit it."

"Yeah, in a perfect world, maybe I would, but we don't live in a fairy tale," she said, wistfully remembering the adventure Emma had been concocting in her head. Brogan had seen the resemblances to their own circumstances, but unlike Emma, she could see the ending. A woman courageous enough to sail across the sea in search of herself wouldn't settle for the tedious life of a village fisherman. She'd learn what she needed to learn to weather the storm, and then she'd sail on. So would Emma, eventually. She was too good not to.

She pushed back from the table. "You said it yourself. You got a degree, you have credentials, you have skills and a personality, but has Lady Victoria ever called you in for drinks?"

He snorted.

"And you're not holding your breath, are you?"

He shook his head. "I'm not her type."

"I'm not either, and it doesn't matter how gay I am, or nice, or hardworking, because at the end of the day, people like her don't fall for gardeners or bartenders or clerks or temporary help of any kind."

"You're much more than you give yourself credit for," Charlie said, "and actually being a little unfair to Emma, too, because if what you say about her is true, she didn't get rich and famous by some accident of fate."

"No," Brogan agreed. "She's smart and creative and passionate about what she does. She has everything going for her."

"Then why do you think she'd be wrong about what she wants, just because what she wants right now is you?"

"I don't think she's wrong about what she wants *right now*," Brogan said, "but I've been wanted before, lots of times, by lots of different women. It always passes, and maybe this time around, being wanted for right now isn't good enough."

"Why?"

"Because with someone like Emma, a moment isn't going to be enough."

Emma examined the black dress that had arrived in the mail and studied her thin reflection in the mirror. Reggie looked up from where she'd been digging around in the lower corner of the terraced garden. Emma suspected the kid wanted something to do in some place she felt welcome and useful, so she didn't point out there wasn't much real gardening left to do. She didn't mind the company or having her youthful energy around every now and then.

"What do you think?" Emma asked her.

Reggie shrugged.

"Not impressed?"

"I don't like dresses much," Reggie said, "but I bet you will look pretty."

She smiled at the simple statement that likely said much more about Reggie than she realized.

"Do you like it?" Reggie asked, standing up and wiping her dirty hands on her jeans.

"I don't know," Emma admitted, holding the dress out away from herself. "I can't decide if it's too plain, or too much."

Reggie frowned. "Can it be both?"

"You wouldn't think so, but it's all one color, and the cut of the front is rather plain, but the back—" She turned it around to show the swooping dip from the neckline to well past studious. "I worry from the front it'll look like I'm headed to a funeral, and from the back it'll look like I'm headed for an—" She remembered who she was talking to and said, "Embarrassment."

Reggie's eyebrows knitted together as she inspected the dress more closely, as if trying to see what Emma was talking about, but in the end, her innocence and tomboyishness combined to block any real understanding, so she offered the best suggestion she had. "My mum likes dresses. Maybe we should ask her."

Emma shook her head. "I'll figure it out."

"Are you sure?" Reggie asked. "She's going up to the pub soon. My uncle Charlie might go, too, and Brogan is always there early. We could take a vote."

She blushed at the idea. She didn't need her evening wear subject to popular approval. And the idea of asking Brogan specifically made the concept even more daunting. She had yet to fully process the kiss they'd shared on Monday. Maybe "shared" was too strong a word. Brogan had certainly leaned into the experience, but Emma had never lost sight of the fact that she'd been in control. Or maybe "control" was also too strong a word, because she hadn't exactly planned the kiss, or thought it through, or even unpacked it after the fact, but she had been the one to start it, and keep it going, and then end it, all of her own doing.

She'd also been the one to walk away, and to stay away, choosing to immerse herself in her new writing project. The world of fiction she'd created, full of turbulent seas and pirates and rocky shores, surprisingly felt much less complicated than her real life, and she'd chosen to hide there. It was a convenient hiding place because it looked like progress. The words spilled out of her in ways she couldn't have dreamed of even weeks ago, and rich worlds filled her waking hours. She stayed busy, both physically and emotionally, and everyone from her old life would've been so proud of the strength and creative fortitude she'd employed to jump back into writing with such complete abandon.

Only she understood the real abandonment was of the feelings Brogan sparked in her.

"Are you okay?" Reggie asked.

"What?"

"Your eyes looked sad, or maybe mad?" The girl observed her with insight beyond her years. "Are you sad-mad about the dress?"

"No," she said quickly, refusing to add that she might have been a little sad-mad about herself. "But I'm not ready to make a decision yet."

"Where are you going to wear the dress?" Reggie asked.

"To a cocktail party at the castle."

"With Lady Victoria?"

"She's the one who invited me, but I'm actually going with Brogan."

Reggie laughed. "Aunt Brogan would look funny in a matching dress."

"I don't know that she'll wear a dress," Emma said, sharing a chuckle at that image.

"What's she going to wear?"

"I don't know," Emma said honestly.

"What's she supposed to wear?"

"I don't know," she said again. "I don't even know what I'm supposed to wear. I've been to book launches and fundraisers, but none at castles. And usually my agent tells me how formal to dress, or the invitation might list a dress code."

"People tell you what you have to wear to their parties?" Reggie scoffed. "Rude. If I had a party, I'd let people wear what they want."

"But then wouldn't everyone want to wear pajamas?"

"Yes! I'd love a pajama party, but my mum likes to get dressed up all posh. She went to a thing at the castle once for something or another."

"Really?" Emma asked, chewing on her lip a little bit. It wouldn't be terrible to talk to someone who'd been to a similar function, but she barely knew Ciara. She did know Brogan, though, which didn't make her feel any better. She either had to ask a near stranger for advice, or the person she knew best, but she wasn't ready to confront how well they'd connected. No, actually, she'd have to face both of them at once, because they were in the same place. A public place. She checked her watch. It was four thirty. Hopefully there wouldn't be much of a crowd at the pub, which didn't start serving food until later, but the thought offered small comfort.

"My mum loves dresses," Reggie added, but she couldn't stop her face from scrunching up, as if she found that fact unsavory.

"Maybe I could Google 'appropriate attire for cocktail parties hosted by British nobility,'" but even before the full sentence left her mouth, she realized the obscurity of those search terms.

"Or you could ask a person," Reggie suggested, the plainly obvious choice.

"Right," Emma said, not wanting to admit to a ten-year-old that she was being silly because she felt silly, for all the things she didn't know and some of things she did, in this situation. She didn't know what to wear to a function the likes of which she'd never imagined being invited to. She did know Ciara, who would probably love to help. She also knew Brogan would be kind and sensitive and affirming. Emma would have to face Brogan eventually, and in doing so, she'd have to face the kiss, and the way her heart still beat a little faster when she recalled the unexpected softness of her lips . . . actually, maybe, a public meeting was the best place to do that. Much less risk of a repeat or complicating behavior in a bar than in a car, and with siblings and coworkers around rather than just the two of them.

"Yeah, maybe that's the best," Emma said as she worked around to the conclusion that facing a bit of embarrassment now would beat having to do so in close quarters and castles next week. She wasn't sure if ripping off that Band-Aid with an audience made her brave or cowardly, but she didn't have time to second-guess herself, because Reggie grabbed her by the hand and, giving a little tug, pulled her out the door.

"Did Isabelle and Simon sell their house?" Will asked, as Brogan poured him a pint of ale. "The sign is down."

"Yup. Edmond had me transfer the keys to them, since Joanne's on bed rest and he doesn't want to be away from her."

"Good Lord, hasn't that woman had that bairn yet?" Tom asked. "I saw her a month ago, and she looked ready to pop then."

"The first one's usually the hardest," Diane said. "They'll get easier after this."

"I don't know," Ciara mused. "Padrig was my last one, and he hung on the longest. The doctor had to drag him out. He gets his stubborn streak from his father."

Everyone laughed in unison, especially Brogan and Charlie.

Ciara feigned offense, but before she could complain, the door to the pub swung open and hit the stone wall with a loud crack. Everyone looked up to see Reggie, her face smudged with dirt, and her red hair disheveled as usual.

"Child," Ciara sighed, "what am I going to do with you, tearing in here like you're on fire, but covered with mud?"

Brogan laughed, undercutting her sister's exasperation. "Hiya, Reg. Way to make an entrance."

Reggie grinned sheepishly. "Sorry 'bout the door, but I got excited."

"Yeah? What's new and exciting in the world?"

"Emma got a new dress," Reggie blurted, and all the air left Brogan's lungs.

"What?" everyone at the local table asked together.

But before Reggie could explain, Emma stepped into the sun-filled doorway and smiled shyly. If Brogan had hoped to get her air back after the unexpected mention of her name, seeing her did little to further that aim. She felt like she was breathing through a straw as a million words and feelings sprang forth.

Emma was stunning in the amber light, her hair long and loose in white-gold strands across her slender shoulders and fair features. They stood frozen, staring at each other for entirely too long to be casual, until Diane mercifully rescued them both.

"Emma, how lovely to see you again."

Emma blinked as if she hadn't yet noticed anyone else in the room, and Brogan knew the feeling. "I didn't know you were open for business yet. Reggie mentioned her mom and Brogan would be here, but she didn't say I'd be interrupting an event."

"Nonsense," Esther said. "We're just a few locals who get together on Fridays before dinner. And you're a local now. You should join us."

Emma shook her head. "I'm not much of a drinker."

"That can be fixed," Tom said, grabbing another chair and dragging it toward the table for her. It didn't go without notice that he placed it right next to his own. Both Esther and Diane rolled their eyes.

Emma turned from him to Brogan, and her cheeks flushed as she clutched something tighter to her chest.

"What have you got there, dear?" Esther asked.

"Her dress," Reggie exclaimed. "She can't decide if she should wear it to the castle when she and Brogan go see Lady Victoria."

Everyone turned slowly to face Brogan, and she smiled weakly. "Did I forget to mention I'm going to miss next Friday because I'll be accompanying Emma up to the castle?"

"Yeah," Ciara said dryly, "must've slipped your mind."

"Oh no," Emma said, her hands rising to cover her mouth the way she did when overwhelmed, only this time she still had the dress clutched in her hands, so it looked like she was trying to use it to hide her face as she said, "I'm sorry, I didn't even think about you having to miss work, or time with friends. You don't have to go."

"Don't be silly," Brogan said quickly. "I work all the time. One night off isn't going to kill anyone."

"That's true," Charlie said. "I'll cover the bar."

"Of course he will," Ciara seconded, then with a little more cheek added, "We'd love nothing more than for you and Brogan to go up to some posh event at the castle."

"But what about her dress?" Reggie asked exasperatedly.

"What about it?" Esther said.

"Is it too plain or too much?"

Emma blushed. "We don't need to worry about that now."

"Why not?" Diane hopped up. "Let's see it."

"I really didn't expect . . ."

"Half the town to be here," Brogan finished for her. "Sorry about that."

"No, it's not your fault," Emma said. "I should've called, or not, and made a decision for myself for once, instead of running to you . . . again."

"It's no problem." Brogan wished she could soothe the panic and doubt in Emma's eyes again. "I'm sure whatever you wear will be fine."

"But this is my first trip to a castle, and I'm so awkward anyway without adding nobility to the mix."

Everyone at the corner booth turned from Emma to Brogan with each comment as if watching a verbal tennis match.

"You're not awkward," Brogan said softly.

Emma laughed, a sharp shot laced with disbelief and embarrassment. "I don't know how you could possibly still believe that after dinner and how I . . ."

Her face flushed profusely, and Brogan suspected she'd been about to mention the kiss Brogan had still been completely unable to wrap her head around. Five days later she still had no explanation that didn't leave her confused. Still, her desire for answers was overridden by her instinct to protect Emma and put her at ease. "No worries. We'll figure something out. I don't know what I have to wear, either."

Reggie sighed dramatically. "That's why I said she should ask my mum. She knows about dresses and fancy parties."

Ciara laughed but added, "She's not wrong."

Brogan nodded. Of all the McKay children, Ciara had got the only real stitch of fashion sense that went past purely utilitarian.

"And you've been to the castle," Reggie added, a hint of pride in her voice that made her mother smile sweetly at her.

161

"I have once or twice. They held a fundraiser for the parent-teacher organization once, and there was also a reception for small-business owners. Neither one was excessively formal, but they were evening events with an open bar and hors d'oeuvres."

Emma nodded. "I expect this will be about the same."

"I've been to a few of them as well," Brogan admitted reluctantly. "If you want me to stop by and look at the dress later, I'd be happy to."

"No," Esther practically whined. "I've never been to the castle for a party. I'd like to see the dress."

"Me, too," Diane said.

"I wouldn't mind seeing the girl in a dress," Tom muttered, earning him a sharp poke in the ribs.

"Can't we please have a look?" Diane asked, then seemed to realize she might be pushing too hard, and added, "if it's not too personal."

Emma smiled nervously, and Brogan could tell she was trying to politely extract herself from the situation. "Leave the poor woman alone. She doesn't need a committee to dress her."

"You hush," Esther said. "I've got bones enough to pick with you later."

Brogan hung her head, knowing she had a proper grilling coming her way as soon as Emma was out of earshot.

"Ms. Volant." Will finally spoke. "Don't let them turn you into a toy doll if you don't want to. What you wear isn't anyone's business but your own, but they mean no harm. They're just excited to have something new and nice to think about."

Emma's expression softened, the worry lines fading from her face. "I know. Everyone here has been so wonderful to me. I feel silly asking strangers what to wear."

"We're not strangers!" Esther exclaimed. "We're neighbors."

"And don't feel bad about not knowing something. I've lived here my whole life, and I'd still have to ask someone what to wear to a party with Lady Victoria," Charlie offered. "That doesn't make you silly. It makes you one of us."

Emma glanced from him to Brogan, then back again. "You wouldn't happen to be Charlie, would you?"

He chuckled. "Was it the hair?"

"Your easy smile," Emma said sweetly, then widened her own smile to include the rest of the group. "You all have been incredibly warm and welcoming."

"Then show us the dress," Diane said, clasping her hands together excitedly.

"Okay." Emma nodded, then took a deep breath before holding out the scrunched-up black cloth at arm's length.

Brogan turned her head, first to one side, then the other, trying to make out the completely formless black sack, then turned to the others for some sort of cue and noticed the same expressions of confusion on all their faces.

"Is it terrible?" Emma finally asked.

"Well," Esther said kindly, "I can't tell."

"It doesn't exactly hold its form when you hold it out like a dead snake," Tom added.

"I think what my husband is trying to suggest is, you might need to put it on to give us the full picture."

Emma sighed resignedly. "I was afraid of that."

"You don't have to." Brogan tried to offer one more exit.

"I'm going to have to do it sooner or later."

"We promise to be gentle," Ciara said, then excitedly pointed her toward the back of the bar. "The loo's through the dining room and down the hall."

"I'll show you," Reggie said, grabbing her hand and leading her off.

Brogan tried to give Emma her most apologetic facial expression as she watched her edge down the bar before she turned and wandered around the corner. Bracing herself for what was sure to come next, she tightened her shoulders and turned back toward the corner booth. "Anyone need a refill?"

Charlie was the only one who managed to look amused. Everyone else stared at her with a range from confusion to accusation.

163

Finally, Ciara spoke for the group when she said, "Talk fast."

Brogan shook her head. "Don't make a bigger deal out of this than it is."

"Why would I make a big deal about my sister going on a date to a castle party with a famous writer?"

"And what about Emma saying she can't run to you 'again'? How many times has she already done so?" Esther asked.

"And there was a mention of dinner," Diane said quickly. "Add that to the sailing we already knew about, and the castle would make three dates."

"Four," Charlie offered. "There was a tea in Warkworth."

"Have you ever had four dates with the same woman in your life?" Ciara asked.

"They weren't dates," Brogan said, a tad too defensively. "We have spent some time together, yes, but as friends."

Charlie's eyebrows shot up under his ruddy mop top, but she silenced him with a sharp look, and he retreated behind his pint glass.

"I don't know if Emma would share that assessment," Esther said almost pensively. "She didn't look at you with the eyes of someone looking for the opinion of a friend. She turned to you hopefully, for support, for affirmation."

"She really did," Will said, as if he found the idea amusing. "If I were a younger man, I'd have felt a little twinge of jealousy."

"Younger man, humph," Tom said. "I'm not young, and I still wouldn't mind being the one to add that little hint of pink to those pale cheeks of hers."

"You lot are so eager for something that isn't there, you're going to paint it into the picture yourself," Brogan said, weary of having this conversation, both with herself and with everyone else. "Emma's in a new place, finding herself in foreign situations, and coming off a hard time."

"You're the one working hard for explanations that aren't there," Esther shot back. "And she doesn't appear nearly as lost or heartbroken as she did a month ago. She's got life back in her body and a little gleam in her eye."

164

"Because she's going to a party at a castle on the personal invitation of the daughter of a duke."

"Exactly," Diane said, "she's getting out again. She's getting back into the swing of things, and aside from her adorable little fuss over the dress, why shouldn't she be there? She's every bit as prestigious as anyone else who'll be on the guest list."

"Absolutely," Brogan agreed, as her chest constricted. "Emma will fall into those circles because that's where she belongs, but we all know I'm no royalist, much less part of the high-end party set Lady Victoria runs with."

Everyone sat back, a few frowns between them, and Brogan was torn between the desire to end this conversation, and sadness that not one of them had even mounted an argument to her last point. "It's the way things are. I know it, and Emma will, too, as soon as she's back on her feet."

"But will she know it in the meantime?" Diane mused. "Have you told her you just want friendship?"

"I don't think I need to state the obvious."

Will leaned back in his chair until the front legs lifted off the floor. "I wouldn't be so sure about yourself there. I don't want to be indelicate, but plenty of women have come through that door looking for something more than friendship from you."

Now it was her turn to blush, but she managed to say, "And every one of them has walked right back out again in a short time. I've never had to tell any of them to head out of town, either."

"Right," Ciara said slowly. She'd been uncharacteristically quiet for the last few minutes. "All of them went back to their own homes and lives, but this is Emma's home now. She chose this place as her sanctuary as much as you have. You're going to see each other. You already have, more than you planned. If that's not going to change, maybe you need to change the way you handle those encounters."

"So, what?" Brogan asked hesitantly, her heart feeling uncomfortably scrunched in her chest at the thought of seeing Emma every day, and the thought of not. Both prospects felt equally fraught. "You don't think I should go to the party with her?"

"We're saying maybe you shouldn't lead her on," Diane said gently. "It could make things complicated later. You might have to face a little awkward conversation straight away."

"We don't want to see any hearts get broken," Ciara added.

Brogan noticed her sister didn't specify any heart in particular, but the way her own had beat in an erratic rhythm since she'd seen Emma shrouded in the golden light made her suspect things had already got further out of hand than she'd intended. She never thought there was much chance of the two of them getting close enough to worry about intentions and misconceptions, but still, there was the kiss.

She sighed at the memory of Emma's lips, so soft and sweet, and could no longer convince herself they weren't quickly approaching heartbreak territory. Maybe the others were right, and it was time to step back. Screwing up all her resolve, she gave one sharp nod and said, "Okay."

"Okay what?" Tom asked. "Okay, you're just friends? Okay, you're going to go where she leads? Or okay, you're going to call this whole thing off right now?"

"I don't know," Brogan admitted.

"You better decide real fast, because here she comes."

Brogan turned to glance over her shoulder as Emma stepped through the doorway from the dining area. Her smile was shy, but Brogan couldn't see why. A woman who looked like her, wearing a dress like that, had nothing to feel insecure about. The black cloth hugged her body loosely enough to accent her subtle curves without begging for attention. The straps covered the tops of the shoulders, but nothing else, and the neckline offered the most tantalizing peek of collar bone Brogan had ever laid eyes on. She was about to offer a comment along the lines of saying such a tasteful option would be welcome anywhere, when Emma turned slowly around, revealing the most deliciously sweeping plunge that gathered at her shoulder before swooping down to her mid-back, then up to the other shoulder.

Whatever inadequate words she'd been about to utter died, parched to oblivion in the desert of her mouth. All she could manage to do was stare at the smooth, creamy expanse between Emma's shoulder blades, as if it were an oasis amid a desert.

Distantly she could make out the voices of other people in the room. Random words floated over her—"beautiful," "stunning," "superb." They were all insufficient.

Then Emma turned to her, lips curled up, eyebrows arched expectantly, blue eyes sparkling with a devastating mix of hope and uncertainty. Brogan realized she was being asked a question, but she couldn't remember what it was. Something about Emma, and honesty, and her intentions. Oh yeah, a party. A party where Emma would wear that dress. The little spark of clarity that realization offered was enough for her to form and say a single word.

"Perfect."

Chapter Eleven

Brogan opened the door to her car for Emma. Emma could see she'd cleaned it since their last driving lesson. Gone were the bits of mud from country roads and gone were the scraps of paper and receipts from the floorboards. The little touch warmed her chest every bit as much as the sight of Brogan in her dark slacks, gray sweater, and black sport coat had. How did the woman always manage to get things right?

Emma felt dull and awkward by comparison, despite the hint of color that appeared in Brogan's cheeks upon seeing her, though she'd admit to not hating the reaction. It had been a long time since anyone had looked at her the way Brogan had in the pub last week. Even before her divorce, Amalie had lost interest in her on nearly every front, including the physical, which, of course, contributed a great deal to the divorce. The thought cooled the heat she'd been basking in.

Brogan slipped into the driver's seat and pulled out of town.

"Will we be the first ones there?" Emma asked nervously. "I never want to be late, so I always get to events too early, and then I end up hiding in a bathroom or something. I don't want to stand there awkwardly by myself, but I don't want to have to make small talk with other awkward, early-arrivers either." She grimaced. "Isn't that terrible?"

Brogan laughed. "Not at all. I'm cringe-worthily familiar with the feeling you so perfectly described there."

"No. You're easy to talk to, and you always say the right thing. I only get the words right when I put them to paper and spend months revising them."

"Not true. You describe things with such vivid detail, like when you talked about the view from my room, or even the process of being socially awkward. I've seen or experienced those things hundreds of times, but I've only ever felt them in the pit of my stomach. I've never even considered the fact that there might be words for those sensations."

"When you've spent as much time as I have hiding in the coat-rooms of events being thrown in your honor, you have plenty of opportunity to inspect and chastise your own reactions."

"Maybe that's it then," Brogan said. "I haven't had many events thrown in my honor."

"It's sort of terrible," Emma admitted. "You feel so unworthy, so ungraceful, and everyone is looking at you, and you don't know what to do with your hands. Then you have to say something thankful, but also self-effacing, because you don't want to come across as patronizing, but also you don't want to seem unappreciative even though you wish everyone would let you get back to your couch and pajamas. And then, once again, you have to make conversation with people who know much more about you than you know about them, and they all expect you to be witty and charming, but I'm not good off the cuff, so I say bland things." She was rambling now, but as the words continued to spill out, her anxiety rose, and it must have shown in her voice or in her verbal flood, because Brogan moved her hand from the gear shift and set it lightly atop her own.

Emma looked up as Brogan took her eyes from the road long enough to meet hers and smile. "It'll be okay."

"Really?"

"I promise you won't have to talk to anyone you don't want to. I'll run interference all night. We could even have a signal."

"Like what?"

Brogan pursed her lips together. "How about if you're talking

169

to someone and you start to feel uncomfortable, you can tug on your ear, and I'll step in?"

Emma's eyes watered, and she blinked away the tears but found the emotions behind them harder to erase.

"Did I say something wrong?" Brogan whispered, as she turned onto a wider road.

She shook her head. "You said something right, again, like always."

"If you don't like the plan, you can say so."

"Not only do I like the plan, I invented it. Early on, after my first book became a bestseller, I started finding myself in these situations more often. I asked Amalie if she could help rescue me when I got overwhelmed. I suggested we could have a sign or something."

Brogan's jaw twitched, but she didn't say anything, giving Emma the freedom to dive deeper into that particular memory. Amalie had laughed at her at first. Then she'd grown irritated. She'd accused Emma of being childish and immature. She'd told her if she didn't want the praise, maybe it should go to someone else. "She always loved the limelight. She had a hard time under-standing why someone wouldn't want to make the most of it. It wasn't easy for her to go to all of those events and watch me struggle with people fawning over me, so eventually she stopped."

"She stopped what?"

"Going to the events. Which made sense. I mean, most part-ners don't follow each other to work, right?"

"I don't know," Brogan said, as if measuring her words. "I sup-pose not every day, but expecting a partner to go to a special function in your honor isn't unreasonable."

"It got to the point where it was easier for both of us if she used that time to do her own thing." The phrase stuck in her throat a little, because doing her own thing had eventually turned into doing someone else.

"Emma, you know it's not your fault, right?"

She smiled weakly, and Brogan slowed the car before turning onto a little farm lane.

"What she did to you, whatever it was, it wasn't your fault."

"She had an affair with another one of her writing protégés," Emma said bluntly.

Brogan nodded. "I'm sorry to have that confirmed, but I'm not surprised, given what you've told me about her."

"No, that's part of the burn. I seem to have been the only person surprised, and the last one to know. Apparently, she'd done little to hide the liaisons, making sure to show off her new girlfriend to as many of our friends as possible before leaving me, which made me feel doubly foolish."

"You were in love," Brogan defended.

"But she wasn't." Her voice cracked. "A fact she made abundantly clear, not just to me, but to the whole world. I wanted to handle everything quietly. Part of me wanted her back, but she had to set fire to every bridge. Did you know she wanted it written in the divorce decree that she had an affair?"

Brogan shook her head.

"I filed for a no-fault divorce, and she made me go back to amend the papers, to list the reason as infidelity." Emma barely held back a sob on the last word. "She wanted, no she *needed*, the public record to show she'd cheated on me. It wasn't enough for me to know. It had to be written down in legal documents I'd have to keep on file for the rest of my life."

"All right," Brogan finally said, clutching the steering wheel so tightly her knuckles went white. "I hate her."

"No," Emma said softly.

"I'm sorry." Brogan pulled the car slowly to the shoulder of the country road and put it in park before turning to face her fully. "I've tried to stay quiet because you clearly loved her, and it's not my business, and I try not to let myself hate any human being, especially one I don't know, but Emma, I hate this woman."

"It's done now."

"It's not, because she's got inside your head. She's affected your sense of self. You're near tears when I offer to do something any friend would gladly do for you, all because someone who was supposed to love you made you feel like you didn't have the right

171

to basic kindness. She was wrong. About everything. You deserve to feel comfortable and cared for. You deserve to know you're secure. You deserve to have your needs and desires taken into consideration."

Emma shook her head again, not necessarily because she didn't believe Brogan, but because she didn't believe someone like Brogan could see those things in her.

"I mean it," Brogan continued forcefully. "You've been abused, maybe not physically, but emotionally, by someone who couldn't handle your success, your talent, or your passion. She was jealous and insecure, and I think deep down she knew she didn't deserve you, but instead of doing her best to be honest and kind and honorable, she set fire to the whole damn building to prove to herself and everyone else that she could."

Emma started to shake her head again, but this time Brogan caught her face in her hands. They were so strong and so tender, and it had been so long since she'd been touched, Emma closed her eyes and leaned into the caress.

"Emma," Brogan whispered, her voice low and thick. "What she did wasn't about you. It was about her and her shortcomings, not yours. You deserve a partner, someone who will share in your success, someone who will never let you doubt that you're cherished and safe, regardless of whether or not you write a million bestsellers or never write again. You deserve—"

The next words died on Brogan's lips, or maybe Emma wiped them away with her own, as she pressed her mouth hungrily to Brogan's.

This kiss was not slow or tentative, and it was not one-sided. This kiss was met and returned by Brogan, and it was as if her will combined with Emma's to explode through them both. The pieces of her shattered heart shuddered as Brogan's mouth opened to her own, hot, commanding, possessing, but also offering so much of herself as their tongues tangled. Emma whimpered as part of herself that had been frozen came clawing back to life. At first, she couldn't breathe. She didn't want to, but when finally forced to break the seal between their mouths to gasp, she inhaled with Brogan, and was aware of the scent of her, the taste, fresh and invigorating, a hint of salt clinging to her from the sea she'd spent the day sailing, the sea Emma sought solace in, the sea she'd crossed to get to here, even if she'd never imagined feeling this way again.

The thought made her open her eyes in surprise.

Again.

No, not quite. She wasn't sure she'd ever felt exactly the same way with Amalie. This was rougher, more raw, less hazy. She felt more awake than she had last time, but there was no denying that the rush pulsing through her stemmed from the same vein she'd let another woman sever. The wound had almost bled her dry. What was she doing risking that kind of pain again? Was she so stupid or weak that she returned to the razor's edge with her first step back into the light?

"Emma?" Brogan whispered, her voice still low and raspy, but now also laced with concern.

She shook her head slowly.

"I'm so sorry." Brogan sat back and pushed her hands through those luscious red locks so that one fell across the smooth skin of her forehead.

Emma reached up to brush it back, but instead twirled it between her fingers, soaking up the cool silkiness as if her nerve endings had never touched anything so satisfying. The contrast of the copper against her own pale skin made her feel as if she were seeing the color for the first time. Something about the kiss had sent all her senses into overdrive.

Then Brogan pulled away, backing up as much as she could in the small Peugeot, so the back of her head rested against the driver's side window. Her chest rose and fell rapidly, and her dark pupils almost consumed their outer rings of green, either in lust or terror, or perhaps the same mix of the two cracking through Emma's chest. "I'm sorry, Emma. I don't know what came over me. I wanted you to know, I mean, you were so upset, and so beautiful, I needed to make you . . . I got swept away."

She said such wonderful things in a way that made them sound terrible. Brogan. Stunning, stoic, strong Brogan. What had Emma done to her? And why should *she* be the one to apologize?

"I didn't mean to overstep—"

Emma held up both her hands. "You didn't. I'm the one who should be apologizing. I got carried away as much as you did. I don't know what came over me. I've never done anything like that before."

"It's my fault," Brogan stated flatly. "I can't seem to stay focused around you, but I didn't come here tonight with ulterior motives. I wanted to be a good friend, not someone who takes advantage of an emotional moment."

Emma wasn't at all sure that was what had happened, or at least not a total explanation. She'd had plenty of emotional moments. Lately her life had been a nightmarish string of them, and she'd never once had the urge to kiss anyone, and yet with Brogan she'd done so, twice. Surely that meant something. "I did feel emotional, but I don't think you, I mean, it's a lot of things, but . . ."

"It's okay," Brogan said. "You don't owe me an explanation."

"Good, because I don't think I have one, for either of us, but I wish I did."

Brogan nodded, then let out a shaky sigh.

That sigh said more than any of the words Emma had used so far. She was confused, disoriented, and awash with emotions she couldn't begin to pick apart, much less process. And while none of that was completely new, she didn't want to drag poor, sweet, beautiful Brogan into her muddled mess. She wasn't ready for that kind of responsibility. She wasn't ready for any of this.

She hadn't given any thought to feeling anything for anyone again, ever, but certainly not so soon.

"My divorce hasn't even been final six months," Emma said aloud, but mostly to herself.

"I understand."

"Three months ago, I thought it was great progress when I could get out of bed without crying." Emma laughed without humor. "And a month ago I was so proud when I started to consume solid foods on a semi-regular basis."

Brogan smiled. "You should. Those are big steps in a long process. I've seen you transform so much from that first night of screaming at each other in the doorway."

Emma laughed a little lighter at the memory.

"I can't imagine how fast all those changes have felt to you," Brogan continued, "and I certainly didn't mean to push you for more than you're ready for. I didn't mean to push you at all."

"You didn't. You've been kind and patient and understanding, and it also bears mentioning that I kissed you, twice." Her chest tightened again as the panic took hold once more. "And now that I say that aloud, I'm more than a little embarrassed because I'm not sure you welcomed that."

"I did," Brogan said quickly. "I don't want you to worry about that, please. I greatly enjoyed both kisses, maybe more than I should have, but I also enjoy your company without kissing. I don't want you to feel pressured."

"I never have around you. Not once. You may be the only person in my life who doesn't seem to want something more from me than I want to give, which might be why I keep making such a fool of myself by clinging to you, then pulling away. You make me feel safe enough to feel things I'm not ready to feel." Emma's voice cracked with the weight of that realization. "I'm not ready. I don't know if I'll ever be ready, but I know I'm not ready right now."

Brogan reached across the car and tentatively took her hand, even while keeping the bulk of her body back. "It's okay. You're all right. I'm all right. I'm not asking you for anything. The only person you have to answer to is yourself."

Emma smiled. "I don't know if leaving everything to me is comforting or terrifying."

Brogan nodded. "I understand, but the good news is you don't have to decide right now. You don't have to do anything, but if you still want to go to this party, I'd be happy to go along with you. Just as we are. No answers, no expectations, no pressure."

Emma sighed and shook some of the tension from her shoulders, then gave Brogan's hand a little squeeze. "Thank you. That actually sounds perfect."

Brogan barely had five minutes to pull herself together in the tight confines of the car before the massive expanse of Penchant Castle came into view. The mammoth stone structure towering over both town and country would certainly offer a lot more space than the close proximity of being in the car with Emma, and she needed that right now. The heat still radiated off Emma's tantalizing skin, compounding the utter temptation of her consuming mouth, and twisting Brogan's stomach into knots, but as she pulled up to an iron gate hanging within a large stone archway, she remembered that space did not equal freedom, much less peace.

Her cheeks had already begun to feel warm even before she climbed out of the car, held out her keys, and locked eyes with the valet.

"Brogan?" Ali asked, his dark eyes wide in a flash of surprise, followed by amusement. Then with a quick glance at Emma, his grin widened. "Good on ya, girl."

An older man in full uniform cleared his throat disapprovingly, and Ali's expression snapped back to neutral before he snagged her keys. "Good evening, Ms. McKay."

She frowned and turned back to Emma, wanting to introduce her to him, but another employee she didn't recognize had already motioned them forward.

"Right this way, Ms. Volant." He indicated the main entrance through another high stone archway, this one inset with a wooden door at least twice as tall as they were. They passed under a massive, wrought iron-chandelier, and Emma didn't seem to know where to look. The foyer was covered in a mix of tapestries and ancient battle armor.

"Wow," she whispered, her lips forming a perfect little *o*.

It had been a long time since Brogan had been impressed by the grandeur of these rooms, but she didn't miss the smug expression on their guide's face. She wanted to smack him upside the back of his head. Who were either of them to take away from the pure wonder in Emma's eyes?

He led them up an immense marble stairway with a lush red runner and past the flags bearing the lions of the Penchant family.

"Do you know when this was built?" Emma asked.

"Construction of the castle began in 1096."

"That's almost seven hundred years older than my country," Emma said, throwing him a smile. He continued to stare straight ahead.

"Has it ever been under siege?"

"Several times."

"By who?" Emma asked excitedly.

"The Scots, King Edward the Fourth, and during the Wars of the Roses it fell twice, once to Yorkists, once to Lancastrians."

"The Wars of the Roses," Emma mused, the same spark in her eyes Brogan had seen there when she spoke of pirates and the open seas.

"What an amazing legacy," Emma added, turning her smile back to the butler or footman or host. Whatever he was, he didn't return the expression. He didn't meet her eyes at all. Brogan watched the fact dawn slowly on Emma, as her smile faded, probably wondering what she'd said wrong, when in reality she couldn't have said anything right. This wasn't Downton Abbey. Most of the staff weren't full time, much less seen as extended family. Most of the people working tonight would have been given unsubtle cues to speak when spoken to, and that didn't happen frequently, at least not at this level. Men like Archie, who wore suits and worked in the land offices, might occasionally have the ear of the duke, but the people who staffed the lady's party were barely even meant to be seen, much less heard. Not that many of the guests ever tried to break that wall, but Brogan knew standard protocol was to answer only direct questions or offer services specific to your employment. Anything else might mean you didn't get called back for the next event. She'd never minded those rules, until she saw the tight set of Emma's lips.

Thankfully, her impassiveness didn't last long. As they reached the top of another, shorter set of stairs and entered a long hallway, Emma let out another little excited "oh." She wandered off the elaborately patterned rug to examine a giant portrait on the wall.

"That's Lady Victoria." She turned back to their stone-faced attendant for confirmation. "She's so little."

Brogan laughed. "She's ten feet tall."

Emma shook her head. "I didn't mean the size of the painting. I meant she's young."

That was true enough. In the painting, the young heiress couldn't have been more than sixteen. She wore an elaborate gown and an impish grin underneath haughty eyes in a mix of teenage-esque rebellion and upper-class superiority. If the papers were to be believed, she'd lost neither quality in the ensuing fifteen years.

Emma leaned closer to read the small glass plaque next to the oil painting. "Lady Victoria Charlotte Algernon Penchant in her service as attendant to the Countess of Wessex on the occasion of her wedding to His Royal Highness, Prince Edward."

"That would've been her coming out-year," Brogan explained.

"A coming-out portrait? How progressive."

Their household overlord blanched, but his reaction only added to Brogan's amusement.

"Not exactly. They used to present daughters of noblemen to the queen when they came of age. Now the occasion is acknowledged more informally with events and portraits like this one. The announcement you're thinking of was mostly documented in the tabloids, much later in Lady Victoria's life. I doubt there's a formal painting to commemorate *that* coming out."

"This way please." Mr. Buttoned-Up finally couldn't contain his displeasure any longer and ushered them along.

Emma grimaced at the polite rebuke, but as she followed him down the hall, she did manage to sneak one last glance over her shoulder at the painting. Brogan's stomach gave a little twist, but she couldn't quite put her finger on why. Maybe it was her general discomfort at their surroundings, or the disdain of a man she really should have ranked below in this situation, or maybe it was

Emma's obvious enjoyment of a place that represented Brogan's inferior status. Or maybe, she thought as they turned into the Penchant family's personal library, it was something more.

Emma froze inside the door, her eyes filled with delight as she examined the room with its floor-to-ceiling shelves of books all awash in the natural light, streaming orange through the full-length windows at either end of the space. She took her first steps in an almost dreamlike state and ran her fingertips over a row of leather-bound volumes closest to them. As she walked along the ornately carved shelves, she murmured the titles and subjects ranging from classic fiction to law and history.

About halfway down the wall she stopped, and Brogan glanced over her shoulder to see, right at eye level, a complete collection of Emma's own books.

Emma stared for a second before turning back to Brogan, then rolled her eyes. "I suppose this is a nice touch to get me to loosen my bank account."

The words were right, but the blush in her cheeks said while she might have seen through the gesture, she didn't hate it. Brogan took in a few more details of their surroundings and began to suspect the move was calculated to influence something other than Emma's bank account.

In fact, the entire event seemed conspicuously catered to Emma. She knew from experience that most official events at the castle were held in the formal living room or the portrait gallery, with the library generally reserved for gatherings of family and friends. This space was always more intimate than the reception areas, but even the details here had been adjusted. Gone was the foosball table, replaced by overstuffed reading chairs. The bar, which used to have a prominent place in the center of the room, had been shifted to a back corner. End tables that had been set with priceless gifts from the wealthy and powerful now all held books whose subjects ranged from local history to strong women's fiction, and the photos scattered about were all of Lady Victoria, dressed down, on motorcycles or walking in the woods. The image this room conveyed was a stark contrast to the stiffness of the rest of the castle without losing any of its impressive scale. The personal invitation from Lady Victoria didn't seem nearly as coincidental anymore.

"Would you like a drink?" Brogan asked, eager for a chance to do something with her hands.

"A glass of wine might be in order here," Emma admitted, her voice sounding small and intimidated.

"Of course," Brogan said, then meeting her eyes asked, "You okay?"

She nodded. "I think so. I mean, it's a bit overwhelming, but books soothe me. As long as I focus on them and not the idea that one family owns all of this, I might be all right."

Brogan nodded. "Good plan. You've got this, but remember, one tug of the ear, and I'll be right there."

Emma smiled sweetly. "Have I told you in the last ten minutes that you're the best?"

"No, but you can make up for that when I return with your wine," Brogan said, then walked quickly away before any of the butterflies in her stomach had the chance to take flight.

The bartender glanced up as she approached, a benign smile plastered on her otherwise inexpressive face until a flash of recognition caused her eyes to widen the same way Ali's had. Brogan only had a second to note how sad their shock was. It probably spoke to the complete unlikelihood of social mobility, but before she had a chance to say anything, the woman looked past her to Emma, and her smile grew exponentially.

"Are you here with Emma Volant?"

"Hi to you, too, Tabby."

"Sorry," Tabby said, without actually appearing to be. "I mean, totally not my place, please don't report me or anything."

Brogan shook her head frantically. "Of course not. You know I'd never . . ."

"I don't know nothing about you if you come to upper-crust fundraisers with world-famous millionaires. That's not social climbing. It's like feckin' pole vaulting," she whispered, then shook her head. "And now I've gone and said 'feck' at work."

"Calm down," Brogan commanded, not wanting to draw any attention to them, for both their sakes. "She's just a friend."

"Maybe you should work on that," Tabby said more quietly. "She's loaded."

The tightness in her stomach ratcheted up another level. She'd never seen Emma that way. Not that she didn't know there was a massive class difference between them. She was aware of that every moment Emma's lips weren't on her mind, but she'd never once considered Emma a possible ticket up or out of her current tax bracket. She never gave much thought to her net worth at all. When she thought of Emma outclassing her, she didn't mean financially. She meant in elegance, grace, poise, worldliness, and a million of the other intangible qualities that made her so appealing. She was beautiful and brave, where Brogan thought of herself as mostly bland. Maybe that's why she'd fallen into the ground-shaking kiss in the car. Emma hadn't made her feel boring. She made her feel strong and seen and needed, but no amount of reconceptualizing her sense of self could balance out their bank accounts. Then again, she wasn't sure even that reminder would've been powerful enough to inspire any restraint.

In those moments she'd forgotten her place. Hell, she'd forgotten her name. The only thing she'd known right then was Emma, and the only thing she'd wanted was more. She'd burned for her in ways she'd never burned for anyone. And no matter how much she tried to regain her composure since then, if Emma so much as inclined her head to her, she'd fall again.

The thought terrified her. She'd never had any trouble backing away. She'd made a life of never wanting what she couldn't have, and the way Emma had been ripped apart by her own emotions after the kiss only showcased, in heart-wrenching detail, that Brogan couldn't have her.

Not really.

She could've pushed for more during the kiss. She could probably push for more tonight, but a series of stolen moments on the side of the road to somewhere else was all Emma had to offer. She couldn't have made it any clearer as she practically choked on the words, "I'm not ready." Emma was in transition. She wasn't where she was a month ago, and she wasn't where she was going, either.

"Hey, you okay?" Tabby asked.

"Yeah," Brogan whispered.

"Sure? 'Cause you sort of seem like you could use a drink."

"Yeah," she repeated, remembering what she'd come over for. "Two glasses of wine."

"What kind?"

"Um." She didn't know. "How about one white and one red?"

Tabby chuckled. "Never mind. You're the same Brogan as always."

She sighed at the truth of the statement, then turned back to watch Emma as Tabby grabbed two bottles and a corkscrew.

An older man had approached Emma, and she smiled at something he'd said, then gestured to her book. His expression brightened, his bushy, gray eyebrows rising into shaggy hair of the same color. She was clearly regaling him with some story about her work. Brogan remembered what it felt like to be given a little peek into Emma's world. She was mesmerizing as she spoke about the things that inspired her.

She was mesmerizing a lot, actually. Despite all of her talk about being socially awkward, no one in this room would ever doubt her place in it. She more than fit here in this light, surrounded by books and artists, in that dress; she flourished. And she was emerging from the cocoon she'd used to protect and heal herself. If Emma had gone from the woman who'd sobbed at their first meeting to the woman standing before her now in such a short time, where would she be two months from now?

As if to answer the question, Lady Victoria materialized out of the corner of Brogan's vision and headed straight for Emma. Instead of pulling back, Emma's face lit up with recognition. The older gentleman clearly got the message and excused himself as their host closed in.

Everything Brogan had observed in Emma over the last few

months told her Emma was happy to see Lady Victoria. From the relaxed set of her shoulders to the genuine smile across her lips, the expression was more than mirrored as Lady Victoria leaned in to kiss her quickly on both cheeks. The move was a little too European for Brogan's taste, but she didn't doubt the glowing regard Lady Victoria exuded was sincere in this case, and when she stepped back, she didn't exactly reestablish a polite distance. Brogan couldn't hear what they said to one another, but they stood close enough to say it in a whisper. Then, as she laughed at something Emma said, Lady Victoria placed her hand on the bare skin of her upper arm. Emma made no move to shake off the touch.

The subtle sign of interest made a small muscle in Brogan's jaw twitch. Then she silently cursed the involuntary response. She wasn't jealous, or maybe she was, but the emotion made her feel stupid. She had no right. She had no desire to play this part. She refused to see the heiress of a duke as a competitor. She wasn't trying to win Emma and, even if she were, she'd be an idiot to go up against a beautiful, rich, literal noblewoman. Just looking at them made her heart hurt on multiple levels. Even she couldn't imagine a more fairy-tale pairing. American ingenuity meets British aristocracy in one classy package with two blond bows on top.

She briefly considered slipping out a side door and leaving them to their happily-ever-after when Emma met her eyes. Her smile turned a little shy again, and she nodded for Brogan to join her. Like a puppy eager to please, she acquiesced to the subtle call.

"Hello," Lady Victoria said, and extended her hand.

Brogan noticed that she didn't get a cheek kiss, not that she'd have welcomed one, but the contrast was clear as she shook her hand.

"Victoria, this is Brogan McKay. I wouldn't be here without her. I might not be anywhere without her right now."

"Then I'm greatly indebted to you." Victoria's smile was warm as it encompassed them both.

"She has a flare for the dramatic." Brogan brushed off the compliment.

"Only in fiction," Emma said.

"Either way, it works well," Victoria said.

Brogan raised one wineclass in salute, then looked at the other, before shrugging. "And it looks like I have a drinking problem here, but one of these is for you, Emma."

"Which one?"

"Whichever you prefer. Or try them both if you like."

"Maybe a sip of each?" Emma asked, taking the white first.

"A woman who shares all the wine is my favorite kind of party-goer," Lady Victoria mused. "And is that a hint of Geordie I hear with a touch of Irish in your accent?"

"Good ear, Your Ladyship."

Victoria's face flushed crimson. "Please, call me Victoria, or better yet, Vic. The trappings of titles are pretentious enough in their formal capacities. I can't stomach them at all among friends."

Friends. Brogan doubted the word extended to her so much as to Emma, but she appreciated the grace of the gesture. She accepted the white wine back and passed Emma the red, watching her expression closely to see which one she enjoyed more, but out of the corner of her eye, she could see Victoria watching her. Was she noticing the same sort of cues Brogan had observed moments earlier?

"This one." Emma curled the glass a little closer to her chest. "You're not getting this one back."

Both Brogan and Victoria laughed, then Victoria said, "I'm sorry. I feel gauche admitting this, but you seem so familiar to me. I know we've crossed paths before, but I cannot place you."

"I'm sure you have that happen a lot with all the events you host." Brogan sidestepped the question she hadn't quite been asked.

"Did you go to Cheltenham?"

Brogan fought back a bitter laugh at the name of one of England's most elite girls' schools.

"Or do you shoot?" Victoria asked, then turning to Emma, explained, "My sister shoots. I hardly compare, but sometimes her friends let me tag along out of sympathy."

Brogan shook her head. "I don't shoot."

"She sails," Emma offered. "Maybe you two met through that."

"Could be," Victoria said, her eyes narrowing as if she were trying to mentally flip through some internal Rolodex of memories. "Wait, were you at Princess Sasha's wedding to Kerry Donovan?"

"No," Brogan said flatly, hoping the flush rising in her core wasn't yet visible around her neck or ears. She was going to have to put a stop to this guessing game eventually.

Victoria frowned. "I thought I had it there. Seems like I remember you from a party of some sort."

"You do." She hoped she managed a tight smile instead of a grimace. "I'm one of your bartenders."

"Excuse me?"

Brogan nodded toward Tabby standing in the corner pouring wine for other guests. "I did that job several times over the last few years. Your thirtieth birthday, your sister's engagement announcement, two Christmas parties for your house staff, and um, your hen party."

Victoria's bright eyes clouded, and suddenly Brogan wasn't the only one blushing. "I'm sorry I didn't remember."

"Don't be," Brogan said quickly. "It's not a regular thing for me, just a way to make a little extra money, mostly in the winter when the tourist traffic dries up in Amberwick."

There was a beat of silence as all three of them stared at each other. It stretched as Brogan's mind began to run away with possibilities of what Emma must be thinking. Or what Victoria must assume about her now that she knew Brogan's rightful place was serving the two of them, not conversing.

"Amberwick is a truly beautiful village," Lady Victoria finally said. "Are you from there originally?"

Brogan nodded. "Yes, born and raised."

"You met her wonderful niece at the school the day we met,"

185

Emma interjected. "Remember, she was the redhead who showed us around the various book projects?"

Victoria's smile softened. "I do remember. I adored her. She's like an adult trapped in a ten-year-old's body."

The astute observation made it harder for Brogan to hold onto all of her resentment. "That's Reggie."

"And Emma said you sail?"

"I do. Not competitively, though."

"Her family gives the puffin tours," Emma said, a hint of excitement in her voice.

"That's one of the small businesses we featured in our tourist initiatives last year," Victoria said. "I meant to get down there to take a tour myself but never got the chance."

"And her brother works here at the castle," Emma said, as if she enjoyed this game of pretending they had meaningful connections when they didn't. Or maybe Emma was embarrassed to be here with the bartender and was trying to use Brogan's family to bolster her social cachet. The thought made her stomach hurt. Emma turned to her. "Which brother works in the office here?"

"Archie," Brogan said. "He's in your land management department."

"I'll have to keep an eye out for him," Victoria said. "I've mostly had my hand in local real estate, but as my father moves closer to retirement, I suspect the land management will fall to me, and I'll need all the help I can get."

"I'm sure he'd be happy to offer his advice," Brogan admitted with a little chuckle. "He's always given plenty of it to me, whether I particularly wanted to hear it or not."

Victoria laughed a little harder than the comment warranted. "Sounds like my sister."

"The one with the guns?" Emma asked.

"The same. And don't think for a minute she isn't afraid to remind you of her crack-shot abilities while telling you how you ought to live your life."

"Why am I feeling better about my only-child status?" Emma

asked, and they were all back on steady footing again, three women talking about their families and their jobs. Only, two of them were millionaires, and this time it would take a lot more than social graces to help Brogan forget that fact.

Still, she was here for Emma, who for some reason seemed interested in keeping her around. Emma tugged on her sleeve to pull her along as Victoria gave them an abbreviated tour of some nearby state rooms, and asked Brogan's opinion on things she had no right to give them on, like history and art, and when they returned to the party, Emma introduced her as her dear friend when Victoria made introductions to the other local artists in attendance.

She probably should have been grateful for the many votes of confidence. It was almost as if Emma didn't realize she should feel awkward about being here with her. Maybe it was her American concept of social class, or maybe she simply wasn't one to put on airs. Or maybe she had enough money and power in her own right, so she didn't ever have to feel insecure about the company she kept. The last option did please Brogan in some perverse way. As much as she didn't want to be Emma's version of slumming it, she liked the idea of Emma having enough self-confidence to blaze her own trail, even if that trail led right into the uppermost echelons of British society.

That thought was interrupted by Lady Victoria looking up as the lights of the large chandelier flipped on. "It appears day has turned to night while I've been chatting your ears off. I think time might have got away from me."

"I think we may have monopolized you all evening," Emma said abashedly. "I'm sorry."

"Not at all." She leaned in conspiratorially. "You two are by far the most interesting people I've talked to in weeks."

Brogan noted that she'd included her in the comment clearly meant for Emma. She had to hand it to Victoria. She wasn't as prudish or pretentious as Brogan might have liked. At least if Victoria had turned up her nose at her, it would've given her a compelling reason to dislike her in return.

"I do worry I'm expected to mingle more, but I'd hoped to give you a tour of the grounds before night fell completely."

"Don't be silly," Emma said. "You can't leave your own party."

Brogan suspected a person who had a castle with grounds and gardens to tour could probably do whatever she damned well pleased, but instead of defiance, Victoria responded with resignation.

"You're right. I have some responsibilities I've probably neglected too long," she admitted, her voice tinged with a hint of sadness. "But I did promise you a real tour, and despite what some people may say, I work hard to keep my promises."

"I believe you," Emma said sincerely, and grudgingly, Brogan did, too.

"Then you'll have to come back," Victoria said resolutely, then turning to include Brogan, added, "both of you, sometime when I don't have any other responsibilities, and we can all be less formal."

"I'd love that," Emma said.

"How does next week work for you?"

"Wow, next week? I suppose. I don't have anything set in stone, but"—she turned to Brogan—"I can't speak for you. Maybe we should check calendars."

"That sounds entirely too stuffy," Victoria pushed. "No need to confer with social secretaries. You tell me what works for you, and I'll make it work for me."

Emma blushed a little. "I guess I could do Thursday or Friday during the afternoon."

"What about you, Brogan?"

She shook her head slightly, still reeling from how easily Victoria had commanded an audience, and how quickly Emma'd accepted. "Actually, this is my busy season. I'd have a hard time getting away any time soon."

"Surely we can steal a few hours of your time." Victoria nudged her.

It was a nice touch, but she'd had her fill of playing buffer or chaperone, and the sooner she let whatever was happening here happen, the sooner she'd be free to move on. Her stomach gave another queasy flip, but she stood her ground. "I wish I could, but I've seen the grounds plenty of times. My youngest brother has actually been doing your landscaping lately, so why don't you two do this one without me, and I'll take a rain check. I could probably get away long enough to drive Emma up Friday afternoon, but that's about all."

Victoria took the out. "I can arrange a car. Say, one o'clock Friday afternoon? Emma?"

Emma frowned slightly, and her eyes swept over Brogan with a hint of sadness she hadn't seen there in a few weeks, but before Brogan had a chance to second-guess her decision, Emma nodded. "I guess I can't think of anything stopping me."

"Good," Victoria said. "It's settled."

Brogan forced a smile as the deal was sealed, but she didn't actually feel anything close to settled.

Emma rested her head against the cool glass of the passenger-side window and stared up at the dark sky lit with the pinpricks of a thousand stars. She hadn't noticed before how much better she could see them out here. She'd never lived in a place dark enough to appreciate their multitudes. She smiled at the thought. In order to see so many lights, she had to step more fully into the darkness.

"It's beautiful here," she said, with a contented sigh, "the sea, the stars, the rolling pastures, the castle. How is everything so picturesque all the time?"

"They say it's God's country up here, but I suppose people everywhere think that about where they live."

Emma closed her eyes and relished the low hum of Brogan's steady path around gentle curves. The emotional rollercoaster and social engagement of the last few hours had taken a lot of energy, but not in the soul-sucking way she'd come to associate with public appearances. The people she'd interacted with were much more subdued with a lot less bravado than the aspiring artists and investors she'd known in Manhattan. Aside from the donation she'd willingly made to the local arts initiatives, no one had wanted much from her. Victoria had set a relaxed tone, and her social graces had put Emma at ease at every turn.

"I did not hate tonight," she mused aloud as she sat up.

Brogan smiled over at her for a second, her eyes seeming as sleepy as Emma felt. "That's a ringing endorsement."

"It is!" she laughed. "For me anyway. That was the biggest event I've attended in ages, and with a different set of people than I'm used to. And in a castle that looked like someone dropped it out of a medieval fairy tale. That might be old news to you, but I can't believe humans still live in places like that."

"No, I'm with you there," Brogan said dryly.

"Well, I could've felt in over my head. I expected to, but I wasn't nearly as intimidated as I feared." She reached out and put her hand atop Brogan's on the gear shift. "I owe a lot of my comfort level to you."

"I didn't do anything special."

"You did. You stayed by my side, you smiled at me when I got nervous, you were beyond attentive. I never even had to ask for a drink. I would merely think it, and you'd appear with a glass in hand."

"Old habits of a good bartender," Brogan quipped.

"It's more than that."

Brogan laughed, but the sound was strained in a way it hadn't been earlier, even in the moments after the kiss when their bodies had burned and emotions had cracked in her voice.

"Did you have a good time?" Emma asked.

"Yes."

"Really?" Emma's stomach tightened at the feeling she'd had this conversation after other events, in another place, with another woman.

"Of course," Brogan said with a smile that barely reached her cheeks, much less her eyes.

"Would you tell me if you didn't?"

"Emma, I enjoyed being with you tonight."

The words were right, but something else wasn't, and she couldn't quite place what. The set of Brogan's shoulders? The way she kept her eyes on the road at all times? The tiniest tinge of something distant in her tone?

Emma's chest tightened with the urge to ask more. She wanted to understand. She wanted to know Brogan, her wants, her needs, her moods, the same way Brogan intuited those things about her. At the same time, not enough time had passed since their last serious conversation for her to forget how that one had ended. A little shiver raced up her spine at the memory of the kiss and the realization that she wouldn't hate a similar result.

Which was why she couldn't put herself in that position again. Despite her body's urging to the contrary, she wasn't ready to feel those kinds of emotions again. She wasn't strong enough, and it wasn't fair to Brogan to keep reeling her in, then pushing her away, but that fact wasn't enough to make Emma ache for her any less.

She used her thumb to swirl little circles on the back of Brogan's hand before she even realized what she was doing. Even as she'd been musing on Brogan's ability to hurt her, she'd still reached out for her. Wasn't that evidence enough that she couldn't trust her own instincts? The last time had nearly destroyed her. She couldn't face that kind of devastation again, not yet. Actually, hopefully, not ever.

She removed her hand from Brogan's and sat up a little straighter as they turned back into the village, the streetlights of Amberwick illumining their way right to Emma's cottage.

"Thank you for going with me."

"It was my pleasure," Brogan said, in a way that felt neither completely forced nor completely genuine. The mix set off another round of warning bells in Emma's gut, and this time the impulse to understand came with an almost equal desire to protect herself from getting too involved.

Maybe Brogan was tired, maybe she had something else on

her mind, or maybe she'd hated the event the same way Emma had used to, or even the way Amalie had. The thought left a bitter taste in her mouth, which she supposed she should be grateful for, in that at least it killed any worries about ending the night with another kiss.

Still, after saying a quick goodbye and walking up to her front door, she did turn around to wave one more time, and maybe wish for something she shouldn't.

Chapter Twelve

"It's been almost a week," Charlie said.

"What part of 'I don't want to talk about it' implied I'd want to talk about it in a week?"

"I don't know. I mean, I thought maybe you were tired, or processing something."

Both statements had been true when she'd got home from her evening with Emma, and the week since then had done little to help on either count. She'd worked nearly nonstop between the boat and the bar and the post office. The arrival of her newest nephew two days earlier had been cause for both excitement and a lot of schedule-juggling to provide key drop-offs and check-ins at a variety of Edmond's rental properties. She hadn't got more than five hours of sleep any night all week, and yet, when she did get a down moment, instead of crashing, her mind ran laps around the inside of her skull.

"If I went on a date with a woman like Emma, I'd make sure everyone knew all about it," Charlie continued. "I'd be like, 'Oh, what's that? You'd like a pale ale? That's like the one time I went on a date with a beautiful millionaire.'"

"I don't doubt it, Charles, but maybe that's why you've never been on a date with a beautiful millionaire."

"Ouch." He laughed and rubbed his jaw like she'd actually delivered a blow. Then he slid his pint glass across the bar to her. "Fill me up, will ya?"

"On your tab?"

"Yeah, but no worries. I'll pay the whole thing before closing time. Nora paid me for a few of the shifts I picked while you were helping Ed."

She pulled the tap and watched the yellow liquid fall into the glass. Then, closing her eyes for a second, she had a little trouble prying them back open again until Charlie said, "Whoa there. Don't waste the beer."

She jerked her head up as something wet hit her hand.

"Sorry," she mumbled, setting the glass in front of him so a little sloshed over.

"Hey, I'm happy for a heavy pour, but if you're falling asleep standing up, maybe I better take over at the tap."

She shook her head and glanced around the bar. The place wasn't packed, but with four tables still occupied at nearly eleven o'clock on a Thursday, she couldn't deny any longer that tourist season was upon them.

Any other time the thought would've injected a little energy into her step, especially with the group of young women getting an early start on their weekend at the corner booth. "We've got too many customers at the inn for me to turn in early."

"Yeah, ya do," Charlie said, following her gaze to the four in the corner. "They all staying upstairs?"

She nodded, aware that meant they'd likely shut the place down.

"And that fact not bringing a little grin to your frowny face brings me right back to Emma Volant," he said. "What gives?"

"Nothing," she shot back, sad to mean it. She hadn't heard from Emma all week, and while that was probably for the best, given all the hard truths she'd had to face last Friday, she didn't have to love it.

"Are you grumpy because the date was terrible, or because it was awesome and she hasn't called you?"

"Neither. Both. It wasn't a date."

"There's three valid options." He smirked. "Must've been a busy night."

She opened her mouth, but before she could even formulate a response, one of the women from the corner table stepped up to the bar.

"Hi," she said, her smile both a little sweet and shy. "Is it too late to get another round for me and my friends?"

"Not at all," Brogan said quickly, even though the clock to her right said ten minutes to closing time. "Two pinot grigios, a cider, and a Bacardi and Coke, right?"

"Perfect." Her smile grew. "We're up all weekend from York. I've only been here five hours, and I don't know how I'm going to leave on Sunday."

Brogan nodded. "Amberwick's not hard on the eyes."

"Understatement. I'm not sure I've ever had a prettier stroll than the walk along the estuary toward the sea."

Brogan smiled and set two glasses of wine on the bar before turning to pour the cider.

"And did I see you coming in on a sailboat earlier?"

She turned back around in time to see Charlie smother a grin behind his pint glass.

"I do sail with the puffin cruises out of the harbor."

"So, you're multitalented," the woman said, leaning on the bar. "Sounds like you're kind of a good woman to know around here."

The exchange couldn't have been easier to peg. She'd had it with many women over the years. Short stay, the need to get away, an outgoing woman, not so subtle compliments, all the pieces were there, and she was pretty. Her long, black hair fell over the shoulders of her white T-shirt and across her bare arms. Her smile was easy and unassuming. All Brogan would have to do is lean in, and she wouldn't have to sleep alone for a few nights.

"I'm Brogan." She tried to sound friendly.

"Caroline," the woman said, accepting the cider Brogan placed before her. "Do you work all weekend?"

"Pretty much," Brogan admitted, as she poured the Coke over a glass of rum. "I'll sail every day, and work the bar tomorrow and Saturday, too."

"Then I'm sure we'll see each other again."

Brogan managed a smile she hoped wasn't completely crinkled with the exhaustion weighing on every other part of her body. "I hope so."

Caroline continued to grin and held eye contact a few seconds longer than social graces would require, then backed away from the bar toward her friends, who immediately fell into whispered giggles.

"Any day now," Charlie muttered when Caroline was out of earshot.

"What?"

"You can tell me how you get women you aren't even interested in to throw themselves at you."

She rolled her eyes. "She didn't throw herself at me. She showed mild interest, and how do you know I didn't return it?"

Now he rolled *his* eyes in a way that made her feel as if she might be looking into a time-delayed mirror. "You barely said two words to her. You didn't offer to take her out on the boat, or to dinner, or show her around town."

She pursed her lips as she considered the fact she'd done everything on his list with Emma. She didn't think that was a coincidence. "I see what you did there."

"Just trying to start a conversation with my older sister."

"You have four older sisters. I don't see you bugging the rest of them."

"The rest of them don't have a wide and varied group of women coming on to them."

"One woman, Caroline is one woman."

"What about Emma?"

"What about her?" Brogan snapped. "What do you want me to tell you? That we had another mind-melting kiss in the car?"

"That's a start." He seemed pleased with himself, as if he had anything to do with it. "Mind-melting is a good start."

"Yeah, a good start to getting my heart broken, because as soon as we got to the castle, it became clear Lady Victoria orchestrated the entire event to win Emma's affection."

"What?"

"She set the whole thing up in the library and had Emma's books in a prominent place."

"That doesn't mean—"

"It gets better. She kissed her on both cheeks and kept touching her bare arm."

"What did you do?"

"I stood there as long as I could while she tried to place where she recognized me from. I waited patiently while she ran through the list of every prep school and royal social event of the last few years before I finally admitted I had, in fact, been at several of her parties, but as the hired help."

He winced.

"Yeah, is that the story you wanted to hear? Or how about the one where Vic—that's what she wants us to call her now—invited Emma for a private tour of the castle grounds, and the two of them are going on a day-date up there tomorrow afternoon."

His shoulders sagged, and the dejection on his face probably matched exactly how she'd felt for days, or rather for nights. Because, when she'd been working, she'd been able to keep her mind busy, but she'd lain awake night after night replaying the memories of Victoria and Emma together. No matter how much she built up the kiss to epic proportions, she couldn't replay the evening in any way that didn't end up with Emma making a date with the daughter of a fecking duke.

"I'm sorry," he finally said. "I didn't know."

Brogan snorted. "I did. I saw it coming a mile away."

"You know it's not too late, though, right?"

"Of course it's too late. The clock struck midnight, and I'm not even a footman. I'm a kitchen mouse."

"Come on, you're at least a footman."

"If you'd seen the way the actual footman at the castle had looked at me, you'd know for sure I rank below him on the social ladder."

"So, what?" he asked. "It's over?"

"Yeah, it's so over it never really began."

197

"Except for the best kiss of your life."

She sighed. She couldn't deny that point. She didn't even want to. As much as she tried not to wish for more, she also didn't regret the little bit she'd had. "Yeah, except for that."

"Which is why you're still forsaking the other women flirting with you. You've still got it for Emma. You're still waiting on her."

The comment set her teeth on edge. "I'm not waiting on Emma."

That would be pathetic. Emma had made it abundantly clear she wasn't ready to move on . . . yet. Brogan knew what that "yet" meant. Brogan was fine for now. She was *always* the *now* for women like Emma, but Lady Victoria was the *yet*. She'd seen a full-color picture of where Emma was headed. When she did get back into the dating game, she wouldn't play in Brogan's league.

Try as she might to bank her entire future on one passionate kiss, Brogan couldn't see any scenario where Emma settled for a barkeep in a cottage when she could have a title and a castle to call her own. What kind of person sat around, falling deeper and deeper while waiting to get the brush-off?

She'd never been that person before, and all the details of her life remained exactly the same as they'd been three months ago—same home, same jobs, same prospects for weekend entertainment. Sure, she might not be a millionaire, but she had a good life. She loved her family, and she loved living in a place so beautiful, people from other places vacationed there. Plus, with tourist season hitting full swing, she had plenty of prospects who didn't need anything more from her than she had to offer.

All of those things had felt glorious last summer. Why should they stop being good enough now?

She was still pondering the question when the group of women at the corner booth all rose and carried their glasses back to the bar.

"Thanks."

"Cheers."

"See you tomorrow," they called on their way up the stairs, but

Caroline lagged a couple of seconds, and as she swept past the bar she slipped her palm across the polished wood. Then with a smile and a little wink at Brogan, she lifted it once more, and there in its place sat her receipt folded neatly in two.

Brogan stared at the paper for a long second before turning back to Charlie. He arched his eyebrows in that mix of curiosity and dare only a younger brother could muster. The conflicting thoughts and emotions assaulting her core didn't offer any helpful advice on the choice in front of her now. And yet, as the thoughts swirled through her mind, every loop whispered a similar refrain, something along the lines of, "Emma has a date tomorrow."

With a heavy sigh, she grabbed the receipt and slipped it quickly into her pocket. The move didn't make her feel any better, and it certainly didn't clarify what she wanted to do. Then again, what she wanted and what she could get had become two different things over the last few weeks. Maybe it was time to try to pull them back together again.

The town car wound up past the gate where Brogan had dropped her car with the valet last weekend. This time there wasn't even a valet at the gate. The driver merely used a remote built into the dash to open the entrance. Emma smiled at the glorified garage-door opener, unsure if it made the approach to the castle more or less formal. She didn't have a chance to ponder the question for long before they crossed what she assumed must have originally been a drawbridge and drove into an inner courtyard.

Victoria stood on the front steps waiting for them, in decidedly dressed-down attire. Still, even her jeans and her cream-colored sweater appeared tailor-made for her, which Emma realized they probably were. And yet, the olive canvas jacket she wore open added a rakish element. She'd pulled her honey-blond hair back into a loose ponytail, giving her a more relaxed and youthful appeal, even within the doorway of an ancient castle.

The car slowed to a stop in front of her, and the driver hopped out, but Victoria stepped forward, intercepting him and opening Emma's door herself. "Good afternoon."

"Hello," Emma said, a wave of bashfulness washing over her as Victoria kissed her quickly on each cheek.

"I'm sorry I couldn't come and pick you up myself," Victoria said. "I'd intended to drive my own car down, but a meeting with the land development board went on entirely too long."

"Sounds serious."

"No. I mean, maybe, in that they are all serious, and they all go on entirely too long," she said, with a slight grimace, "but it comes with the job."

"Does it?" Emma asked, as the town car pulled away. "I have to admit, I have no idea what goes into being a lady, in any sense of the word, really."

Victoria laughed. "I hate to disappoint, but day to day it's not a glamorous existence. Of course, I get to attend some formal events like the arts reception, or ceremonial outings like presenting the book awards at the school, but most of the time I wake up and go to work in an office like everyone else. I spend my days analyzing the real estate market, trying to balance budgets and pay the rent like anyone else."

Emma looked around the castle courtyard, from the high turrets to the wrought-iron torch stands jutting out below gargoyles and a lion-emblazoned crest. "Must be a lot of rent."

"We actually own this, but no, it's not cheap to maintain, which is why everyone in the family bears the responsibility of working to earn our keep."

Emma eyed her skeptically. Even after meeting Victoria twice, she hadn't given any real consideration to how the daughter of a duke would spend her time. If pressed, she would've guessed at a life of leisure. She wasn't sure she believed the hardworking, middle-management picture Victoria was trying to paint.

As if reading her mind, Victoria said, "It's true. Google my family if you have to, but I'll give you all the inside information. My dad was a barrister until he inherited the title. My mother was in international banking. I also have a younger sister who lives here with her husband at least part-time, and they are both in pharmaceuticals."

Emma relented. "Okay, that's surprising."

"I don't want to overstate our situation. None of us are struggling financially, but we don't ever take for granted that all this"—she gestured around the courtyard—"will even be ours in twenty years."

"Wow," Emma said, a little saddened by the thought. "Nobility ain't what it used to be."

Victoria burst out laughing, the sound unexpectedly rich in its lack of restraint. "Don't feel too sorry for me. There are a few perks to the position." She pointed to a nearby four-wheeler with muddy wheels and a large picnic basket at the back. "Want to go see them?"

Emma smiled, her nervousness gone. "I do."

They rode slowly out of the courtyard and around the back of the main castle residence. Then, passing several large cannons atop an earthen battlement, they drove down a ramp over a rough, stone embankment. Emma held a little tighter to Victoria's waist, feeling the warmth of her body even through the canvas jacket, until they reached another stone wall. She released her grip as Victoria hopped off to swing open another heavy metal gate and called, "Pull on through."

Emma's shoulders tightened at the suggestion. "I've never driven one of these."

"It's on. Just twist the throttle on the handlebar."

She scooted forward on the black leather seat, and holding her breath, gave the handle a gentle turn. The engine noise flared, but she didn't move."

"More revs," Victoria called.

She nodded, and with more gusto spun the throttle open. The ATV shot forward, and she lurched back across the seat. Victoria jumped out of the way as Emma buzzed through the opening, then threw up her hand, shouting, "Brake, where's the brake?"

Thankfully she didn't really need one as a slight incline past the gate slowed her progress gently enough, and with her hand off the throttle, she stopped in a short enough space that Victoria was able to swing the gate shut and jog to catch up.

"Are you okay?"

Emma nodded uncertainly, her chest rising and falling with each deep breath. Her heart beat rapidly and pumped the excess blood right to her head.

"Are you sure?" Victoria sounded genuinely concerned, and her deep blue eyes filled with worry.

"Yes," Emma finally managed, "are you?"

"Quite."

"I thought I was going to hit you."

"It would serve me right," Victoria chastised herself. "I can see the headline now, 'Heiress attempts to impress American literary genius and gets flattened, literally.'"

Emma opened her mouth to respond, but as the words sunk in, she closed it again.

"Did my compliment fall flat, too?" Victoria shifted from side to side, her boots sinking slightly into the damp earth. She then shrugged and wiped her dirty palms across the front of her jeans.

The move was so unabashedly unladylike that Emma's smile sprang back to life.

"What?"

"You don't need to impress me. I'm no one special."

"Are you kidding?" Victoria stepped forward. "After we met at the school, I read all of your books—"

"All of them? That's, like, almost a book a week."

"I couldn't put them down. You create the most amazing worlds filled with women I can't even imagine meeting, much less being."

"Says the woman with a castle."

Victoria laughed, but it wasn't the same sound that had vanquished Emma's nerves earlier. "The only thing interesting about me was completed about eight hundred years before my birth."

"Not at all," Emma said. "I find plenty interesting about you.

You juggle nobility with a day job. You're equally engaging to sculptors and schoolchildren. You were an attendant to a countess on her wedding day, but you wipe dirt on your jeans."

Victoria glanced down at the faint streaks of mud across her light denim and rolled her eyes. "My mother would be appalled."

"So am I," Emma admitted, "in the best possible way."

The tension slipped from Victoria's shoulders. "I like the sound of that."

"Good. Shall we continue this tour you promised me?"

"On one condition."

"What's that?" Emma asked.

"I drive."

Emma laughed. "Yes, please, and slowly."

Victoria sighed contentedly. "I'm good with slow."

They rolled at a moderate pace along the castle's outermost wall, then down to a winding brook. Following the path of the water, they went past elaborate flower beds terraced up a sharp slope back toward the battlements. Serene garden paths wove amid flowering bushes Emma wished she knew the names of, before dipping under ivy-laden arches.

"Those are my mother's doing. She loves a proper garden," Victoria explained. "Hers have become a major tourist attraction in the area."

"I can see why," Emma said.

They hugged the bank of the babbling stream as it fell over smooth stones until they came to an old, arched bridge.

"This is Lion Bridge," Victoria said. "My great-great-great-grandfather built it so my great-great-great-grandmother could ride out and inspect her orchards without getting her skirts wet."

"How chivalrous," Emma said, as they crossed the stream safe and dry, then climbed steeply upward.

"Don't get any ideas. The chivalry faded from the gene pool about the time we started needing day jobs."

Emma laughed, but the sound died as they crested the hill. Verdant pastureland rollicked and rolled out in three directions, a sea of green blanketing hill and dale until, off in the distance, a tall forest rose majestically to create a natural wall of oak and Scots pine.

"Is this the land you were managing at your meeting today?" Emma asked, when she found her voice.

"No. This is still family land. Well, technically it's all family land, but in other places it comes with zoning and estate details and grants and trusts. This is one of the few places I don't have to worry about regulations or etiquette or responsibilities."

The explanation sounded wistful, almost mournful. Emma had never considered that someone who lived in a fortress might need to escape to someplace safer, but it was clear that's what Victoria saw here.

"Is it lonely?"

"The forest?"

"No, the title."

The air left Victoria's lungs. Emma wouldn't have heard it over the low drone of the ATV, but she felt it in the places their bodies connected. The intimacy of realizing something she'd said had taken someone's breath away made her feel an incredible weight of protectiveness.

Victoria finally said, "Yes."

"You don't have to tell me if you don't want to. I understand."

"I know you do," Victoria said. "I saw it in your eyes the first time we met. The way you looked at those kids with such a mix of interest and fear. You know what it's like to be looked up to, you know how it feels to fall short of people's expectations, and you keep putting yourself out there because you care."

"I'm afraid you've misjudged me. I don't put myself out there. I'm actually quite the hermit. I only went to the school because the event meant so much to Reggie."

"Exactly." They were nearing the tree line now, and Victoria lifted her hand off the throttle completely. "You didn't want to be there, you didn't want them to put their unabashed faith in you, and yet you tried to be honest and open with them all the same."

Emma shook her head. "You make me sound much more valiant than I felt."

"I know the feeling," Victoria said, climbing off the ATV and unlatching the large basket. "Shall we sit awhile in the shade of an ancient forest once filled with knights and ladies?"

"I'd like to sit for a while in the shade with a friend, regardless of titles."

Victoria's cheeks flushed a delicate shade of pink, but she carried on unlatching the picnic basket and removing a large plaid blanket from inside. Unfurling it and setting it on the ground, she motioned for Emma to make herself comfortable. "That's my family tartan."

Emma glanced down as she stepped on the emerald and navy wool. "Are we allowed to put something like that on the ground?"

Victoria shrugged. "It's not the national flag or a family standard."

Emma squinted at the towers of the castle rising in the distance, where both of those things flew high in the baby-blue Northland sky.

Victoria followed her gaze and smiled sadly. "There's no escaping them around here."

"That must carry a tremendous weight of responsibility."

"No one feels sorry for the poor little rich heiress," Victoria said, in a self-deprecating tone, as she dropped down next to Emma with a sack of fruits and cheese. "But yes, there are days when I've entertained fantasies of burning the whole place down. Or, at the very least, voted with the republicans in the hopes they'd make good on their promise to abolish the monarchy."

"Really?"

Victoria smiled in a way that didn't make Emma any more certain about the seriousness of her claims. "Would you like some Stilton?"

Emma blinked at her and then down at the block of blue cheese on the small cutting board in front of them. "Um, sure, but is that whole 'abolish the monarchy' thing a possibility?"

"A girl can hope," Victoria said, then frowned down at her hands as they clutched tightly to the cheese knife. "I'm sorry. I don't mean that. Please don't tell anyone I even joked about it."

"Of course not," Emma said, "and you were right earlier when you said I understood those feelings. There have been plenty of times I cursed the day I ever wrote that first book."

"But they are so good."

"And you are, too," Emma said, gently prying the dull knife from Victoria's hands. "You're a natural with people. I'm sure you're adored by everyone in your . . . What do you call it, kingdom?"

"Dukedom," Victoria mumbled, "but it's not mine, and probably won't ever be, and I didn't want to make today about the complexities of my family line. I wanted you to think I was normal."

"I do," Emma said quickly. "You're by far the most normal member of the aristocracy I've ever met."

"Those other aristocrats you hang out with must be real numpties, then."

"See, that's what I'm talking about," Emma said, as she arranged a few Stilton crumbs on tea crackers. "You're funny and self-effacing."

"And you like that?"

"Doesn't everyone?"

"No," Victoria said flatly. "None of my advisors find it amusing. The local press is split down the middle between finding me comic relief or a complete example of why the British have lost prestige in the world. I somehow manage to be both out of touch with my average countrymen and too irreverent for the duties inherent in my station."

"Americans love that sort of character. You'd play very well there."

"I'll never forgive my great-, great-, great-, however many times, grandfather for failing to jump on the great American land grab when he had the chance. Alas, I am fated to live in limbo here. Not quite part of the past, but not quite part of the future, either."

Limbo.

Emma understood the feeling, and for some reason it made

her think of Brogan. She couldn't quite say where she fit, either. Was that why Emma hadn't found the courage to go speak to her all week?

"I envy the freedom that comes with being self-made," Victoria continued, relaxing back and staring up at the few wisps of white clouds overhead. "It must feel good to know you're responsible for getting to where you are. You don't have to worry if you can succeed, because you already have."

Emma shook her head. "No, it's terrifying. There's no direction. There are so many ways to go wrong, and so few ways to go right. And everyone's watching you and waiting and dying to know what comes next, and what comes after, and what about after that, and it's never a yes-or-no question."

"But at least you get to chart your own path. No one else is standing over you with rules and protocol to remind you that whatever you want to do isn't the way your great-times-fourteen-grandfather did it, and he was Percival the Great. You're just Victoria the Placeholder."

Emma could hear the strangled quality of Victoria's voice as she choked out the last word. "Hey, you're not a placeholder. You're a person. You're the rightful heir of Percival the Great."

"I'm not," Victoria said, then jammed a whole cracker into her mouth.

"What do you mean?"

"I'm not male."

"But your father doesn't have a son. You said you've got only a sister, and she's younger. The powers that be might not like it, but you will inherit your father's title."

"Actually, I probably won't. I mean, I almost certainly won't. The rules for passing down titles are still very much based on a male heir."

"I thought the rules had changed. I remember a big to-do over the last royal baby."

"The rule changes to the line of succession apply only to the monarch."

"So, wait. Who becomes duke when your dad dies?"

"Hopefully that won't happen for a long time, but there's no clear answer. They might find a male cousin, but, more likely, the title will cease to exist."

Emma looked across the fields, over the river, back toward the stone castle that felt so much farther away. "What happens to all of this? What happens to you?"

Victoria smiled sadly. "All excellent questions."

"There has to be a way. This is not *Downton Abbey*. You have to have rights as a woman. You have to have some recourse."

"I might have, once upon a time. There are plenty of cases throughout history of Parliament allowing a title to pass to the husband of a duke's daughter."

Emma let those words sink in. "But you don't have a husband."

Victoria shook her head. "Not anymore. What's the phrase you Americans use? Strike two."

"And strike three." Emma did the mental math. "The fact that you don't want a husband?"

"Maybe I should let go. My sister might make a legitimate claim if I stepped out of the way, but it's an awful thing to ask of her, the weight of an entire region. The castle is the biggest tourist attraction in Northland, sustaining almost every family within a fifteen-mile radius in some way or another. What if everything crumbles on my watch?"

"It won't," Emma whispered. "There has to be a way. We're living in a new millennium. The laws have to change sometime. You can fight them."

Victoria sat forward, her blue eyes dark and intense. Emma couldn't tell if the storm clouds swirling there were born of inner turmoil or inner strength, but the ferocity stirred something that made her heart beat faster. "There might be a way, but it won't be easy, and I can't do it alone. And I didn't mean to bring all of this up today, but since I've failed miserably at normalcy, I can at least offer honesty. I need a partner, someone who understands, someone I connect with, and can rely on, and trust."

The two of them stared at each other for a long, heavy second, Victoria's blue eyes intensely focused, almost pleading. Then with a soft exhale, she leaned in and kissed Emma. The move wasn't aggressive so much as hopeful, a silent request. Emma registered the emotions every bit as acutely as the physical sensations, though those were not unpleasant. Victoria's lips were as soft as Brogan's, and the caress of her hand as gentle as Brogan's. The yearning behind the kiss was every bit as compelling as the woman who'd delivered it, and yet Emma felt nothing.

Maybe not nothing. She felt an affection for Victoria and a connection to her loneliness, but compared to the emotions Brogan's kiss inspired in her, that didn't feel like much, and she couldn't help but compare. The first kiss with Brogan had been gentle, too, sweet and subdued, and yet it'd caused a warmth to spread through her chest, down her limbs, and all the way to her toes. Brogan's kiss had awakened long-dormant parts of herself. Maybe that was why she'd let herself fall so easily into the next kiss, the one that had consumed and terrified her, the one that had sent her heart into overdrive and scrambled her brain to the point she had considered things she was in no position to consider yet, or ever, but Brogan had made her want to in ways Victoria didn't.

The reminder made her pull back.

Biting her lip, she blinked open her eyes. When had Brogan's kiss become the one she compared others to?

Victoria's blue eyes fluttered open as a flush spread through her checks. "I think I may have made a mistake."

"No," Emma said quickly, not wanting to make either of them feel more awkward than she already did.

"No?"

"I mean, maybe. It wasn't quite right, but not a mistake."

"It's okay." Victoria tried to fake a smile before turning away. "I make mistakes. A lot of them, actually."

"Something else we have in common," Emma said, her heart breaking a little bit for each of them. "I understand."

"I know you do," Victoria said. "It's one more thing that drew me to you. I won't lie. I've seen the papers."

It was Emma's turn to blush.

"I didn't mean that to sound bad. I'm terrible at this." Victoria rubbed her face with her hands. "I only meant we've been through some of the same things. We work with some of the same pressures, and we've both put our trust in people who couldn't handle the realities of our lives or work. For what it's worth, my mistake took the same escape route yours did, but he got to tell the world I wasn't straight to begin with, so no one could blame him."

Emma winced. "A betrayal of trust is still a betrayal, and you faced two of them."

"I've wasted a couple of years wondering which hurt worse. In the meantime, I've grown lonely and tired, but I don't trust anyone to see me for me, instead of who I was or who I might be."

"Vic." Emma placed her hand on the sleeve of her jacket, feeling the heat and the uncertainty radiating off her. "It's going to be okay. You aren't alone. You aren't even the only person on this blanket who feels that way."

Victoria smiled. "I'm sorry. You're right. It's just, the pressure can be a bit consuming sometimes. I wish I didn't have to carry it all by myself."

"You don't. I'm here to listen. I'd like to help. As you said, you've read the papers. I'm in no position to turn down friendships, but if you're looking for something more, I'm willing to bet at least a thousand women in the UK would gladly murder me for the chance to be where I'm sitting right now."

"I won't deny that," Victoria said, without a hint of cockiness, "but I'd rather take you up on the offer of friendship, if you don't mind."

"It's not an either-or equation. You can have me as a friend, *and* have women throw themselves at you."

Victoria sighed. "It's not everything it's cracked up to be. The types of women who do that are always the ones who want all the trappings of my life with none of the realities, and the women who are smart enough and sensitive enough and poised enough to understand what they'd be signing up for aren't the type of women who chase after flash and glitter. It takes a rare breed of woman to take on the total package."

Emma nodded, and pictured Brogan, the image of her so clear in her mind's eye she had the urge to reach out and touch her, to anchor herself to Brogan's steadiness, to her easy confidence, to the way she made Emma feel safe and exhilarated at the same time.

"Worst of all," Victoria continued, "I don't trust myself to recognize a person of that caliber if I meet her. I've shown such poor judgement in that area in the past. How can I ever be sure again?"

Emma nodded solemnly. She'd known that fear before. She'd felt it worm its way into her brain and temper even the beat of her heart, but as much as she could empathize with the uncertainty Victoria expressed, she no longer shared it. She had met exactly the type of woman Victoria was describing, and she'd pushed her away.

Chapter Thirteen

Brogan wiped down the bar at the Raven for the second time. She was still almost an hour from closing time, but the last of the weekend tourists had paid their tab and moved slowly toward the door. Maybe she could clean up and cut out a little early tonight. Then again, it wasn't as if she had anything to rush home to. She'd hardly made enough use of her empty bed lately to find any solace there. Her last week of nights had been restless and filled with frustrated dreams she'd had to work hard not to examine. And tonight, she'd have the added fuel for the fire that came from knowing Emma's house was still dark when Brogan had walked to work at six. Brogan had assumed that meant the date with Lady Victoria had gone well enough to extend into the evening. Would she be tempted to check if Emma was home at eleven? There'd be no way not to notice if a light was on as she walked back to her own place, but would she tell herself Emma had simply gone to bed, or would she torture herself with the possibility of a castle sleepover? Either way, she'd likely have to wait until tomorrow to know for sure.

Brogan gave the bar a little kick as a way of kicking herself. She wasn't waiting for Emma. She couldn't. Aside from the fact it would make her pathetic, she'd also drive herself mad.

Thankfully the door swung open, interrupting thoughts she didn't want to have. She was aware enough to realize that just a moment earlier she'd been hoping not to have any more customers, only to feel relieved when some arrived.

"Good evening," a woman called jovially, as she pushed through, followed by three more, all laughing and waving.

"Good night out?" Brogan asked.

"Indeed," one of them called, causing all of them to laugh. "We've been up to a bonfire at Sugar Sands with some local blokes."

"Sounds fun," Brogan said, without meaning it. She suspected the local guys would feel the same way, given that all four of the women were back to the inn before midnight.

"Fecking freezing is what it was," the last woman through the door admitted. Brogan racked her brain for the name she'd scribbled on the back of the receipt earlier in the week. Christine? Catherine? Caroline.

"If you'd had more of the whiskey, you'd have stayed warmer."

"I had to drive you lot home." She pushed a few strands of long, dark hair from across her forehead then rolled her eyes at them before casting a smile toward Brogan.

"Then have one now, to catch up before you come up," one of the other women said, as she bounded toward the stairs. The two others followed enthusiastically if not gracefully.

"Like a bunch of drunk Labradors, the whole lot of them." Caroline took a seat at the bar instead of following her friends. "I had to drag them up the dunes, or you'd have had to call the lifeboats out and search for them off the shore."

Brogan took a glass from overhead and set it upright on the bar between them. "Then this one's on me, because I wouldn't have had to make the call. I'd have been driving one of the boats."

Caroline's smile turned sly as she shed her coat, revealing a deep purple sweater. "I suspected as much, which is why I did let Marla get a little close to the water a time or two. I wouldn't have let her drown, mind you, just splash around enough to get you to ride in on that amazing sailboat I saw you commanding earlier today. Do I lose my free scotch for admitting to that, or do I get extra for not giving in to the fantasy?"

Brogan's heart beat a bit louder for a few seconds, as if trying to stir itself up again. It should be easy. She wasn't given just a little opening; Caroline had swung the barn doors open wide and asked her to sail inside. Brogan could say basically anything. She didn't even have to be clever. A simple "yes, please" would likely suffice, and yet she merely took a bottle of scotch from the rack behind her and poured a healthy stream into the glass.

Caroline seemed to get the message she wanted. Whether or not it was the one Brogan wanted to send might have been a different matter, but she didn't resist, and Caroline said, "Drinking alone is the sign of a problem. You might have to join me."

Again, Brogan wordlessly poured another glass from the bottle already in her hand. Then she walked around the bar and flipped the closed sign over in the doorway. *In for a penny, in for a pound.* She sat down on the stool next to Caroline and clinked their glasses together. She'd done this before. She could do it again.

"So, how are you enjoying your trip to Amberwick?" Okay, not her best come-on or conversation starter, but she'd managed to speak, and Caroline ran with it.

"I'm having a blast. It's funny to say, but I feel like I've got younger since I've been here. The weight of the city has lifted off my shoulders, or maybe the salt air is invigorating me somehow. Is that why you spend time on the water?"

Brogan raised her eyebrows at the second allusion to her being affiliated with the ocean.

"I'm not stalking you or anything," Caroline quickly said, laying a hand lightly on Brogan's arm for emphasis, or maybe to undercut her own statement. "I've seen you sailing in and out of the estuary two days in a row now when on walks along the beach. It's hard not to stop and watch you work the riggings. You have an amazing presence out there, strong and confident."

Brogan took a sip of her scotch, its warmth spreading through her in ways the compliment hadn't. It wasn't that she didn't appreciate the ego boost, but she didn't feel strong or confident anymore, and she didn't know when that had changed, which wasn't quite the same thing as not knowing why it had changed.

"Have you been sailing long?"

"All my life," Brogan said, grateful for an easy question.

Caroline smiled again, relaxed and carefree. "I like the image of a redheaded girl racing around the deck of a sailboat. Did you run barefoot on the beaches and scramble around the dunes, too?"

"I did, indeed. Sometimes I still do."

"Sounds glorious," Caroline said. "I work for an insurance adjuster in York, and before that I lived in Leicester."

"That's pretty enough country."

"Yes, but there are no sailboats, no dunes, and no pirate women to run off with."

The comment made Brogan remember Emma's character, the one who would cross the high seas, which of course made her think of Emma.

Why couldn't she stop? She'd never been the type to pine for something other than what she'd had in the moment, especially in moments when she'd had more than enough. Caroline wanted her. Caroline was interested in her. Caroline would never require more than Brogan could give. Well, maybe not never, but at least for the rest of the weekend, Brogan would be enough.

And yet something was missing that hadn't been in previous interactions. Maybe the sense of lacking came only from comparison to something better. Maybe comfort and ease simply paled when cast in the shadow of the spark she felt for Emma.

Damn her. How dare Emma come in and ruin Brogan's contented life by making her wish for more? Anger burned now where the scotch had been. She'd done enough moping and wavering and feeling sorry for herself. She might not be of Emma's caliber, but she wasn't helpless or worthless, and there was a vibrant, bright, attractive woman right in front of her, waiting for her to take what was being offered.

With a surge of defiance, she leaned forward and captured Caroline's mouth with her own. They collided with a suddenness and fervor neither of them seemed quite ready for. Lips pressed against teeth, but what the kiss lacked in grace, it made up for in gusto. Caroline took hold of Brogan's face, running her fingertips into her hair. The touch was possessive, affirming, and laced with a need Brogan could fill for her. She grasped Caroline's hips, pulling them forward, up off the stool until their bodies pressed flush. Desire radiated off the woman in her arms like heat shimmered off pavement. She parted her lips, urging Brogan onward with insistent strokes of her tongue. Brogan obliged, pressing herself into the physical sensations that had comforted and stimulated her so many times before.

She fought to keep her mind on the steps, the basics, the tangible. Stealing a breath, she kissed along the corner of Caroline's mouth, tasting the drink they'd now shared in more ways than one. She tried to lock onto the connection as her mind started to wander. Scotch, they both liked scotch, they both drank it to warm themselves, Caroline from the chill of the night, Brogan from the chill inside herself.

No. She wasn't going back there.

Redoubling her efforts to stay present, she flattened her palm against Caroline's back and tried to soak up the softness of her breasts as they pressed against her own. This woman's body was every bit as supple as any who'd come before her, and responsive, too. She melded herself to Brogan, and Brogan tried to slip more fully into the oblivion that body offered. God, how she tried. Like a dancer who'd rehearsed the steps or an actor whose marks had been taped to the stage, why did it feel like she was ticking boxes on a list someone else had written for her?

She swept her tongue along Caroline's ... again. She'd already done that. Not that deep kissing had a maximum quota. Normally she wouldn't rush this stage, but tonight it felt like a bridge to somewhere else, somewhere she wasn't sure she wanted to go. She hooked an index finger through a belt loop on Caroline's jeans, tying herself to the present, to the woman in her arms. As Caroline's hips rocked forward against her own, she knew the next step would be welcome, and if she tried harder to focus, she might be able to pull it off, but the harder she had to try, the worse she felt. Instead of heat or urgency building in her chest, an aching disquiet began to spread. She could still sleep with Caroline tonight, but she began to fear if she did, she wouldn't be able to live with herself for a long time afterward.

The thought jolted her back.

"I'm sorry," she whispered.

"What?" Caroline mumbled, kissing her again.

Brogan's lips moved against hers one more time, but she couldn't go back. She might not be the person she'd been before, or the person Emma needed, but she wasn't this person, either.

Leaning back to open her eyes, she waited until Caroline's eyes fluttered open as well before whispering, "I can't."

She watched the bewilderment play across her features, as dark pupils narrowed. "Why not?"

Brogan shook her head, slowly. Then as guilt and confusion mingled inside her, she turned her head away from Caroline's eyes, and right into the baby blues of Emma Volant.

Standing in the doorway, cheeks red, eyes wide, her lips parted as the lower one quivered, Emma shook her head slowly.

Reaching out, the instinct to protect too strong to even allow complete thoughts to form, Brogan moved toward her. "Emma."

She shook her head more frantically now, so long strands of gold hair fell across her face. "No. I, um, I shouldn't have. I'm sorry."

Then she turned and fled, not even pulling the door closed as she went. Brogan took two steps before realizing one of her fingers was still hooked in Caroline's belt loop. Glancing back at her for the first time, she saw confusion and embarrassment and hurt in her eyes, too. She sighed. What was she doing?

Untangling herself more deliberately, she sat back down on the stool and exhaled a shaky breath. She needed to offer some sort of explanation. She owed Caroline at least that, but how could she even begin to put into words what she herself couldn't understand? And if she did find a way, would admitting what she'd done make either of them feel any better?

Thankfully, Caroline spoke first. "So, is she your girlfriend?"

Brogan snorted. "No."

"Maybe you should go fix that."

217

Her chest ached. If only she knew how. But she didn't. That's what had got them all into this mess to begin with, and nothing had changed. She rested her elbows on her knees and let her face fall into her hands. She couldn't go after Emma without anything to say, without anything more to offer. Doing so would only perpetuate the cycle that had landed them here.

Straightening up with a new resolve, she managed to at least meet Caroline's eyes. "I'm sorry about tonight. I didn't mean to mislead you."

"You didn't. We didn't really get far enough before you pulled back." Caroline shrugged as if the fact didn't bother her, but then she grabbed her scotch glass from the bar and downed the remains of the drink in a way that made Brogan suspect she'd had some practice at managing her expectations. "I appreciate you being honest with me before we did. But a word of unsolicited advice?"

"Yeah?"

"Maybe you should give her the same consideration." Then, without waiting for a response, she grabbed her coat and headed upstairs.

Brogan put her head on the bar. At least she didn't feel any overwhelming need to chase after Caroline. She was right. The two of them hadn't got far enough for Brogan to feel anything more than mild embarrassment, thank God. What would she have done if they'd slept together?

She groaned as she realized that's probably exactly what Emma thought was happening, and the longer Brogan sat here, the more that idea would entrench itself in Emma's mind. Would she be upset? Hurt? Or more likely relieved, if she'd just got back from her date with Victoria.

Brogan lifted her head to confirm the time was now past eleven. Past closing time and, unlike Cinderella, well past time that Emma should have returned from a castle if she'd had no intention of playing the role of princess, or rather duchess. Maybe that's why she'd come up to the bar so late. She'd probably wanted to tell Brogan she'd had a great time, that she was sorry, but she'd fallen for Lady Victoria. Maybe she'd wanted to explain straight away, so Brogan wouldn't get too attached. Her mind was running away with itself, but there was no mundane explanation at the ready. Introverts like Emma didn't come to pubs so late unless they had a pretty compelling reason.

Brogan had been in this business long enough to know that women who burst into bars at closing time did so because they were excited or desperate. In Emma's case, neither of those options held anything good for her.

She rubbed her face a few times and stood. When she'd set out to prove whatever she'd wanted to prove with Caroline, this ending wasn't the one she'd pictured, but it probably still served her purpose.

Brogan sighed as she remembered Emma's eyes, wide with a myriad of emotions she couldn't bring herself to try to decipher tonight. She suspected she wouldn't be able to avoid the task forever, but for both of their sakes, she prayed she could at least hold off until morning.

Emma stared out at the glittering waves of high tide as they rolled nearly up to the sandy dunes. The vista hadn't changed since the morning before. The sea still shone sapphire. Gulls still arced high over a distinct ridge. Her garden continued to grow, verdant and fragrant from fertile soil. The outside world hummed with potential and possibility as spring hit its stride in the English borders, which was why Emma pulled her shades tightly shut. She couldn't handle the stark contrast between what she saw outside her conservatory window and the internal winter she'd been plunged back into.

She sat curled on her couch in a blanket and stared at the book in her lap without actually reading. She hated being up all night. She hated not being able to eat. She hated the way her hands shook when she tried to turn a page. Maybe that was some sort of metaphor. She couldn't turn the page in her life, either. No, that was maudlin and overly self-indulgent, two more things she hated about herself right now. That kind of thinking had let all the progress evaporate simply because she'd seen Brogan kiss another woman.

She squeezed her eyes tightly shut, as if the childish gesture could somehow wipe the image from her memory or the emotions from where they'd settled heavily across her shoulders. It didn't work. All the hurt and humiliation and crushing sense of betrayal she'd worked hard to banish had come roaring back. Only now, the sense of naiveté that accompanied those feelings was compounded by the fact that she had no right to feel them.

Brogan's actions shouldn't have this kind of power over her. They hadn't made any promises. On the contrary, Emma had repeatedly pushed Brogan away. She'd told her emphatically she wasn't ready and never asked her to wait until she was. Why had she expected her to? Because the kiss they'd shared had been life-affirming? She'd learned the hard way that just because she had strong feelings for someone didn't mean they'd be reciprocated. Maybe Brogan kissed women like that all the time. Emma thought back to the conversation she'd overhead at the post office. Brogan clearly didn't suffer from any lack of opportunity where women were concerned.

She tossed her book to the floor and curled into a ball on the couch.

"Stupid, stupid, stupid," she muttered. She'd been dumb to believe someone like Brogan would have interest enough in someone like her to forgo other women. Who in their right mind would choose someone so broken, so sad, so timid and weak, when they had lines of hotter, more confident options lined up every weekend? The saddest part was, she couldn't even summon any anger at her. If Emma were in Brogan's shoes, she wouldn't have taken the risk, either. Hadn't Victoria made it heart-achingly clear yesterday that women of Brogan's caliber could write their own tickets? Why would she sit around waiting or trying to chase someone who said she didn't want to be caught?

Her pity party was interrupted by a knock at her door, and her first response was to pull the blanket up over her head like a kid hiding from a noise in the night. Huddled in her self-imposed darkness, she found one more reason to hate herself. She was a coward, a pathetic coward. Okay, two reasons.

The knock sounded again, accompanied by Brogan's muffled voice calling, "Scone delivery."

She smiled in spite of herself and added the reaction to the growing list of things to hate.

"Maybe you're busy," Brogan called, "or sleeping, in which case I'm an arse for waking you up."

Emma snorted from under her blanket.

"I can leave them on the doorstep, but the gulls will probably eat them, which will probably make them happy, except flour isn't good for them, which is not your problem. I'm rambling now, and your neighbors are probably listening to this, too."

"Why does she have to be so damn disarming?" Emma asked aloud as she sat up and threw off the blanket.

"Um, hello?"

"I'm here," she admitted grudgingly, as she opened the door.

"Good morning?" Brogan said as she looked her up and down quickly. "Did I wake you?"

"Sure, let's go with that," Emma said, glad for the logical excuse for her appearance, which, judging from the concern in Brogan's eyes, probably wasn't good. She didn't imagine her hair was in great shape after hiding under a blanket, and she hadn't slept, so the dark circles were probably back under her eyes, not to mention the fact that she wore a ratty gray sweatshirt and some paint-splattered sweatpants. "I'm not much of a morning person."

"No worries." Brogan accepted the charade and ran with it. "I'm sorry I came over so early. I forget other people aren't up with the sun every morning."

Emma nodded, not mentioning that she'd been up with the sun, which had actually risen about three hours earlier. "Come on in."

"Thanks." Brogan entered, scones first. "I'm sorry I can't stay long. I've got a morning sail, but I wanted to check in."

"No need." Emma tried to sound casual as she plopped back onto her corner of the couch.

"Really?" Brogan asked, taking a seat in a chair close enough to be conversational, while maintaining a healthy physical distance. "I haven't seen you all week."

"We've both been . . . busy."

Brogan nodded. "Tourist season is in full swing, but I did want to hear how your date went."

The thickness in Brogan's usually smooth voice made Emma examine her more closely. She was so busy noting the dullness of her eyes and the way she slowly rubbed her palms together as if trying to wipe something away that it took a moment to actually process the words she'd spoken. "I'm sorry, date?"

"Yesterday."

"What date?"

Brogan shifted in the chair. "With Lady Victoria."

"I didn't go on a date with . . ." Her voice trailed off as she remembered the picnic, the gardens, the kiss. "Oh my God, did everyone think that was a date but me?"

"Aye."

She rose and paced around the living room. "I'm so stupid."

"You're not," Brogan said calmly.

"I am. I totally misread the entire outing. I made such a fool of myself. I gave her the wrong impression, and I gave you the wrong impression. And this isn't the first time I've missed some pretty major clues in this department. I'm so naïve. How many times am I going to make the same mistakes? Maybe I'll never learn."

"Hey." Brogan spoke softly as she stepped into Emma's path, stopping her loop around the living room. "You aren't stupid. You're sweet and open and amazing."

"I don't believe you."

Brogan laughed softly. "You think I'd lie about something like that?"

Emma's face flamed, and she took a step back. Was that what she really thought? Brogan would lie to her? It didn't fit the picture she held of Brogan, and yet neither did the image of her kissing someone else. How could she say such wonderful things to Emma, make her feel safe and seen and desired, then kiss her with such passion, only to turn around and do the same with someone else a week later? Was Brogan a liar, or had Emma simply misread the situation, which, to be fair, she seemed prone to doing?

"Please tell me what's going on."

"I don't know," Emma admitted. "I don't think I can trust myself to know."

"Of course you can. Come on." Brogan nudged her toward the couch and this time sat beside her, though still without allowing their bodies to touch.

"What happened yesterday?"

"Apparently, I went on a date with Victoria, only I didn't get the memo."

Brogan smiled in a way that didn't carry any warmth. "Did you have a good time, though?"

"I guess. I mean the grounds are lovely, and she is lovely, and we had some conversations that were quite . . ."

"Lovely?" Brogan offered.

Emma swatted at her. "Don't."

"What?"

"Be funny and disarming when I'm trying to have a crisis of confidence."

"Why not? I thought that's why we were friends. I disrupt your crises."

"Friends." Emma repeated the word. It's what she'd asked for and what she honestly believed she'd wanted, right up until the moment she'd seen some other woman in Brogan's arms.

She shook her head, realizing that wasn't completely true. It might have been what she'd told herself, what she'd told both of them, but she'd gone to the bar last night hoping for more. That's why it had hurt so damn bad then, and now.

"What?" Brogan asked softly.

"It's what I said I wanted."

"A friend?"

"Yes."

"And you have that in me. Always. I like you, maybe too much at times, but you're the first new friend I've had in years. I've missed you this week. There've been so many times I've wanted to tell you something about my day, or show you something around town, or stop in and see what you're up to."

"But you didn't."

"Because we've blurred some lines in the past. And I didn't want to make you feel pushed or pressured. I know the back and forth between friendship and something more is tearing you apart, and to be honest, it's hard on me, too. I wanted to give us both a chance to move on."

"Move on?"

"Yes, you with Lady Victoria, and me with . . . whoever."

Her cheeks flamed again. *Whoever.* Brogan didn't have anyone particular in mind. Just not Emma. She was too hard, too complicated, with too much back and forth. "I see."

"Do you?" Brogan asked, her voice a little higher.

"I shouldn't have put you in that position. I had no right to ask you to wait for me. It was unfair."

"No," Brogan said quickly, "that's not what I meant. That's not even what happened. You didn't ask me for anything, much less something unfair."

"Then what happened?"

"We became friends. I crossed a line a time or two."

Emma held up a hand. "I kissed *you*, twice. I'm unsure about a lot of things, but I'm not going to let you take responsibility for my actions."

"You're in transition. Your life has been one massive upheaval after another."

Emma couldn't argue.

"You're still finding your stride. You're trying things out in a new place with new people. You need space and freedom to do that. You don't need someone to tie you down, or rush you, or push you into making decisions you aren't ready to make."

Again, she couldn't disagree with the statement.

"It's been hard for me to know what's right in any given moment, and not because I don't care or I'm not patient enough."

"Because you're not interested."

"Because I can't be your rebound, Emma." The words came out in a rush, and before Emma even had the chance to process them, Brogan forged on. "You're amazing. You're making such fantastic progress. Watching you come back to life has made me so happy. Having you around these last few months has meant more to me than I should have let it, which is why we have to stop. I don't trust myself not to fall for you while you're on the mend, and I'm not sure I could survive being some fling until you get back on your feet and get back to women of your own caliber."

Alarm bells sounded in Emma's brain. "Women of my own caliber?"

"Of course, and I don't begrudge you that. I've tried to make it clear I don't hold any claim to you."

"Obviously," Emma said, unable to empty her mind of the way Brogan's mouth had claimed someone else's.

"It's only natural that, as you get your strength and confidence back, you'll gravitate to women who understand your way of life, women as smart and as powerful and talented as you are. When you're back on top, you'll want someone like Lady Victoria by your side."

Emma snorted. "Well, that's ironic."

"Why?"

"Because yesterday I told Victoria I wanted someone like *you* by my side."

"When? Why?"

"Yesterday. She kissed me, and all I could think about was you. All I could compare her to was you, and despite her being all those things you listed—powerful, strong, intelligent, wealthy, talented— I judged her as lacking when set up against you. But I guess that serves as a reminder of what a terrible judge of character I am, because it seems I made the same mistake I made last time."

"What?"

"After all the pain and shame and swearing I'd see the signs

225

next time, I missed them again. I went and fell for someone exactly like my ex."

Brogan flinched and turned her head as if Emma had struck her. "I'm sorry if what you saw last night hurt you, but I'm not at all like your ex. I'd never intentionally cause you pain. I only wanted to release us both. I thought it would be better if we moved on."

"But you didn't ask me what I thought was best for me. You made that decision because of my success, my money, my fame, and that makes you exactly like Amalie."

"I'm not." Brogan jumped to her feet. "I'm not resentful of your success. I'm in awe of you. I'm not jealous. I'm inspired by you. I only want you to have someone worthy of you, and anyone with eyes or half a brain can see that person isn't me, not by any measure. Why drag things out?"

"I'm not sure your motives make much difference on the practical end of things. Amalie couldn't take the discrepancies between us, so she slept with someone else. You can't handle the same discrepancies, so you kissed someone else. I can't believe I'm going through this again."

"It's not the same thing," Brogan pleaded, her voice sounding near frantic now.

"In some ways, that hurts worse. If you'd just been attracted to someone else, I could've lived with that. It would've been something different, something normal, something that happens to regular people all the time." Her pride made a twisted attempt to assert itself. "Can you say that? Could you look me in the eye and tell me you're not attracted to me? Or you're more attracted to that other woman?"

Brogan stared at her for a moment, her jaw tight, her breathing labored, before she shook her head. "No, God, Emma, you're so beautiful, sometimes it hurts to look at you for too long. I've wanted you so much I haven't slept in a week, but I wanted to give you freedom and space to chase your own desires. I couldn't stop myself from falling in love with you in the meantime, though. That's why I pulled away."

The words she would've welcomed last night offered no comfort now. "No, you didn't pull away. We could've talked about that like adults, like friends. Instead, you pulled someone else close, and that makes you exactly like Amalie." She was pacing around the room again, wearing the cream-colored carpet thin as her brain worked faster than her feet. Hurt and confusion had given way to anger, first at herself, then at Brogan. "Both of you assumed I was too rich or self-centered or influential to judge a partner on factors like heart or personality or shared values. Both of you assumed you knew what I would want or do in a relationship based on things I never said or felt. And both of you went ahead and acted on your fears rather than putting faith in me."

"Emma," Brogan whispered and reached for her, "I didn't mean—"

"It doesn't matter what you meant." She jerked away. "It doesn't matter whether kissing someone else was born out of resentment or some sort of misplaced chivalry. Both scenarios ended up with someone I trusted in the arms of another woman."

Brogan hung her head. "I'm so sorry."

"Me too."

"You have nothing to apologize for."

Emma sighed. "I leaned on you too much. I put too much faith in you. It wasn't fair. I shouldn't have put either of us in a position where we needed to act out of fear or hurt."

"You didn't."

She threw up her hands in exasperation. "Clearly I did, because here we are. Despite every ounce of logic and reason I've tried to employ, I'm a romantic at heart. Maybe I wanted too much to believe in the hero across the sea who would restore my faith in myself and in love."

"You deserve that."

"Deserving and getting are two different things. It was foolish to think anyone could ever see me as a whole person, flawed and scared, yet smart and strong." She thought back to Victoria's comments about the type of women who would chase the trappings not being worthy partners, and the women who were worthy partners not wanting the trappings. Maybe Victoria had been right. Maybe that hybrid simply didn't exist. "Apparently there's no one out there who can handle the conflicting parts of me as both powerful and vulnerable. I thought you could be a partner to me in every aspect, not a savior and not a detractor, but it was too much to ask and too much to believe in. That's why I write fiction instead of memoir."

"Please don't. Emma, it's me. I messed up. I failed you."

"You did." Her voice sounded cold even to her own ears, but the fire had gone out of her, replaced with the numb chill she'd carried with her for so long. "But at least you were honest with me early on. You could've dragged this out for years. I'm grateful you didn't. I've wasted enough time, felt enough betrayal to last a lifetime."

"What are you saying?"

"Maybe you were right to do what you did. Maybe it saved us years of pain, because you clearly aren't the type of person I want to tie my life to, just not for the reasons you initially thought."

"Emma," Brogan whispered.

Emma glanced at her watch, as if resetting some clock on grief. "It's time for you to go."

Brogan stood and reached out to her, but Emma walked purposefully toward the door. She had to end this. Now, before she fell apart again, before she began to question herself, before she did something she'd regret.

Brogan followed her, and when Emma swung wide the door, she stepped through, but then turned back to stare at her, green eyes so full of sadness Emma's knees nearly buckled. "What do we do now?"

Emma shrugged and swallowed a lump of emotion before she could speak. "You said yourself, we have to move on. That's probably the only thing you were right about all week."

Then she softly closed the door, before Brogan had a chance to see her cry.

Chapter Fourteen

Brogan stood staring at the door for entirely too long. Or at least it felt like a long time. Then again, the last few months had felt like minutes, so what did she know, except that by the time she managed to turn around, several tourists were casting concerned glances at her as they walked slowly by. Could they sense her despair? She wasn't crying. She was too stunned to form that cohesive of a response. Instead, she simply turned in a circle, searching for answers in streets she'd walked since childhood and in skies she'd gazed into her entire life. They suddenly felt more foreign than the American on the other side of the door. How could that be? Why did someone who'd spun her around for weeks seem so clear this morning? Or maybe Emma wasn't clear so much as her assessment of Brogan had been.

Brogan had messed up. She'd misunderstood. She'd hurt Emma. There was no room for disagreement there. She felt her failure in her bones. Somehow, she'd always known she would come up short for Emma. She'd been holding her breath since their first meeting, expecting it to happen at every turn, and now it had. She should've at least been able to relax. The worst had happened, and she'd had her initial assessment of her own unworthiness confirmed. However, instead of feeling relieved or vindicated, she felt bereft.

She'd never wanted this, never wanted to hurt Emma, never wanted to fall for her, never wanted to kiss Caroline in the first place. She certainly hadn't wanted to feel the hollowness that was now spreading through her chest and into her limbs. She wiggled her fingers in an attempt to keep the dread from paralyzing her fully. She'd only meant to rip off the Band-Aid, or cauterize a wound before it had a chance to bleed them dry. Instead, she'd opened an old one, for both of them.

She covered her face with her hands as if trying to wipe away the memory of Emma's expression when Brogan said she'd "move on with whoever." Or the betrayal in Emma's eyes when Brogan said she'd pulled away because she was in love with her. In doing so, she'd confirmed Emma's worst fears. She'd made her feel like she wasn't good enough for Brogan when clearly the opposite was true. The complete mess she'd made over the last twenty-four hours proved Brogan wasn't worthy and she couldn't be trusted with someone so precious. She still tasted bitter bile in the back of her throat at the comparison to Amalie, but Emma was right about the bottom line.

Maybe that's what ultimately mattered. Emma had seen the truth. Emma was free now, but Brogan had a sinking suspicion she never would be. The fear hammered in her chest as the grief of what she'd lost clawed at her insides. Despite her best efforts at distance and denial and self-restraint, she'd lost the battle and fallen in love with Emma Volant.

Emma stood in her small kitchen. How long had she been frozen by indecision? Minutes? Hours? The sun that had been high over the North Sea when she'd come in had now passed over the cottage and out of direct view. Beyond that, time had become a vague concept for her. She had no real use for a clock or watch. She hadn't left her house in a week. She didn't need to now. She had enough canned soup in her cabinet to survive the apocalypse. That would've been enough when she'd first arrived here, or the first time she'd grieved a mistake about who to trust. As the burn of shame and chill of inadequacy oscillated inside her now, at least she had some frame of reference. She didn't really find that comforting. She didn't appreciate the reminder that she'd done this to herself not once, but twice. Still, she took a cold sort of solace in knowing the humiliation of losing Amalie shouldn't even be compared to Brogan's betrayal. If she'd survived the former, she'd survive the latter . . . probably.

She'd been married to Amalie. She hadn't laid even a casual claim to Brogan. She'd spent years of her life with Amalie and only a few months of friendship with Brogan. Amalie had dragged her name, reputation, their solemn vows through the gutters of New York. Brogan had merely kissed a stranger in an empty pub. The two shouldn't even compare.

And yet, here she sat, day after day, night after night, replaying the way all her hope and faith and emotional progress had come crashing down around her, and the whole thing felt eerily similar. Grief kept her sluggish all day and restless all night. It ached in her muscles and joints. It undercut her ability to focus on work or reading or watching TV. She spent hours curled up under a quilt in her conservatory watching the waves and clouds roll in. How long would she have to mourn before she could restart the healing process once more, and did she even want to if she was merely destined to make the same mistakes time and time again?

Her stomach growled, reminding her what she'd come in here for in the first place. Food. Soup. She didn't want any. And yet she was hungry, the real kind, not the empty kind she'd grown used to before. Furrowing her brow, she realized she missed real food. The fact might not have surprised most people, but it was the first difference she'd felt since showing Brogan the door a week ago. She missed something. That wasn't exactly new. She missed so many things, but at the moment scones were definitely on this list, and safer to address than any of the other pieces of broken heart rattling around in her chest.

Scones would never hurt her. And she could get some any time she wanted. Right or wrong, she'd run away from all her problems in America and chosen to hide out in England. Scones were everywhere in England. She'd seen them in several places

231

around town. Then again, Brogan had been in all those places, too. Even the place where she'd had scones in Warkworth was awash in memories of Brogan. Still, there had to be places that delivered scones. She smiled faintly at the memory of the local women huddled around a plate of scones on her doorstep.

The ladies delivered scones. They had to have gotten them somewhere. Or did they make them? She leaned back against the nearest countertop. Why hadn't that occurred to her before? People made their own scones. She could make her own scones. She could fill one of her more basic needs. In theory. She laughed, a little bubble of a sound, but she liked the way it rumbled up from her chest and out of her mouth without an effort or strain. So, maybe she couldn't make her own scones right now, but she could learn.

She'd learn.

The idea made her almost giddy.

She crossed the small kitchen in two steps and snatched up the note the ladies had left on their first visit. Then, picking up both speed and purpose, she headed to the living room and dug around the couch cushions until she located her long-dormant cell phone. She quickly dialed an unfamiliar number.

"Hi, Esther?" she said when the ringing stopped. "It's Emma. Emma Volant, from the village. Yes, you said I could call if I needed anything . . ."

Within two hours, her kitchen was full of people and food and warmth and life.

Not only had Esther gladly rushed over, she'd brought Diane and Ciara and little Reggie. Not to mention flour and raisins and the culinary miracle of clotted cream.

"So, we whack them with this thing?" Emma asked, holding up the rolling pin.

"No," they all called in unison, then burst out laughing. Emma got the sense they were wondering how she'd managed to stay alive without basic survival skills, but she didn't feel judged. She felt . . . she didn't know. Not quite happy. Her other problems weren't solved or gone, but standing there with the heat of the oven, and the warmth of friends, and flour on every visible surface, the pain felt more bearable.

"What about the book club?" Reggie asked, apropos of nothing.

"What about it?" Diane asked, taking the rolling pin from Emma's hand and nodding for her to watch as she ran it smoothly across a rough rectangle of dough.

"Aren't we going to start one?"

Everyone sort of looked at Emma sheepishly. "What did I miss?"

"Well." Ciara drew out the word until a bit of Irish accent came through, reminding Emma of her sister. She had to fight to keep her face neutral and her ears from echoing Brogan's voice. "We're all big readers, and we were thinking it might be nice to start a book club, but . . ."

"But?" Emma asked, wondering where this was going.

Ciara's cheeks flushed nearly as red as her hair. "We don't know how."

Emma smiled. "Is that all?"

"We thought maybe you did, and you could show us, but we didn't want to impose on you."

"Or take advantage of your contacts," Esther added.

"I'm not sure I understand how asking me how to start a book club would be taking advantage."

"We aren't either," Diane admitted, "but we've never had a book club in the village, at least not that I remember. Do we have to order things or work through a store? Do we need to inform the author? Or get workbooks? Or have a board or publicity?"

"You certainly could," Emma said. "Some book clubs function formally with dues and events and speakers, but the best ones I've been a part of consist of a few friends who agree to read the same book on their own, and then go someplace casual to talk about it."

All three of the older women relaxed visibly, and Reggie excitedly offered, "We could meet at Barter Books. They have books and scones."

233

"Books and scones?" Emma asked, genuinely interested. "Why have I not heard of this place?"

"Oh, it's just up the road," Diane said with a shrug, then passed Emma a silver ring with flour all over the rim. "Now use this to cut as many circles as you can out of the dough."

"It's a big bookstore in an old train station," Reggie continued, while Emma tried to cut through the scone dough without smashing it too flat. "And they have a café with scones and bacon butties, and a full English breakfast."

"What's a full English breakfast?"

"The full English is what we call having everything you could want to start out right on one big plate. There's eggs and bacon and bangers and beans and tomatoes and mushrooms."

"And they serve all that in a bookstore?" Emma asked, her excitement building.

"I could get lost in there all day," Ciara said wistfully, then tousling Reggie's ginger mop added, "or at least I could before I had kids."

"It does sound like everything I would need to be happy for a day," Emma admitted.

"I'm surprised you haven't been there," Esther said, as she placed the last of the cutouts on a baking sheet.

"I didn't know it existed. I don't know much about the area outside the village."

"Surely you've been up to the Holy Island of Lindisfarne," Diane said as she collected the scraps of dough and gently rolled them out again.

Emma shook her head.

"Oh, they have replicas of stunning illuminated gospels and an exhibit of how the monks used to make them."

"And a Viking museum!" Reggie added.

"Plus, it's beautiful," Ciara said. "But not as beautiful as Cragside."

The other two women made little hums of agreement.

"What's Cragside?" Emma asked, realizing it wasn't just scones she needed a lesson in.

"It's a manor house built by a great inventor. It was the first house in the whole world to have hydroelectricity, but as impressive as the house is, it pales in comparison to the gardens."

"You could be there for days and not see them all," Diane agreed, as Emma cut a few more scones from the remaining dough. "I make Tom take me down there every spring. If I'd known you'd never been, I would've asked you along."

"It's not too late for her to go," Esther said, finally sliding the baking sheet into the oven. "Though for summer walks, I do love Hadrian's Wall."

"I've heard of that one," Emma said, with a little prick of excitement. "Is it far from here?"

"You're less than an hour from some of the best stretches."

"And forts, and a Roman Legion museum with real weapons." Reggie hopped around excitedly, like she had a sword in her hand.

"I didn't know," Emma admitted. "I never thought about Northern England being part of the Roman Empire, and I've never left the village except to go to the grocery store, or the two trips to the castle."

"You haven't even been to Edinburgh?" Ciara asked, sounding surprised. "I'd have thought someone like you would enjoy visiting all the Harry Potter sights and do some proper shopping."

Emma realized she would indeed enjoy taking that trip, and wondered why she hadn't even considered it until now. Depression? Lack of knowing what was available? Or had she simply been too afraid to branch out of her cottage and beach? She didn't feel right mentioning any of those options in the midst of such a lively conversation. She didn't want to slip back into the darkness that had paralyzed her all week, so she tried to offer a more practical excuse. "I don't have a car."

"You could take the X18 bus right to Barter Books," Esther offered, "and the trains to Edinburgh run from north of the estuary every half hour."

"I hadn't even considered taking a train to Scotland."

Diane chuckled. "You Americans never do, but you'd need a bus to get to Holy Island."

"The X18 North will get you up to the causeway," Ciara said. "That's the one I take up to Berwick, but even with the tide out, I don't think you'd want to walk all the way across."

"Unless you're a pilgrim." Diane giggled. "But I think there's a shuttle."

"Only in the summer," Esther added.

"Are you sure? I think they got so tired of numpties getting stuck out there at high tide that they started running it year-round. I could do a little research for you," Diane offered.

"Or she could buy a car," Reggie said matter-of-factly.

They stopped their bus planning and turned to Emma, eyebrows raised.

She bit her lower lip and pondered what did seem to be the obvious solution. "I hadn't thought about it before."

"Why not?" Reggie asked.

"I, well, I don't . . ." She didn't know the answer. Since driving with Brogan had gone better than she'd feared, she probably should have considered becoming mobile much sooner. Why hadn't she tried to drive? Why hadn't she tried to explore?

Brogan.

The answer hit her chest like a hot poker. She'd relied on Brogan. She'd assumed Brogan would always be there to help, to teach, to show her things filled with magic and wonder.

"Maybe Emma doesn't want to go through the hassle of buying a car until she knows for sure she's staying here," Ciara told her daughter softly.

"Don't you want to stay here?" Reggie asked, a twinge of hurt and fear in her voice.

Emma's heart constricted, and not just at the emotion behind Reggie's words, but at the emotions it sparked in her. She glanced around her kitchen, at the women who filled it with food and kindness, then out across her garden to the sea, set in gray and green as the afternoon light faded behind the village. Did she want to leave?

This place wasn't without conflicts for her. The pain she had felt thinking of Brogan only seconds earlier should have given her more pause. She'd come here to get away from feelings like those. She'd run away from her home and her friends and the life she'd built there, all to escape the feelings that shot through her in that moment. Closing her eyes she could still isolate the hurt and the embarrassment and the sense of betrayal she'd felt at seeing Brogan kiss someone else, or hearing Brogan say she was attracted to her but didn't trust her enough to share those feelings. The anger and shame and sadness still swirled inside her, but this time she felt no desire to run.

That was different. That was new. That gave her hope.

Opening her eyes, she smiled faintly and threw her arm around Reggie's shoulder, turning the girl slightly until they both faced the window overlooking her garden. "See that lavender growing out there, and the way the chives have already sprouted? Or the little shoots of green on the rosebush we moved out of the shadow from the hedge? They remind me I have roots here. They run generations deep, and I have to believe they still carry a bit of wisdom for me. I don't want to lose those ties any more than I want to sever the roots we put down ourselves."

The boat cut smoothly through the easy, rolling waves where the narrow river met the vast expanse of sea. Brogan barely noticed the little rise in the bow, or the titter of giggling children as the sloop slid down the backside of the crest.

"I'm going to hoist sail," her dad called.

She nodded absently and kept her hand light as a slew of kids hopped up, all clambering to help. She was glad for the extra hands. Lily and James were both old enough to find their way around the boat, or at least keep an eye on the younger ones, which allowed Brogan to keep a hand on the tiller as she turned to look back over her shoulder at the village growing smaller behind her.

Without meaning to, her gaze found its focus on the white peak of Emma's conservatory. Was Emma enjoying the sun in there? Had the warmth of it helped melt the lines of anguish

Brogan had caused to crease her forehead? Would the graceful glide of gulls overhead help her find some of the peace Brogan had shattered? Would the subtle scent of salt on the air soothe the raggedness that raked Emma's voice as she called herself stupid, or would it only remind her of the tears Brogan had seen shimmering in her eyes before she closed the door?

The thought sent another sharp pain through her chest, and she jerked back as if she could somehow escape the point of some invisible knife.

"Brogan!" her father shouted in a tone she hadn't heard out of him in ten years or longer. Pure dad voice, raised in fear and frustration, was the first thing to cut through the haze she'd been shrouded in all week, and she looked up to see a literal boatload of family members staring at her.

Her mother clutched her twin nephews, one in each arm. Nora had a sleeping baby strapped to her chest. Charlie and Archie stood at the bow, staring back over their shoulders, while Arthur and Ginny sat stock-still between Neville and Marcus. No one appeared hurt, but then she noticed James and Lily still frozen in a half crouch in front of her dad with the boom to their back.

Looking slowly down at the wooden bar clutched closely to her side, she realized what she'd done. While trying to pull away from her internal pain, she'd jerked them all off course, causing the boom to swing wide and wildly toward her niece and nephew.

"I'm sorry." She said the words that had circled through her mind ever since that morning at Emma's.

"What were you thinking?" Liam asked, residual fear making his Irish accent burn through forty-plus years of living in England.

"I . . . I didn't . . . I got distracted."

"Not good enough," he said, a little softer. "Not like you, either. You know better. The water's no place to lose your head."

She nodded as her voice caught in her throat. He was absolutely right, and she did know better, but she'd sort of come out here hoping for a distraction. She'd hoped some time at play with the people she loved most would help her think about something, anything, other than the mistakes she'd made, and the hope she'd lost.

Now, looking at her siblings, their spouses, their children, she was struck once again with a wave of grief at the thought that she'd likely never have a family of her own. She took a deep, shaky breath and stared down at her hands, not trusting herself to speak.

"Brogan?" her dad asked, "what's got into you?"

"Liam," her mother said softly, "not now."

"What's the matter with Aunt Brogan?" Wendell asked, or maybe it was Seamus.

"Not a thing, boyo," Liam said, his usual affection back in his voice. "Want to go take off your shoes and swing 'em off the bow?"

"Yay!" All the smaller kids shouted in unison and began tugging on trainers and socks.

"Go help the littles," Margaret urged the older two kids, and then waited for them to all scramble away up front before turning back to Brogan. "Now you hand your brother the tiller. He'll manage until you pull yourself together."

Even if she'd had the inclination to argue, she knew better, so she wordlessly switched places with Neville.

She eased onto the low bench along the starboard side and closed her eyes. Tilting her chin toward the sun until its light illuminated even the back of her eyelids, she took several slow, deep breaths. She had to tell her family something, but how could she possibly explain what she didn't fully understand? She could barely even make sense of what had occurred, much less why. Everything that had seemed clear in the heat of the moment felt muddled and murky upon reflection. Shouldn't it have been the other way around?

A strong hand clasped her shoulder and squeezed.

"It's okay to have an off day," Neville said.

"Lord knows you've earned one," his wife Claire added.

"Kind of makes me feel a little better about myself, actually,"

Nora said with a hint of teasing in her voice. "If Brogan can miss a swinging boom, I don't feel as bad about putting the baby's diaper on backward this morning."

Brogan snorted softly and blinked open her eyes. "Thanks."

"Honey, we all have hard times," her mum said. "We all make mistakes."

"I've made a lot of them this week."

"Nah," her dad said. "So you nearly knocked my grandchildren into the North Sea. I've got plenty more of them."

Her mum smacked him on the shoulder, but the others all laughed.

"That wasn't even the mistake I meant," Brogan admitted.

"How'd you mess up with Emma?" Nora asked.

Brogan didn't stop to ask how Nora knew her anguish centered on Emma. She'd rather not hear what the village rumor mill had to say on the subject. "The fact that you know it has to do with her proves things had gone too far. I let her go."

They all stared at her for a second before her mother finally said, "Did you ask her first if she wanted to be let go of?"

Funny how that seemed like such a logical question when phrased that way. Why hadn't she thought to ask it herself sooner? She shook her head.

Several people around her groaned.

"I blame myself," her dad said solemnly. "I spent too much time fishing with you as a kid, but I never liked to clean them, so I didn't teach you the right lessons, I suppose. You see, women aren't of the catch-and-release variety. Some of them want to be caught."

"I just assumed she would—"

"There's your first mistake," her brother-in-law Marcus said, with a chuckle. "You shouldn't assume anything with women. I mean, I thought you'd have understood that, seeing as how you are one."

"Right?" Neville asked. "I sort of suspected the whole playing for the same team would be easier. I'm with you, Nora, kind of glad to know Brogan doesn't have a one-up on the rest of us."

"You two," their mother scolded. "Can't you see your sister's upset?"

"She's always been her own worst enemy, though," Nora said matter-of-factly. "Too perfect for her own good."

"Too industrious, too," Neville added. "Sets the bar too high for the rest of us. Your standards are too high."

"Come off it," Brogan grumbled. "That's not true. I'm not perfect. That's the whole point. She deserves better, she deserves someone perfect, and she looked at me like I was. I couldn't take waiting for the other shoe to drop. I couldn't sit around waiting to disappoint her. I'd only lead her on by making her think I could be what she needed when I knew deep down I couldn't."

They all stared at her for several more long seconds before Nora got up, pushed her husband aside and wrapped her in a hug as tight as the sleeping infant between them would allow.

Brogan sagged into the embrace. All the strength and denial and distraction she'd tried to use to keep herself upright drained from her bones and muscles, and she nearly went limp as her mother joined the hug. She breathed deeply, the smell of salt and baby shampoo filling her senses, and the soothing touch of people she loved enveloped her. How long had it been since she'd let herself accept affection without wondering when it would end?

"You are the biggest numpty of the whole family. You know that, right?" Nora asked after several long minutes. "I thought it was Charlie, but it's definitely you."

"Mum," Brogan pretended to whine, "Nora called me a numpty."

Her mother smoothed her hair with a gentle caress. "Nora's right, dear."

Brogan sat back from the hug. "What?"

"I've never known a single woman in my whole life who went into a relationship expecting perfection," Claire said.

"Some women get lucky and find it, though, right?" Neville asked, causing his wife to laugh outright.

"Nice try, but no." Then turning back to Brogan, she said, "I don't love your brother because he's perfect. I love him because

241

he's perfect for me. He's kind and hardworking and he makes me laugh, and most of all because he loves me even through all of my own imperfections . . . of which there are very few."

Brogan turned to Neville, who shrugged and smiled. "She's right on every point."

Claire caught his chin in her hand and planted a kiss on his cheek.

The move was so sweet and easy, Brogan felt another pang of regret at what she didn't have.

"I'm not one to be doling out relationship advice," Marcus cut back in, "but I can add that while you McKays are an intimidating clan to marry into in a lot of ways, I've never met a more fiercely loving group of people in my life. And you McKay women in particular come with a special brand of strong will and soft heart. I've never met Emma Volant, but I can't imagine she'd be any more immune to that combination than any other mortal."

Nora eyed her husband lovingly, then glanced down at their newborn daughter before grinning. "Do you see how these babies keep happening?"

Liam puffed out his chest. "That's right. I've heard all the jokes about the McKay's propensity for breeding, but it's not because I'm Irish. Well, not totally. It's because we love each other. We have plenty of love to go around, so we keep expanding the circle."

"But who says Emma wants to join that circle?" Brogan asked. "She's got other options. Lady Victoria is trying to woo her."

"And?" Liam asked.

"Lady Victoria has a title, and a castle, and—"

"A tight-ass family," Neville cut in.

"Neville," his mother chided.

"Language aside, Mum, it's true," Nora said.

"It doesn't matter," she said, in her mum tone. "Brogan, it doesn't matter what anyone else has. It matters who you are and whether or not you're happy with the life you're leading."

"Are you happy with your life?" her dad asked, staring back across the water toward the village.

Brogan followed his gaze and pondered her answer. The vista was still as stunning as ever, and the sea as familiar as it was exhilarating. Nothing about this place or her own place in it had changed, but maybe she had. "I still love this place, and I still love all of you." Brogan managed a weak smile toward her nieces and nephews, all dangling their feet over the front rail. "I'm proud of where I live and where I come from, and I'm content with what I do, but for the first time, I let myself wish for something more, for someone to share it all with. Now, for the first time, I feel truly and pathetically lonely."

Her dad sighed. "That sounds . . . pretty . . . human."

"Human?"

"Yes," her mum agreed. "Human."

"It doesn't make you pathetic," Nora added, "or maybe we're all pathetic, but I think it's safe to say every single one of us is in the same boat . . . figuratively and literally."

The others all nodded before their mother smiled. "And maybe if you can let go of all your preconceived notions about wealth or fame or jobs, you might find that Emma is human, too."

Brogan smiled faintly, but the emotions clogging her throat made it hard to breathe, much less speak. The truth of that statement should have made her feel better. Emma was human. She'd been open about her humanity, her weaknesses, her fears, her sadness, and also her hopes. She'd been open and honest every step of the way, and Brogan hadn't believed her. She'd let her own insecurities overcome all evidence that she had a real chance at happiness, and she'd blown it. The realization hurt even worse than thinking she'd never been in the running at all. Before, the forces against them had seemed random and distant. Now, as she faced the prospect of a lifetime wishing for a second chance that might never come, she also had to live with the consequences of knowing she had only herself to blame.

Chapter Fifteen

"Left side!" Diane and Esther called in unison, their voices having taken on a singsong quality as they'd raised the chorus at every intersection between Newpeth and Amberwick. Then they all giggled, giddy with the excitement that infused the entire adventure of Emma buying her first ever new car.

Emma smiled as she signaled, shifted, and made the turn. She wasn't doing terrible, which was probably also a broad statement for her life in general. She'd gone another week without seeing Brogan, and in that time, she'd managed to shower regularly, eat massive amounts of scones and one or two vegetables, and most importantly, she'd written. Oh, and of course she'd bought a car.

"I still think you should have gone with a zippy little Beamer," Diane said as Emma worked her way through the gears on her way back up to speed. "But I suppose a Mercedes what-do-you-call-it isn't exactly slumming, is it?"

"It's an A-Class," Esther said. "Like Emma, it's class-ay."

Emma shook her head. She hadn't considered the name or even the brand much in her research. "I wanted something safe, and powerful enough to make it up these hills without me having to suck in my stomach and pray for the best."

"Plus, it's got a big back seat," Diane added, patting the leather seat on either side of her. "Plenty of room for . . . whatever."

Esther snickered, and Emma shook her head. "For folding down and hauling some furniture. I'm tired of living in a furnished holiday let. It's time to buy some more comfortable chairs."

"Goodie, more shopping," Diane said excitedly, as Emma downshifted and entered the roundabout that signaled the turn toward Amberwick.

She white-knuckled the curve, but managed not to grind any gears as she exited the turn.

"Left side!" her passengers sang again, but to Emma's surprise, she hadn't needed the reminder. She really hadn't needed their help at any part of the process, but she'd enjoyed having someone to share the big moment with. Again, her heart constricted as she couldn't quite ward off the mental image of who she would've rather shared the first drive with, but she held the sadness at bay.

"I still don't know why you got a manual transmission when you could've easily afforded the automatic."

Emma smiled faintly. She'd pondered the choice extensively over the last week. All the logic pointed to her making the opposite decision, and when the time came, she simply didn't. She didn't want to try to explain it to herself any more than she knew how to explain it to her friends, so she simply said, "Maybe I wanted to remind myself I could do it."

They crossed a picturesque stone bridge over the river and into town, and Emma slowed to make another turn. "Now I just have to make it into my own driveway, and I'm done for the night."

"No, you're not," Esther said. "It's half 4 on Friday. We've got to get to the Raven."

Emma shook her head as the tightness in her chest ratcheted up a few turns.

"No two ways about it," Diane said frankly. "You're a local now. You're obligated to the full English lifestyle, which means time to join Friday Club."

Emma started to shake her head again, as both women sang, "Left side!"

The comment jolted her back into the moment, and she realized for the first time she'd actually pulled onto the right-hand side of Northland street.

She gasped and nearly killed the engine, barely saving it from a shuddering, sputtering death-lurch at the last second. Her cheeks burned and her eyes watered.

"Come come," Diane said softly. "No worries. It's a one-way street. There's no harm in taking your half out of the middle."

Emma swallowed painfully, grateful for the excuse for clamming up. At least outwardly, she could pretend she'd merely gotten flustered by the driving and not the prospect of seeing Brogan again.

She'd been doing so well. She'd mostly managed to function like an adult human for two weeks, and she'd even managed to have fun a few times, but she'd also steadfastly avoided Brogan. She was struck by the sudden fear that if she saw her now, all the progress she'd made would evaporate. Of course, that thought made her wonder, if all the strength and sense of security she'd fostered could be erased at the sight of someone, did it really count as progress, or did it simply count as avoidance? She didn't want to go back to pain and shame and depression, but more than that, she didn't want to go back to doubting herself. She desperately needed to know what was real and what was illusion, and as she turned into her driveway, she figured there was only one real way to find out.

As Diane and Esther flanked her like some flight risk, she allowed herself to be nudged down the street toward the Raven. She must have done a passable job of hiding her apprehension, because the two of them chatted amiably, giving no indication they could hear the throbbing bass beat of Emma's heart pounding against her ribs. Still, she couldn't prevent her feet from faltering as they reached the door to the pub. It felt as if the memory of what she'd seen the last time she'd opened the door had imprinted on her muscles, and she stopped short. Unfortunately, neither of her friends had any such trauma to resist, and swung open the door wide.

Emma didn't have to cross the threshold. She didn't have to

let her eyes adjust to the dim light inside. Apparently she didn't even have to breathe. All she had to do was freeze where she stood in order to lock eyes with Brogan McKay.

She stood behind the bar, tall, broad shoulders, a pint glass in one hand, the other resting casually atop a tap. Everything about her posture spoke to her strength and her competence, her efficiency, but her eyes told a different story. Their captivating green was laced with hints of red and underlined by dark smudges against pale skin. Emma recognized the tells of sleepless nights, and her heart lurched in sympathy.

Time stopped as they stared at each other, wordlessly relinquishing wishes and dreams that had never had a chance to fully form, until her need for air overrode all her senses, and parting her lips slightly, she took in a painfully sharp inhale. At the slight movement, she saw Brogan exhale, the breath she'd been holding released in the fall of her chest and the slump of her shoulders. Push and pull, inhale and exhale, a mirror image, a complete cycle in equal and opposite reactions.

Emma managed a faint smile, then freed herself from Brogan's gaze only to see everyone in the pub staring at the two of them. Had the whole world frozen along with them? How long had they been standing there with everyone watching? Her face flamed under their scrutiny. The urge to flee welled up behind her embarrassment, and she gritted her teeth against her flight instinct. She couldn't give in. She might not be sure of much, but this time she was sure. She didn't want to run or hide anymore.

"I bought a car." She blurted out the only thing that came to mind, but it worked. The simple statement brought a round of cheers and exclamations ranging from praise to surprise, and all at once conversations returned all around her.

Diane's husband, Tom, grabbed a chair from another table and put it between him and the bar, then motioned for her to join him.

Emma managed to make her shaky legs take her to the table before flopping rather ungracefully into the seat.

"Tell us about the car," Ciara said.

"It's a Mercedes A-Class." Emma found her voice. "Sort of like a little crossover, half-car, half-SUV thing."

Ciara shrugged.

"I think you'd better go a little more basic for my sister here," Charlie teased. "What color is it?"

"Shut up." Ciara slapped her brother playfully. "Get me a drink. Get Emma one, too."

"Hey Brogan," Charlie called, without moving from his spot on the booth's bench seat. "Give Ciara another glass of wine, and ask Emma what she wants to drink."

Emma's face flamed once more as every person turned to her. Why couldn't this be easy? Or better yet, why couldn't she be invisible?

"Sure, um, Emma," Brogan said behind her. "What can I get for you?"

"Water," Emma managed, then turning toward her, tried to smile, but the way all the color had drained from Brogan's complexion made her stomach turn.

"Sure, I'll, um, actually—" Brogan turned almost frantically to her brother, "Actually, Charlie, will you man the bar for a bit while I run out to the storage room?"

Charlie frowned. "For a water?"

Brogan closed her eyes, and then nodded. "I'll be right back."

Then before waiting for an answer, she walked at a pace just short of a jog out the door.

Emma's heart broke at her retreat. The only thing harder than being close to her was watching the pain send her away. She knew what that felt like, and no matter what had happened, she didn't wish it on someone she loved.

Loved?

Why had it gotten so hot in this tiny room? Or so hard to breathe? Or so dizzy? No, the room wasn't dizzy. That was just her. She didn't love Brogan. Or maybe she loved her in that hypothetical way, or like a friend, or like a lost love.

She shook her head. The last option was too much, and it must have shown because Ciara reached across the table and patted her hand.

"Give her time."

Emma shook her head again, still unable to find her voice. Brogan's eyes haunted her. She understood pain like that. She recognized the doubt and regret in them. Time didn't make those things go away. It made them fester, it made them grow, it made them move and shift like an emotional cancer.

"Well, I really need the loo." Ciara got up from the booth, everyone at the table watching her go.

Emma realized she shouldn't be here when they Brogan back. She couldn't take this. She didn't want to run or hide, but she was strong enough to face her life alone. All her progress came into sharp contrast with what she felt for Brogan now. She could handle cooking and writing and car buying on her own if she had to, but she wasn't strong enough to cause Brogan pain.

"I should go." Without waiting for an argument, she rose and headed for the door, but before she'd taken two steps, Tom spoke.

"I told you all this was a bad idea."

"Not now," Diane snapped.

"I'm just saying, you shouldn't meddle in other people's lives."

"That's not what you said," Esther shot back. "You said Brogan couldn't keep her, and you were right about that, but you were as keen as the rest of us to make her happy."

"No," the other man, Will maybe, said softly. "Happy was never part of the equation as far as I heard."

"Right," Diane said indignantly. "You didn't care about her happiness. You just wanted to keep her here, and you got poor Brogan mixed up in it all, too. Now they're both heartsick."

Emma turned slowly, unable to break away from the conversation, but also not quite sure she understood.

"Ahem." Charlie did the fake throat-clearing sound that couldn't have been more obvious, and everyone turned to look at her.

"Oh honey," Diane said soothingly to Emma. "It's not your fault."

"What's not my fault?"

"Whatever happened with you and Brogan. It was a bad idea from the outset."

"A bad idea?"

"Throwing the two of you together."

"Who threw us together?"

"No one," Esther said. "We merely talked about the possibility of you and Brogan as a couple."

"When?" Emma asked, afraid of the answer.

"The first time we met you," Diane admitted, "months ago."

Months ago. The words echoed through her brain. Why was this the first she'd heard of it? Had the secret also been kept from Brogan, or worse, had she been in on the plan? Was that all it had been, a plan? Humiliation caused the acidic taste of bile to rise in her throat, and her knees wobbled. Several people reached out to steady her, but she righted herself on her own.

"You have to understand, this was all before we knew you," Esther said. "We thought you might be lonely or need someone to help you, but as soon as we got to know you, we realized it would never work."

"I said you were too good for her all along," Tom grumbled.

"Hey now," Charlie cut in.

"No offense, Charles." Tom waved him off. "Brogan's a fine person, but she's not the settling kind. She doesn't have any staying power. She's attractive enough, though."

"She's more than that," Will defended. "She makes people feel safe and comfortable."

"For a weekend," Tom cut in. "We all know she's good for that long, but no one's ever seen her manage more."

Emma winced.

"Stop it right now," Diane said sharply.

"I'm sorry," Tom muttered. "No one meant any harm. We only wanted you to stay here, and Brogan's women always leave. They throw themselves at her for a few days, but Monday rolls around and they go back to their real lives, their real homes, their real jobs, their real relationships. She must be doing something wrong."

Emma's face burned red hot now, but this time not from shame. Her insides felt like water coming to a boil in a kettle as she heard the echo of Brogan's own words in Tom's condemnation.

"Maybe Brogan's a different sort," Will offered.

"A different sort than what Emma deserves, and there's nothing wrong with that. We've all got our types, and Brogan's a good type. Pretty, sweet, short-term entertainment. She's like most of the town, really, a holiday let."

"How dare you?" Emma seethed. "How can you even think that, much less say it, in front of her brother, in front of me? Dear God, have you said it in front of her?" She looked helplessly from person to person, but their averted eyes confirmed her suspicions. "I can't believe this."

"Honey," Diane whispered. "This all came out wrong. We all love Brogan."

"You should," Emma shot back. "Brogan McKay is the kindest, steadiest, most generous person I've ever met. She singlehandedly pulled me out of a sea of grief when all I wanted to do was swim down. She helped restart my career. She helped me regain my sense of self. She gave me my life back."

The whole weight of the truth hit her only after she'd spoken the words, and she swayed again, but this time her righteous indignation kept her upright. "The only reason I am not curled in a ball on my couch right now is because Brogan convinced me I would do better. Why didn't I understand that sooner? Everything good I've done in the last few weeks can be tied directly back to Brogan."

"Now don't give all the credit away," Diane said. "You've both got your strengths."

"Yes, but because of her strength, her faith, her example, I remembered who I was, or at least who I wanted to be. My money didn't do that. My talent didn't do that. My fame has never done anything to save me from a crushing loss of self-worth. Brogan did. She showed me who I am, who I could be, again." Saying that felt freeing and painful all at once. How could both emotions take up so much space inside her heart at the

251

same time? She felt like she might crack down the middle if she didn't rein herself in, but she didn't want to stop now. Not when she'd finally found her passion again, not when she knew at her very core she was right.

Tom opened his mouth, but Emma raised her hand and cut him off. "Brogan is literally the best thing that's happened to me in years. I'm sorry she let ideas like yours undercut her sense of self, and I'm sorry I didn't understand what sort of insecurities she was having fed to her, but now that I do, I won't listen to anyone repeat the trash Brogan so painfully internalized."

She turned to go, prepared to storm out of the pub, but she didn't even take a full step before she saw Brogan standing behind her, eyes wide and wounded, lips parted, and clutching a bottle of water in each hand.

Emma's heart seized in her chest. How much had she heard? It didn't matter. It wasn't enough. She hadn't ever done enough for Brogan. The thought hurt, but she didn't know what else to say. She didn't know what to do. The anger and helplessness she'd directed around the room moments earlier all turned inward now.

She hated that people made Brogan believe these awful things that couldn't be further from the truth, but she hated it more that she'd confirmed them by pulling her close in one minute and pushing her away the next. She must have made Brogan feel like that's all she'd wanted, a moment. Emma had been so insecure about what she'd wanted, she'd fed Brogan's worst fears. As much as she wanted to blame everyone sitting around that table, she couldn't deny she'd done as much, if not more, to put the shadows of doubt in Brogan's eyes, and she couldn't live with that anymore.

Reaching out on impulse, in need, she cupped Brogan's face and kissed her full on the mouth. Hard and fast, Emma poured all her emotions into the kiss, hoping it could express what she had failed to. Then, before she had a chance to linger in a place she didn't deserve, she broke away.

"I'm sorry," she gasped. "For everything. You're better than the whole lot of us."

And then she ran.

Brogan stood there, mouth agape, head spinning, as Emma flew out the door, her blond hair merely a blur by the time Brogan managed to even blink.

What the hell had just happened?

Her face burned, her lips tingled, her heart hammered, so clearly all her nerve endings were firing, and yet her brain couldn't make any sense of the mixed signals they were sending. Everything had happened so fast. She'd only meant to take a moment to compose herself, to get a little fresh air, but when she'd slipped back in, Emma had launched into a tirade aimed at the entire Friday Club. The tone, her body language, the wording, everything about it seemed discordant with everything Brogan knew about Emma. For several seconds she couldn't figure out what Emma was so passionate about. Then it hit her. Emma was defending her.

All the things Emma had said swirled in her head. She'd said Brogan had pulled her out of a sea of grief, helped restart her career, helped her regain her sense of self. Was that true? The force in Emma's delivery hadn't left much room for doubt, but all the things she'd said today flew in direct opposition to everything Brogan had heard from her the last time they'd spoken. That conversation had been laced with pain and regret and betrayal.

But the kiss still burned on her lips. Even as the rest of her body had gone cold with confusion, the kiss still burned. What was she going to do with it all? What was she going to do with herself?

She blinked away the red tint from her vision, desperate for clarity, and noticed everyone staring at her. The weight of their expectations bore down on her, but she couldn't decipher them any more than her own indecision. Finally, the emotions overcame her, and she shouted, "What can I do?"

The answer was unanimous and full of force as her friends and neighbors took up one voice and shouted, "Go after her!"

This time Brogan didn't argue or even hesitate. Still clutching both water bottles, she sprinted out the door and down Northland street. She reached Emma's cottage just as Emma was closing the door, and practically hurled herself into the house. Emma let loose a little yelp of surprise, and Brogan doubled over at the near perfect reversal of their first meeting.

Or maybe she'd doubled over because she was out of breath and at a loss for words, but either way, when she straightened up and met Emma's eyes, so beautiful and so beautifully open, she no longer felt the need to say anything. Instead, she kissed her.

She barely had the time to process Emma's initial surprise before it disappeared. First she relaxed, melting into Brogan, so supple and soft in her surrender. Then, as if someone had ignited a flame too close to paper, the fire rose up between them, consuming and uninhibited.

Emma was on her, all over her, in an instant. With one hand behind Brogan's neck and the other clutching her T-shirt, Emma yanked her fully inside. Brogan dropped the water bottles she'd absurdly clung to, and they hit the carpet with a heavy thud. Or maybe that sound came from Brogan's heart hitting her ribs when Emma's tongue slipped into her mouth.

Kicking the door shut as she moved, or rather let herself be dragged into the living room, Brogan refused to break the kiss. Emma's lips tasted amazing, sweet and hot, and soft and demanding all at once, embodying the world of contradictions that made Emma so alluring. Why had Brogan ever tried to resist this?

She took hold of Emma with both hands, sliding them up over slender hips until they settled in the subtle curve of her waist. Brogan's head spun, either from the lack of air or the high of finally touching the body she'd craved for so long. She couldn't process anything but her need. It pulsed through her now, no weaker for being satisfied.

She'd known it would feel like this. No amount of Emma would ever be enough. No kiss, no caress, no amount of making love could fill the soul-deep need for this woman.

Emma broke away from Brogan's mouth and ran her parted lips across Brogan's cheek, her breath hot and rapid against already flushed skin. Then with gentle pressure on the back of Brogan's neck, Emma bowed her low enough to take an earlobe between her teeth before rasping, "I want you."

Brogan's knees almost buckled at the simple statement of fact, delivered with such certainty. Emma's tone, combined with the press of possessively strong fingers, vanquished Brogan's remaining doubts, or at least replaced them with a certainty that whatever was happening between them was stronger than her fears. There would be time for conversations and explanations and apologies later, but for now, a dam had burst inside her, and all the desire she'd held back for months rolled forth.

She turned her head toward the heat of Emma's mouth until they were kissing frantically once more. The passion ran away with her as their tongues tangled. She placed a hand firmly at the small of Emma's back, pressing them together until they couldn't find a clear line of separation between their bodies. The fit was intoxicating, Emma's slightly smaller frame folding flush into her embrace. She wanted to cover her, surround her, press into her. Drunk with desire, Brogan slowly walked Emma through the living room until her back hit the wall to the dining room. Brogan should've turned, should've pulled herself together enough to make a plan, or at least make it to a bedroom, but her brain couldn't process *should* anymore. Her body had only one gear, and it screamed *go*.

She pushed up Emma's shirt, sliding her hands over smooth skin until she reached the satin that barely managed to restrain Emma's breasts. Palming them with one hand, she felt a hard nipple pressing through. She used her thumb to tease, and thrilled as Emma arched her chest into the touch. She moved over the other, eager for the same response, but as she rolled the nipple through the thin cover, Emma upped the stakes by taking hold of Brogan's shirt and tugging it over her head in one fluid movement.

Brogan barely had the chance to comprehend the separation

between them before Emma had a skillful finger under her sport bra, pausing only a second to place warm hands over taut skin before continuing to remove the barrier entirely. Brogan groaned at the fleeting nature of the touch, but her frustration faded instantly as Emma replaced her hand with her mouth. With a slight pull on her nipple, Emma elicited another moan from Brogan, who let her head roll back as she arched into the pleasure.

Emma moved to the other side, this time growing bolder, and gently grazing her teeth along hypersensitive skin. Brogan's body bypassed her brain in its response as her hips rocked forward, pinning Emma to the wall as she pulled away from her mouth only far enough to slide down her body. Dragging her parted lips down the center of Emma's torso, she skipped over the navy-blue silk of the bra, then sank to her knees and kissed a line to the clasp of Emma's gray slacks. She flipped open the top button and kissed the newly exposed skin before drawing the zipper down, until the trousers were loose enough to fall, revealing the perfect navy bikinis matched to the bra above.

Smiling mischievously, she raised her eyes to meet Emma's. "Please tell me you haven't been dressed like this for four months, and I've missed out."

Emma laughed and ran her fingers through Brogan's hair. "I bought a car today. I wanted to feel confident."

Brogan hooked a finger in the delicate waistband and peeled it away from the beautiful body before her, murmuring something about how much she liked confidence.

Emma curled her fingers more tightly at the back of Brogan's head and held her close. "Good, but I like showing more than telling."

Brogan rose to the challenge and back to her feet. Taking command of Emma's mouth with her own, they were off again. Brogan hiked Emma's leg over her hip, then used her free hand to cup Emma's ass. With one fluid movement, she managed to lift Emma off the ground, pivot, and sit her on the edge of the dining-room table.

Emma gasped at the abrupt repositioning, or maybe the cool

wood surface against her bare backside. Still, she kept her leg tightly around Brogan's waist. Their lips locked as Brogan moved a hand between their bodies and then between Emma's legs. Finding all the encouragement she needed in the wetness pooling there, she pushed slowly and steadily inside Emma.

"Brogan," Emma called, breaking the kiss as her head fell back. "Yes, Brogan."

She loved the sound of her own name in Emma's mouth, on her lips, rumbling through her throat, with so much raw need. Her chest expanded with the knowledge that she could fill that need. The power surged in her again, and she pulled back only far enough to push forward again. This time she ran her thumb around Emma's clit. Emma in turn stroked her ego by tightening her thigh around Brogan's hip, trying to hold her closer. Brogan increased the pressure with each forward thrust, but then she'd pull back teasingly, to experience the physical sensations of Emma's body trying to draw her back in. She warred between the desire to fill her completely, and the thrill of playing this beautiful body for more, but her better—or baser—instincts won out each time. Her hips rocked toward Emma, pushing her hand forward as they went.

Emma leaned forward again, resting her forehead against Brogan's for a steadying second before her hands and mouth set to work covering Brogan's torso in kisses. Kneading a breast, biting her ear, scratching her nails down the taut muscles of Brogan's back before sucking on her neck, their movements became a frantic blur. Brogan lost track of who was touching what as her heart pounded out a bass beat to match a single word. *"More."*

Gradually Emma's rasps took on a high pitch as each breath grew shallower. Brogan gave a fleeting thought to holding back. No part of her wanted this to end, but like every other time she'd tried to restrain herself around this woman, Emma merely had to breathe her name plaintively, and Brogan's resistance shattered.

With one emphatic push, she stilled against her, inside her, and basked in the pulse of Emma around her.

Slowly, the shivers of orgasm subsided, and tense muscles

uncoiled in their still intertwined bodies. Emma went slack with Brogan still inside her.

Brogan closed her eyes and rested her head on Emma's chest, trying to regain her composure, but all she could manage to do was say, "This feels too good. I want to stay inside you."

Emma kissed the top of her head. "That sounds as good as it feels."

"Yeah?" Brogan asked.

Emma tugged on her hair, tilting Brogan's head back until she could kiss her again. Then sliding her lips over to whisper in her ear, she said, "Stay inside me while I stroke you."

She lifted her leg to press one heel into Brogan's ass again. Holding her close, she worked her hands between their bodies.

She unsnapped Brogan's jeans, loosening her hold on her waist only enough to push the denim roughly to the floor. She kissed her again, scooting closer to the edge of the table, her body pulling Brogan's fingers deeper as she slid her own palm down tightened abs and into the waistband of Brogan's boxers.

Brogan's body was on overload. Too many nerve endings fired at once. She couldn't decide what to focus on until Emma found her clit. They both tightened at once, Brogan in every major muscle group, and Emma around Brogan's fingers.

Brogan dropped her head to Emma's shoulder again and planted her free hand flat on the table, bracing herself securely enough to stay upright. Or at least she hoped she could stay upright, but as Emma ran her fingertips through the evidence of Brogan's desire, she wasn't at all sure she wouldn't cave under the perfect pressure.

Emma ran one finger along the length of Brogan's desire and groaned. "How long have you been so wet for me?'

Brogan bit her shoulder, her mind rebelling at the math before her honesty overtook her. "About four months."

Emma's hips jerked up, driving Brogan even deeper.

"God yes," one of them said, but she didn't know which. Emma circled her now, her pressure becoming more insistent, causing Brogan's knees to shake.

"I don't know how much more I can take," Brogan admitted through clenched teeth.

"I think we've waited long enough," Emma said. Her hips undulated, and she nipped at Brogan's ear. Then with each stroke of her fingers, she added, "You can take whatever you want . . . whenever you want . . . as often as you want it . . . from here on out."

The words, combined with the skillful touch, sent Brogan's mind into oblivion and her body crashing into Emma.

Pushing inside Emma and up against her, Brogan rode waves of release, the sheer force of her arousal the only thing keeping her upright. Her vision flashed white, and her muscles screamed, but she held on until she could shake every excruciating shudder of pleasure from her core, and from Emma's.

Then when she finally had nothing left to give, she slipped toward the floor, but Emma was too fast. She wrapped her arms around Brogan, holding her steady, even as both of them trembled. She urged Brogan's arm over her shoulder and led her toward her room, her knees wobbly enough only to get them to the bed before they both collapsed.

Chapter Sixteen

Emma straddled Brogan's naked body, rocking against the two fingers inside her, and watching hazily as the ab muscles beneath her contracted. They'd made love in various stages of lust throughout the night and again as the morning reflected golden over the North Sea. Brogan looked golden, too, bathed in the light streaming through the back windows. Emma wanted to memorize this moment, from the play of the sun across her light skin, to the way her hair curled across her forehead damp with perspiration, to the way she felt moving inside her. Even as she ached to surrender to the oblivion of her impending climax, Emma wanted to keep Brogan right where she was, always.

The power of the thought struck her in the chest, but it didn't terrify her now. Nothing could make her afraid with Brogan's strong, steady hands on her. And that thought tipped her back into the moment and right over the edge. She arched back in one beautifully toe-curling moment of bliss, then fell forward onto Brogan's chest.

They breathed slowly and deeply as she listened to the sound of Brogan's heartbeat regaining a more even rhythm. Then with a sigh, Emma rolled off her only enough to settle into the crook of her arm. "Do you know how long it's been since someone touched me like that?"

Brogan shook her head against the pillow. "No one has ever touched me like that."

"I find that hard to believe."

Brogan eased onto her side to view Emma more fully. "Don't. I mean it. I won't lie and say I haven't been with other women. We've both seen how our pasts can shape our futures, but this is something different for me. No one has ever made me lose my inhibitions like you did, because no one has seen me the way you do. Not even myself, Emma. The things you said about me back at the pub . . ." Her voice caught, and Emma's heart broke a little again.

"I meant every word of it."

"I believe you. Or I at least believe *you* believed you, and I want to believe it, too."

"How could you not?"

"Because until you came along, I didn't have any reason to. No one has ever seen me as anything out of the ordinary before, especially someone like you."

"Someone like me?" Emma laughed. "Someone who screamed at you upon first meeting? Someone who hid and cried and was totally planning to wither away until you came along?"

"I didn't do anything special."

Emma shook her head. "You don't get to decide that. I do, and I say you helped me back on my feet. You helped me find my way and my path."

Brogan kissed her forehead. "You had that in you all the time."

"That's probably true, but I didn't see it until you showed me how much you believed in me. You came into my life, and you weren't like any of the hundreds of other people who wanted something from me, or tried to tell me how to live, or whispered behind my back. You just showed up and showed me something better. You acted like my recovery was a foregone conclusion. You talked about spring and new life, and then you showed me a new way to live, like I deserved it."

"You do deserve it. You deserve all those things and much more."

"I do," Emma said, "but so do you."

Brogan's smile grew tight, and Emma took hold of her face, so close Brogan had no choice but to meet her eyes. "Listen, I spent the last two weeks fighting to stay present, to be the person you showed me I could be. I filled every need from my stomach, to my career, to friends, to a new car, and I did all of those things on my own, but there was still something missing. I shouldn't have just been fighting for me. I should have been fighting to get you back."

Brogan's jaw tightened under Emma's fingers. "No one has ever fought for me before."

"I'm sorry for that. I didn't realize what you'd been led to believe about yourself. I let my own insecurities cloud my vision. I only ever saw you as beautiful and competent and strong and sexy and steady, whereas I saw myself as the opposite of all those things. I didn't see what someone like you would want in a mess like me."

"And I saw you as a stunning, successful, talented, poised, and powerful woman of the world, while I was so ordinary, barely worth noticing, much less, wanting."

"I hope last night put to rest some of the fears about wanting, but I'm sorry I was too wrapped up in the pain caused by someone else's opinion of me to see that you were dealing with the same sort of delusions."

"They aren't easy to see," Brogan admitted, "and that makes them harder to fight."

Emma nodded. "And they aren't going to go away overnight, for either of us."

"So, what do we do?"

Emma sighed. "We have to trust each other."

"I do trust you," Brogan said.

"Then trust that I love you," Emma said softly, "because I get to decide that."

Brogan nodded slowly. "Can I be in awe of that even if I believe it?"

"Yes." Emma kissed her. "Awe is good."

"Can you do the same for me?"

"Stand in awe of you?" Emma grinned. "That could be arranged."

"Good, but I actually meant could you believe I see you? Believe I know who you are, and that I love you, too?"

Emma's heart did a little happy dance in her chest, but tears sprung to her eyes. "Yes, and I see what you mean about the awe of surrendering to that."

"Feels better than the fear, doesn't it?"

Emma nodded. "Much. I'm sorry I couldn't work around to that sooner."

"Me, too," Brogan said, "but let's try to add guilt to the list of things we're letting go of. No more apologizing. We can't undo our past, not with other people, and not with each other."

"See, that's such a Brogan thing to say." Emma kissed her again. "But yes, I'm trying to pack guilt away right now, so I'll confess there's one thing I'm not sorry for."

"What's that?"

"I am not sorry that none of the other women ever realized what a treasure they'd found in you, because I crossed an ocean to find you and claim you for myself."

Brogan smiled brightly. "Just like the pirate woman in your story."

"Similar concept, but when my pirate finds her treasure, the story's over. For me, finding you is only the beginning of my big adventure."

Epilogue

"Emma," Reggie called as she burst through the door so hard it hit the stone wall of the Raven with a loud crack. "I'm a pirate."

"Girls can't be pirates," Seamus shouted as he ran past.

"Yes they can." About seven women swooped down on him in unison, but Emma turned to Reggie, who stood proudly in the doorway, hand on her hips, wooden sword at her side and her unruly hair falling down over an eye patch.

Emma beamed at the girl, tousling her red curls affectionately and effused, "You are, and you look proper rakish."

Reggie puffed out her chest with pride. "Can I read your new book, then?"

"No," her mother called from across the room. "We've been through this."

Reggie folded her arms across her chest and stuck out her bottom lip, but Emma turned to Brogan and smiled.

Brogan froze, her heart expanding slowly in her chest until it pressed against her ribs. It'd been a year since the first time Emma had looked at her like that, her eyes dancing, her lips curled, her entire expression directed at her and only her. Clearly, Brogan hadn't grown immune to the connection, though, because as the seconds stretched on, Emma finally said, "Ahem."

She frowned, vaguely aware she should remember something.

"The gift," Emma whispered, and nodded toward the booth.

"Oh yeah." Brogan shook herself out of the schmoopy love

stupor and grabbed a stack of books from the bench. "Here you go, kiddo."

Reggie uncrossed her arms and accepted the peace offering. "There are six books about a redheaded pirate girl."

"Pippi Longstocking?" Reggie asked, her eyes lighting up.

"And while they are smaller than my book on their own, when you add them all together, you have more pirate words there than even I wrote. Hopefully it'll hold you over for a while."

"Until I'm old enough to read yours?"

Emma laughed. "Maybe not that long, but I promise Aunt Brogan and I will keep you stocked in adventure stories for as long as you want to read them."

Reggie didn't respond verbally. She simply threw her arms around Emma's waist and squeezed.

"What about me?" Seamus called as he ran by, chasing Wendell, or maybe it was the other way around.

"You, too," Emma called. "Books all around."

"Someone's vying to be the favorite aunt," Charlie called. "You better watch your back, Nora."

"She can have the title until they have bairns of their own. Then we get to spoil them and send 'em home." Nora lifted baby Maggie to her shoulder and cooed at her daughter, "Isn't that right, Mags? Auntie Emma will learn all these things when it's her turn."

"Thanks, Aunt Emma." Reggie released her and ran off, calling for her cousins, and the rest of the adults in the room resumed their normal conversations, but Emma stayed still, as if rooted to her spot near a table full of her books.

Brogan grinned, slipping her arm around Emma's shoulder, and pulled her close enough to kiss her temple. "Doing okay?"

"Aye." She nodded slowly. "Did I just get upgraded to 'Aunt Emma'?"

"I think you did. How do you feel about that?"

"Good," Emma squeaked, then met Brogan's eyes, tears shimmering in her own. "Really good."

"And the part about us having kids of our own? That sort of got dumped on us."

Emma laughed. "No, that's good, too. You'd be adorable pregnant."

"Me?" Brogan started to pull away, but Emma hooked a finger through her belt loop and tugged her close again. "Don't worry. We've got plenty of time to work out the details of my next full English adventure."

Then she kissed her, a light, teasing kiss as playful as her tone.

"Hey now," Charlie called from the corner. "We get it. You're happy together. No need to rub it in."

"Hear, hear," someone called from a table to the side, and Brogan noticed Lady Victoria had taken a break from her conversation with Diane and Esther. Brogan still hadn't got used to seeing her in the pub or joining them on the boat, but she had to admit, Victoria was much more than her title might suggest, genuine, fun, and with a self-effacing sense of humor that was hard to keep at arm's length. Plus, she'd been a good friend to Emma and seemed to enjoy being included in normal village life. "Charlie and I are united in our membership of the Singleton Club. I'm sure Singleton Awareness Week is coming up."

"You should issue a formal decree," Charlie said. "Maybe host a fundraiser or speed-dating pool to raise awareness."

"Perhaps public funding for matchmaker services," Victoria added.

"Don't say that too loud," Tom grumbled. "My wife will start to get ideas."

"Ideas that worked out pretty well," Diane shot back with a nod toward Brogan and Emma.

"You can't take credit for them," he groused. "We did more to muck it up than make it work. Don't start down that road again."

"Oh no, please do," Lady Victoria said, turning to the group of women who'd been attached to her hip since she'd walked in. "Tell me all your secrets."

"We'd be happy to," Esther said. "Now that you're coming down to visit more often, maybe we could also give you a quick tour of the village."

"Or how about we eat?" Margaret called from the dining room.

A chorus of voices called, "Eat! Yes! Let's go."

Chairs scraped against the wooden floor as half the town rose and wandered into the next room, but Brogan and Emma stayed behind.

"You know they're going to want you to read to them next, right?" Brogan asked.

Emma blew out a shaky breath and nodded.

"It's the first book launch in the history of Amberwick."

"I've been told. I've already signed twenty copies."

"You did give them away for free."

Emma laughed. "They earned them. Your family, our friends, this whole town, I couldn't have done it without them."

"Not true." Brogan put her hands on Emma's shoulders and turned her until they faced each other. "You wrote this book. You had it in you all along."

"Maybe," she admitted with a half-smile, "but having you by my side helped bring out the best in me. And if in return the locals want to throw the first book-launch party, who am I to begrudge them that?"

Brogan kissed her forehead. "First of many. I know your publisher is going to host receptions in New York and LA next month, and then London, and who knows where."

"Life is about to get busier," Emma said with a little shiver, "for both of us."

"Yes," Brogan said, "for both of us, together. I'll be right beside you every time you tug your ear."

"Have I mentioned lately how much I love you?"

Brogan smiled because she had indeed mentioned it many times. "I never get tired of hearing it."

"I love you."

"I love you, too."

"And we all love that you love each other," Charlie called from the doorway. "Now, get your arses in here and read to us while we eat."

Brogan stepped back and rolled her eyes at her brother before turning to Emma with a shrug. "No one promised your first book launch for this book would be the most formal."

"No, I can assure you, it's not, but it's by far the best."

Then, before Brogan could argue, Emma kissed her again, this one lingering a little longer, and laced with the promise of more to come.

About the Author

Rachel Spangler never set out to be an award-winning author. She was just so poor during her college years that she had to come up with creative ways to entertain herself, and her first novel, *Learning Curve,* was born out of one such attempt. She was sincerely surprised when it was accepted for publication and even more shocked when it won the Golden Crown Literary Award for Debut Author. She also won a Goldie for subsequent novels *Trails Merge* and *Perfect Pairings.* Since writing is more fun than a real job and so much cheaper than therapy, Rachel continued to type away, leading to the publication of *The Long Way Home, LoveLife, Spanish Heart, Does She Love You, Timeless, Heart of the Game, Perfect Pairing, Close to Home, Edge of Glory, In Development, Love All,* and *Full English.* She is a three-time Lambda Literary Award Finalist and the 2018 Alice B. Medal winner. She plans to continue writing as long as anyone, anywhere, will keep reading.

Rachel and her wife, Susan, are raising their son in Western New York, where during the winter they make the most of the lake-effect snow on local ski slopes. In the summer, they love to travel and watch their beloved St. Louis Cardinals. Regardless of the season, she always makes time for a good romance, whether she's reading it, writing it, or living it.

For more information, visit Rachel online at www.rachelspangler.com or on Facebook, Twitter, or Instagram.

close to home
a darlington romance

"Ms. Spangler's characters are deep and multidimensional."—CURVE

"Spangler's novels are filled with endearing characters, interesting plot turns, and vivid descriptions. Her readers feel immersed in the worlds of her novels from start to finish." —THE OBSERVER

Close To Home by **Rachel Spangler**
Print 978-1-61294-081-6
Ebook 978-1-61294-082-3

www.bywaterbooks.com

At Bywater Books we love good books about lesbians just like you do, and we're committed to bringing the best of contemporary lesbian writing to our avid readers. Our editorial team is dedicated to finding and developing outstanding writers who create books you won't want to put down.

We sponsor the Bywater Prize for Fiction to help with this quest. Each prizewinner receives $1,000 and publication of their novel. We have already discovered amazing writers like Jill Malone, Sally Bellerose, and Hilary Sloin through the Bywater Prize. Which exciting new writer will we find next?

For more information about Bywater Books and the annual Bywater Prize for Fiction, please visit our website.

www.bywaterbooks.com